My
not so
Wicked
Ex-Fiancé

Dedication

To Aunt Berta, my cheerleader and friend. I love you.

Chapter One

OH MYLANTA, MYLANTA. This cannot be happening. I scanned through the article my second cousin Arlene had sent me on my phone, hardly able to comprehend what I was reading.

Edenvale welcomes Prescott Technology, the up-and-coming software company started by owner and CEO Ryder Prescott. In the past five years, Edenvale has become one of Colorado's premier technological centers due to its . . .

How could this be? I couldn't breathe. I needed to talk to Emma.

I walked out of the boutique's back offices to find only a few customers browsing our new summer line. Macey and Marlowe were taking care of them beautifully. Until the summer months began, weekdays were slower than weekends. At least that's what the sales data said that Mr. Carrington had provided me when I bought M&M on Main last year. Now it was M&M'S on Main. Memaw had loaned me the money to take on this new adventure. She, more than anyone, knew how much I wanted out of my family's business and my family out of my business.

"Ladies, I will be right back." I waved as I walked out the door into the beautiful late May day. I loved the Colorado sunshine and less humid days than I was used to in Georgia, but I was happy to see the snow go. This Southern girl had missed her mild winter, but it was worth it not to have to worry about running into my ex-fiancé, Ryder Prescott, cheater among men, love of my life, and crusher of my soul.

I scooted my heels down the cobblestone sidewalks of Main Street. Carrington Cove was a darling town that belonged on the Hallmark Channel. Close-knit shops and boutiques with brick storefronts, some with cute awnings like my store. Most of them had welcoming display windows. Some of the cafés had outdoor seating when it was warm enough, though the natives around here walked around in shorts in two feet of snow.

The sun's rays felt good on me as I hustled to Carrington Cove's Eye Center, owned by some of the best friends I had ever had, Emma and Dr. Sawyer King. They weren't open for business yet but would be in the next two weeks. Carrington Cove was happy to finally get their own optometry practice. Not as happy as the newlyweds were to be fulfilling one of their dreams.

The eye center was two blocks down from us on Willow Street. They were renovating an old coffee shop nestled between a family practice and an old-fashioned candy shop. I peeked through the Frameport glass door with Carrington Cove Eye Center etched into it to find the lovebirds painting—more like kissing and pretending to paint—the reception area wall. I tried not to be jealous of the sweetest couple I had ever known.

I knocked before letting myself in. "I'm sorry to interrupt."

The happy couple was covered in paint from head to toe as if they had rolled around in it, which wouldn't have surprised me. They gave each other one last peck before turning my way with big grins.

"Hey, Shelby, what's up?" Emma set her paint brush down in the rolling tray.

"I'm having sort of a dilemma and I need someone to talk to."

"Is this female related? Should I leave?" Sawyer asked.

I shook my head. "No. Actually it might be good to have a male perspective." I approached their reception desk, trying not to inhale too many paint fumes.

Both Emma and Sawyer hopped on the plastic covered desk, ready to hear my tale.

"Remember when I told you I was engaged?"

They both nodded.

"Well . . ." I paused, hardly able to say it, "it appears my ex-fiancé has started his own company and is moving to Edenvale."

Emma's mouth dropped. "Does he know you live nearby?"

"I don't think so. I haven't talked to him since, well, since I left town and never said a word to him." Not to mention I had done my best to keep my whereabouts secret from him, everything from deleting my social media and email accounts to changing my phone number. Momma and Daddy had convinced me it would be better this way. And after seeing those pictures of him with that woman on his supposed business trip, I had agreed.

"Maybe it's a coincidence," Sawyer offered.

Emma patted her husband's cheeks, adding more paint to his scruff. "Hmm," she considered what he had to say. I loved that about them. "I don't know, babe."

He took her hands and kissed her as if I wasn't there.

I cleared my throat.

They broke apart with apologetic smiles.

"Sorry." Emma grinned. "This is interesting."

"Ryder Prescott—" I almost hated to say his name. It used to be the most wonderful bits of alphabet to escape my mouth. Now I felt like wiping my tongue off each time I had to speak it. "—moving to Colorado is more than interesting. I'm not even sure he's been west of the Mississippi."

Emma squinted her eyes. "Ryder Prescott? That name sounds so familiar."

"You probably remember me talking about him."

She shook her head. "No. It's more recent than that." Emma thought for a second. "Holy crap!" She jumped off the desk. "A Ryder Prescott from Georgia booked one of our cabins at the Ranch for the entire summer. It caught my attention yesterday when I was going through our reservation site because of the length of his stay."

I reached for my heart, the one Ryder broke. "Please tell me this is one of your practical jokes."

I was living at Carrington Ranch in the main house until I could secure a place in town. It was part of the deal when I bought the store since my parents had cut me off for leaving the family business. Real estate was expensive in Carrington Cove, so I was waiting until after the busy summer months to move into my own place. How could I avoid him if we were both there? And why out of all the places in the world had he chosen the Ranch? It was forty-five minutes away from Edenvale where his office would be.

"I'm sorry, Shelby," Emma interrupted my thoughts.

Not as sorry as I was. I fanned my face. "It's fine. It's all fine." I stood tall and proud while lying. My heart raced faster than the Talladega Superspeedway.

Emma tilted her head. "It's not fine. Maybe I can find some legitimate excuse to cancel the reservation."

I shook my head. "Goodness no, don't do that. You and your daddy have a business to run. I'm sure," I cleared my throat, "Ryder's money is as good as anyone else's." Though I had to wonder how he'd come into all this money. An entire summer at Carrington Ranch would be well into the thousands of dollars.

Emma bit her lip and approached me in paint coated cutoffs and one of Sawyer's old T-shirts. I wished I were more like her, comfortable in anything—including her own skin. I loved how she was able to throw her hair up in a ponytail and not wear any makeup. She was naturally beautiful, whether she thought so or not, her confidence and personality made her more so.

I was taught growing up to never leave the house unless you were looking your best, not even to go grocery shopping. I knew that was a turnoff to some people. But it's not like I had to do a lot of those type of domestic things growing up or for most of my adult life. That's what delivery services and the help were for, Momma would say. As silly as it sounded, I liked strolling through each aisle of the store. It reminded me of . . . well, different times. A time when I wanted nothing more than to be blissfully domestic and even clip coupons if I had to. What an evil thought for a Duchane.

Emma got close, but not too close as she was covered in wet paint. "Shelby, we don't need the money and we always have a waiting list."

"I appreciate your offer, but Ryder Prescott means nothing to me. If I saw him today, I would . . ." My breath got caught in my chest. What would I do? Slap him? Ignore him? I knew one thing that would not happen. I would not let his dark chocolate eyes capture mine and melt into my soul. My breath came out in a rush thinking about that first moment four years ago when our eyes had locked. "Excuse me." I turned on my heels.

"Shelby," Emma called. "Let's go grab lunch. My treat."

I waved from behind; my whole body was shaking. "Thank you, but I have to go." I opened the door and ran into the bright sun. I soaked in the rays of warmth, letting that feeling settle my heart. I silently berated myself for allowing him to affect me after all this time while I took a seat on the nearby bench under the gaslit lamppost.

Ever my momma's daughter, I crossed my legs and smoothed out my pencil skirt. I could hear Momma now, chiding me to keep my shoulders back and head held high. For once I didn't listen to her as I sank against the wrought iron. That was a lie—it wasn't the first time. There was a time, a beautiful time, almost like a dream, now, where I didn't worry about the expectations of my family. It was the first time in my life that I could be me, with *him,* curled up in his arms, nestled under a blanket of stars out in the hay field on his momma's and daddy's dairy farm. It was not befitting of a lady, or a Duchane, Momma would have said. But I thought it fit me perfectly. How wrong I had been.

At least the man left me with something. He made me see I was more than my name. I forgot that for a while last year when I came running here under the thumb of my family, but once the shock of his betrayal wore off, I realized I was right back where I had promised myself I would never be, living under the Duchane law. As much as I hated to admit it now, Ryder was right: I needed to be my own person. The question now was what was I going to do?

And why was he coming here?

I stared down at the phone in my hand and pulled up that article one more time, reading it more carefully and trying to breathe while I did so. Oxygen, I found, was helpful for comprehension.

I can't think of a more fitting place to grow the Worlds Collide app and software than Edenvale. The college town atmosphere paired with local venues, attractions, and the outdoor recreation Colorado is known for made it an easy choice. Not to mention the incredible businesses we've been able to partner with in Edenvale and the surrounding areas.

I stared at the phrase *Worlds Collide*. How many times had he used that phrase to describe what we had together? The debutante and the farm boy. While staring at the name of his product and the phrase I once adored, I did something I shouldn't have. I tapped on a folder that I should have deleted long ago. Why I saved the emails, I didn't know. Perhaps, at first, I thought I would wake up from the bad dream to find Ryder as true as I thought he was. When my wakeup call never came, I scoured them to see if I'd missed something. Surely I had missed the clues. But no. There wasn't any hint in any of his daily "Chief" emails to indicate he was planning on breaking my heart. Maybe that was his plan. Perhaps he was one of those men who wanted his cake and to eat it too. Had I not seen those pictures, he would have gotten quite the cake—a seven-layered rum cake with orange blossoms, white roses, and gardenias. Ryder thought it was over-the-top. He'd wanted a simple chocolate cake made with his momma's recipe, topped with a tacky plastic bride and groom. No way was my momma going for that. We'd compromised and decided that would be the groom's cake.

I shook my head. I shouldn't be thinking of all this nonsense. I should be deleting this file folder. My thumb hovered over the trashcan icon. I closed my eyes. Just do it, Shelby. I was really going to do it this time. Really, I was. Then I heard Ryder laugh at me and say, "What are you so afraid of?" He'd asked me the same thing when I'd hesitated to give him my number the first time he'd asked for it at the concert where we'd met.

I thought back to that summer night at the outdoor amphitheater where the sultry air landed on my skin, making it glisten and cling to my sundress. The country rock band gave the night its own pulse. The darker it got, the more intoxicated people became. Inhibitions lowered and strangers began to dirty dance with each other in the aisles. Some of my coworkers from the hospital I used to work at as a midwife decided to partake in not only the abundant alcohol but the sensual aisle dancing. It just so happened that they hooked up with some of Ryder's friends. Being the only sober people in the crowd, we were left to stare at each other. His brown eyes penetrated mine. Even from a distance I could tell he spelled trouble, with his dark blond hair that fell just below his chin and his tanned skin decorated with several tattoos. Oh, did Momma hate those, but I loved to trace their lines with my finger, to watch his skin raise, especially around the one of my name across his heart.

I blew down my blouse, trying to cool off. I should stop thinking about him, but my mind refused to. It went right back to the night where it all began. He had flashed me a crooked grin when he caught me staring at him from two rows up. I bit my lip and pretended I hadn't noticed. He wouldn't be ignored. He jumped over the seats that were separating us and landed next to me with a smile that said *I know you like what you see*. Did I ever, but he was not the sort of man I was used to. He wasn't bred to live and breathe boardrooms. No, he was wild and unfettered, born to live life on his own terms. But he was smart. Even that night, he knew not to push it with me. He stood close by singing along with the band and seducing me with his crooner voice without speaking directly to me. For an hour he said nothing other than to glance my way and smile between songs. He let me come to him.

"I'm Shelby," I'd finally said.

For that I was rewarded with a seductive grin. Momma called that grin of his wicked. Said it was going to ruin my reputation. I told her a thousand times she didn't know the man behind the smile. He wasn't all that wicked. In fact, when he wanted to be, he was sweeter than the homemade strawberry wine he used to make that we drank out of Dixie cups. But in the end Momma was right, and that pleased her more than anything. I should have ignored him at that concert when he responded, "Miss Shelby, I'm Ryder and I'd like to get to know you."

Oh, I had tried to pay him no attention, but that man knew how to sweet talk the devil right out of hell. I gave myself credit for only giving him my email address that night. No matter how much I hated him now, it still made me smile to think about him slack-jawed and sputtering. Not sure a woman had ever denied him her number, or possibly anything. After the initial shock he took it all in stride. "You'll be hearing from me, Miss Shelby."

Bright and early the next morning I received his first email of many.

Dear Chief,

You're in charge. I'll let you make the next move. I hope to hear from you very soon. I look forward to the day our worlds collide again.

Ryder

Did our worlds ever collide, like when hot air meets cold air and a twister forms, threatening to rearrange everything around you. That was never my intention, but I knew dating him would brew up a storm I'd want to take cover from. That's why it took me several days to respond to him. But I kept dreaming about his eyes and how they touched me physically. How when he said my name there was a whisper of familiarity as if I already knew him. Now I wondered if I ever knew him.

My thumb hovered over the delete button one more time.

"Do you really want to do that, Chief?" Ryder sounded in my head.

Yes! . . . No.

Chapter Two

MY HANDS WERE shaking so bad I could hardly write out the deposit ticket for the nightly bank drop. I wished I could say it was because I was overcome by the amazing sales day we'd had. Today kicked off Memorial Day weekend—the unofficial start to summer. Don't get me wrong, I was tickled with the store traffic and record-breaking sales day, but this weekend represented much more.

Emma had been good enough to break the Ranch's privacy policy to tell me that a certain someone would be checking in this weekend. I'd waited on bated breath all day for Emma to tell me when he had. She was doing double duty now, running the Ranch and helping Sawyer get his practice ready to open. She'd decided to quit working for the steel factory at the beginning of this year since her duties as a metallurgist weren't exactly conducive to a pregnant woman. The fumes she was exposed to daily there concerned her. Not that she was pregnant yet, but they were trying their hardest to become so. Two weeks ago, Emma had burst through the doors of the Ranch's main house to announce to Sawyer, who was watching a baseball game with Emma's daddy, Mr. Carrington, that she was ovulating, and it was time.

I'd never seen a man jump up so fast. Sawyer ran to her and swept her off her feet. He probably carried her all the way back to their cabin on the property in Shannon's Meadow. It was actually temporary housing for them. They were staying in her mom's and biological father's old cabin while theirs was being built nearby in the meadow.

Her family was an odd thing. Emma, come to think of it, had the weirdest family connections of anyone I knew. Not only had her momma married her biological daddy's best friend, the man who ended up raising Emma, but then Emma married her stepbrother.

That's right, her stepbrother, though they no longer held that distinction. Emma's daddy finally got that settled with Sawyer's mom, his ex-wife. What an ugly affair that had been. Josephine, Sawyer's momma, was even more overbearing than my own. And my goodness was she determined to get every penny she thought she deserved, which was way more than a year-long marriage necessitated. I think in the end, though, Mr. Carrington paid her more than he should have just to be done with the ugly affair. Not sure how much she got to keep of it, considering she'd hired every lawyer from here to Denver trying to overturn the prenup she'd signed.

But that was nothing compared to the way she'd behaved at Emma's and Sawyer's wedding last fall—the chilliest wedding I'd ever been to. Emma and Sawyer were determined to marry under the same pergola her parents married under. The same one that Mr. Carrington had placed in Carrington Ranch's outdoor amphitheater. So romantic. Emma and Sawyer also didn't want to wait until spring to get married after getting engaged in September. The lovebirds made it as far as October before they tied the knot. It started snowing during their nuptials. For most brides, it would have ruined the moment, but not Emma. She looked up smiling as if it were a sign from heaven. Sawyer kept brushing snowflakes off her hair and face between kissing her any chance he got. The sizzle between them was apparent and warmed all our hearts amid the freezing temperatures.

Everyone's heart but his momma's.

Right before the pastor pronounced them man and wife, Josephine yelled out, "Wait a minute, you never asked if anyone objected, because I do." She was escorted off the property while the snow swirled around her. Sawyer hadn't talked to her since, as far as I know. I had a feeling my own momma might have done the same if Ryder and I had ever made it that far. More like she would have made Daddy do it because appearances were everything to her. It's one of the reasons she hated Ryder so much. She wanted class and refinement; Ryder was in a class of his own.

Speaking of the awful man, had he arrived? I looked at my phone. Still no call or text from Emma. I'd kept trying to tell myself that I would remain unaffected by his presence, but I was having a hard time making myself adhere. I mean, I was planning to marry the man. I still had his ring. The one he sold his prized possession—his motorcycle—for.

Why did I feel a twinge of guilt? The man was a liar and a cheater. I should go home and toss the vintage wide-band byzantine diamond ring into the lake. At the very least I should sell it. There was a thought—I could use the money to go toward the down payment on the little place on Downing Street. The house I wanted reminded me of back home with a wraparound porch and a small balcony off the master bedroom that gave the best view of the nearby mountains. The white shutters against the buttercup yellow siding made this Georgia girl's heart sing. Mr. Jacobsen promised me he wasn't putting it on the market until the fall. He currently rented it out as an Airbnb and wanted to keep it one more summer season to maximize his profits. I only hoped the boutique made enough money for me to afford the down payment and secure the loan.

Memaw had offered to loan me more money, but I already owed her more than I liked to think about, though she said she was just deducting it from my inheritance. More than anything, she gave me the money because she loved needling my momma, her daughter. And nothing got to Momma more than me going against her wishes. She didn't talk to me for a week after I announced my engagement to Ryder. She and Daddy had gone as far as bribing Ryder with a lot of money to walk away. Ryder had not taken kindly to that and begged me to elope. As much as my parents and I didn't see eye to eye, I couldn't imagine being without my family and friends on what should have been one of the happiest days of my life. I'd dreamt my entire life of getting married at the old white Presbyterian church with the bell tower that rang after every wedding. I couldn't wait to hear them ring loudly telling the world that I was Mrs. Ryder Prescott.

Instead, I had been left with a shattered heart and a new address. The only loud ringing came from Momma hollering that she knew all along that she was right about him. Maybe it would be good to see him one more time. I could throw that perfect ring in his face and tell him exactly what I thought of him and his cheating ways. I'd lie to him and tell him I was over him like the Golden Gate Bridge and that he'd done me a favor. He thought so highly of himself that he would probably laugh and say something like, "Sure, darlin', you keep telling yourself that." Oh, I would. And I'd tell that dark-haired hussy he was with in the pictures that it was better her than me. After that, I would do my best to never see him again, even though we would be living on the same property all summer.

I still couldn't get over the fact that he was going to live at the Ranch all summer. Out of all the places in the world, why had he chosen it? Emma thought there was nothing coincidental about it. But why, after all this time, would he choose to be near me? Momma and Daddy said he'd never even come by the house looking for me after I'd left. I had a place of my own in Georgia, but when he found it vacated, I thought he would have at least tried to look for me. My parents' place seemed like a logical choice. Maybe he never even came by my place— I meant so little to him, he hadn't bothered to come tell me he'd moved on. None of my friends from back home had seen him around either. That wasn't too surprising considering he didn't live in Roswell—said it was too high class for him. Yet, now he was going to stay at a swanky dude ranch all summer. That just proved what a liar he was.

The man grew up in Eatonton on a dairy farm over an hour away from Atlanta where he worked. The fool commuted every day. It was a source of contention. He wanted to live in Eatonton after we got married, but I wanted to be closer to the hospital and civilization. Don't get me wrong, I loved going to visit Eatonton any chance I got. He had a sweet little place near his parents. And his momma and daddy were the kindest, most down-to-earth people I had ever known.

I felt terrible that I never said goodbye to them in person. I sent his momma a note telling her I loved her and I was sorry things didn't work out.

I mourned the loss of her almost as much as her son. She had mothered me in a way I had never known. She thought everything I did was wonderful, even when I put my elbows on the table and had two pieces of her pecan pie. She never reminded me about manners or expectations. She loved me for me and because I loved her son. "Many women have loved him for what they could see, but only you have loved him for who he is," she used to say. He did have a pretty exterior. A little too pretty, based on his indiscretion. I'd wondered if the brunette was the only one.

Macey opened the back-office door and popped her pretty head in. My mind welcomed the distraction.

"Hey, Shelby, Marlowe and I have finished restyling the mannequins in the display window. Come and look."

I was always excited and pleased to see what they came up with. Macey and Marlowe, Emma's identical twin sisters, originally ran the boutique, but they weren't all that business savvy. Unfortunately for them, Mr. Carrington was, so he decided the best course of action was to sell the store. Part of the deal when I agreed to purchase it was that I kept Macey and Marlowe on as employees. We had to work out some kinks at first. I knew it was hard for them to give up control and their hefty salaries, but as it was my name and livelihood on the line now, I had to take charge.

Macey and Marlowe knew fashion, but they didn't know anything about making a business plan or sticking to it. I may have decided to get a master's degree in nursing, but I minored in business. It was the compromise I made with my parents when I told them I wanted to be a midwife. They thought I would "outgrow" the silly notion and come to my senses. They agreed to hold off on grooming me to become the heir of Hobbs Inc., which owned over a hundred Hobbs Eye Centers across the country. More like they were waiting for me to marry a metaphorical crown prince to do the honor. Preferably someone we could merge dynasties with. That way my husband could rule the business world while I took over Momma's socialite duties and charities. From the age of eighteen, I was paraded around on the meat market of the future CEO's of America. I had my fair share of interest, even a proposal or two, but I knew I would only ever marry for love.

My parents may have had my entire life planned out for me, but I was never letting them choose my husband. It made them hate Ryder even more—not only did he not have the right credentials, but he made me see I didn't want the life of a Hobbs or a Duchane, two influential families brought together by greed and a lust for power. According to Momma, I didn't need to worry about it now because until I came to my senses and sold the boutique—or as Momma called it, a waste of time—I would not be inheriting Hobbs Inc. They could keep it all, as far as I was concerned.

I stood from my desk with an encouraging smile, happy to think about anything but Ryder or my parents. "Show me what you got."

Macey flashed me her beautiful smile and led the way.

Marlowe was climbing out of the display window when we approached. She brushed back her long ebony hair and adjusted her crocheted halter top, the same one we sold in the store. She looked stunning in it. I'd had the sisters model several of the pieces we sold in the store and plastered them all over our social media pages. It brought in plenty of men. I was sad to say how many of them left with items for their girlfriends or wives after they undressed the twins with their eyes. I was beginning to think that Aspen, one of the friends I had acquired from being friends with Emma, was right—most men were vile pigs. Her favorite thing to say to me was, "At least you found out he was a douche bag before you married the jerk and had a child with him." There was that.

Macey took my hand. "You have to look at it from the outside."

I smiled and played along, following her out into the warm evening air, hinting at cooling down. It still amazed me how warm it could be in the day here, but how chilly it could be at night, even in the summer. I took a second to soak in a bit of the evening sun. I hadn't been outside since lunchtime when I picked up food for the three of us. Though, I had barely touched my salad. My stomach was in knots thinking Ryder could be nearby. I closed my eyes and ran my hands through my curled blond hair.

"What do you think?" Marlowe had joined us outside.

I opened my eyes and turned to see the revamped window display. The array of neon hit me full force. It wasn't my favorite fashion trend but judging by how much we sold of the bright clothing, I was in the minority. Earth tones and neutrals for me, please. I blamed that on etiquette school. One of my instructors there always said, "Clothing should never speak louder than your presence."

I stepped closer to admire their handiwork. Though I didn't love neon, the window display was eye catching and inviting. I loved how they made the mannequins look like they were getting splashed with water. The sign behind the mannequins, dressed in everything from summer dresses to swimsuits, said, "Suddenly Summer. "

I faced both women who were anxiously waiting for my approval. "This is darling, ladies. I love it. Do you want to get a drink or dinner to celebrate the start of our summer season?" Anything to not have to go home and face what, or who, could be lurking on the property.

"Sorry, Shelby, I have a date with Jaime tonight." Macey blushed.

"The new guide?" Marlowe raised her right brow. The Ranch was offering guided backpack excursions this year for their guests since it bordered some of the most pristine Colorado hiking trails.

Macey bit her lip. "Yeah."

Marlowe's nose wrinkled. "He's not very attractive and he's shorter than you."

My eyes widened. I still wasn't used to Marlowe's bluntness. She never finessed a thing.

Macey scowled at her sister. "He's nice."

Marlowe rolled her eyes. "You could do so much better."

I gave Macey a comforting smile. "I would take a nice man over a handsome one any day of the week."

Marlowe flashed me a look as if I'd lost my mind. "You both can hang out with your *nice* men tonight. I have a hot date with Lance."

I was sorry to hear that. Lance was the owner of one of the local bar and grills. He was a womanizer. I would have thought that after

Marlowe's and Macey's unfortunate relationship with Sawyer's brother Ashton last year, she would have learned her lesson. Yes, this was another odd family connection of Emma's. Not only had Emma married her stepbrother, but Macey and Marlowe had, let's say, *carnal* knowledge of the other stepbrother. Neither of them knew they were both seeing the same stepbrother at the same time, but what a mess it all was when it came out last summer. Ashton still had a warrant out for his arrest stemming from him stealing several thousand dollars from the boutique. Hence the reason I now owned the store.

I guess that meant I was on my own for the night. "I hope you ladies have a good evening."

Marlowe wagged her brows before jetting off. "I know I will."

Macey gave me a sheepish grin.

I placed my hand on her arm. "Don't let what Marlowe said get you down. I've met Jaime and not only does he seem nice, but he's well-spoken and adventurous." The man had traveled around the world hiking some of the highest mountains and living among native cultures in places like Bolivia and Paraguay. "You'll have a great time."

"Thanks. He's going to make me a traditional Guatemalan dish called chicken *pepian*."

"Sounds interesting. You'll have to let me know how it is."

"Thanks, Shelby. Maybe we can go out another night."

"I'd like that."

Now I had to figure out if I should brave going home or see if any of my other friends were available. But first, I decided to walk to the bank after locking up the boutique since it was only a couple of blocks away and the temperature was mild enough that I only needed a sweater over my camisole. Also, it was a good excuse to avoid going home.

After dropping off the deposit in the night depository, I leisurely walked past the shops of Main Street, casually glancing at the storefronts. I stopped in front of Cove Café and contemplated going in. I hated eating dinner alone, but if this last year had taught me one thing, it was that I could be alone and okay. Especially after my little failed rebound attempt with Sawyer. Oh Mylanta, I know how wrong that was, but in my defense, I thought Sawyer and Emma were only stepsiblings and friends. I was grateful we had all moved past that, and that it made me realize I needed to let the dust settle and my heart heal before I attempted to have another relationship. Ryder had unfortunately stolen my heart and the battle for custody was still being hard fought.

I decided a dinner alone with a good book was the ticket. I headed for the café door and reached for it when a loud voice boomed, "SHELBY! SHELBY DUCHANE!"

My heart seized. I would recognize that voice anywhere. The question was, what was he doing here? I stepped away from the door and slowly turned toward the drawl so Southern it was dripping in biscuits and butter. An overgrown, slightly overweight man was barreling toward me, his arms outstretched. Before I knew it, I was in those big, burly arms being squeezed half to death.

"Shelby Duchane, girl, it has been a day since I've seen you. You're as pretty as you ever were."

"Bobby… Jay," I barely breathed out against his chest. He still smelled like muscadine wine. I swore he bathed in the sweet liquid. "What in the world are you doing here?" He was not the Prescott cousin I was worried about running into today.

He leaned away from me all smiles. His mop of dark hair ruffled in the breeze while his blue eyes danced. The man always looked like he was hiding something up his sleeve. "You haven't heard, huh?"

Oh, I had heard some things, but based on his mischievous grin, I wondered if there was more. But there was no way I was admitting to knowing a thing. That would have only meant that I was still taking an interest in his lying, rotten cousin. I stepped away from him. "Heard what?"

"I'm the new VP of Sales for an *upcoming technology company* in the area." He wagged his bushy brows.

I faltered back. He had to be talking about Prescott Technology. Why didn't he just come out and say it? And what was Ryder thinking making him the VP of sales? Last I saw Bobby Jay, he was the sales manager for a small appliance store outside of Eatonton.

Bobby Jay took pleasure in my shocked reaction. "Don't look so surprised, girl, you know I can sell mud to a mire."

I shook my head at the cocky man. It was a Prescott trait.

"You should see the deals I've closed for—" He looked up over my head.

"For who?"

"Me."

I froze on the outside while my insides ran hotter than a summer night in Georgia. Bobby Jay's eyes were daring me to turn around and face the man who I was fighting for custody of my heart.

When I didn't turn around for fear of acting unladylike, Ryder decided he wasn't done hurting me. "Miss Duchane," his smooth voice taunted me, egging me to turn around and face him.

He had only ever called me that once, during our first fight when I'd broken up with him a few months after we started dating. I had been tired of feeling like I was being torn between two worlds. He took that as I didn't think he was good enough for me. It wasn't that at all— I hadn't wanted my parents to hurt him anymore. But in his anger, he used the term only used by my parents' maids when they spoke to me. I acutely felt the slight and the meaning behind it immediately that night. When the tears had welled up in my eyes, he took me in his arms and apologized. He promised never to call me that again.

He was a liar.

I spun on my tan heels and faced the inconsiderate, arrogant man. Mylanta, was that a bad idea. Ryder had transformed from bad boy to business man, and I hated to say it, but it suited him well. His long, dark blond hair was replaced with a clean textured top, faded on the sides. He looked more boardroom than farm boy, right down to his crisp dress shirt with sleeves rolled up to his elbows and pressed slacks. I'd never seen him wear anything but jeans or . . . never mind.

I tucked some hair behind my ear before I remembered to act unaffected. I showed off my etiquette classes by standing tall with my shoulders back. But regardless of how proud I stood, my tongue was stunned into silence.

For a moment, Ryder also seemed to be at a loss for words while he perused me from head to toe. That was, until he did something far worse than insult me by calling me Miss Duchane. "Chief," he stuttered before shaking his head.

That stirred something fierce in me. How dare he use that term of endearment? He was no longer worthy of it. I fired back with the only thing I could think of. "Hello, Carroll."

Bobby Jay bent over in fits of laughter while Ryder's face turned redder than the radishes in his nana's garden.

That's right, two could play his game. Ryder's God-given name was Carroll Ryder Prescott and he hated it with all he had, but his momma had insisted on it, on account it was her granddaddy's name.

Ryder recovered quickly with a crooked smile that said he was ready to play any game I threw at him. But this wasn't a game, and we were never playing together again.

Chapter Three

I SAT IN a catatonic trance on Emma's baby blue floral coach obsessing about my encounter with Ryder and Bobby Jay. Not much more was said after the whole Chief and Carroll thing, except Bobby Jay invited me to have dinner with them. He was obviously out of his mind. Ryder must have been too because in a taunting tone he'd said, "Yes, Miss Shelby, why don't you have dinner with us? It's been so long. A lot has happened in a year."

How dare he mock me like that after what he'd done to me? I gripped the iced tea Emma was kind enough to pour me tighter. Wonderful Emma knew I loved sweet tea. I'd never had the heart to tell her that she was making it all wrong. Putting sugar in iced tea did not make it sweet tea. There was a process that involved steeping, baking soda, and adding the perfect amount of sugar while it was still hot until every last bit of it had dissolved. Then it was time to cool it. But I was so rattled after seeing Ryder and Bobby Jay that I couldn't think about putting anything in my stomach.

All I could do was look around the small cabin that used to be Emma's parents' place. My lands, did her momma love floral and pink. Her daddy must have loved her to live in such a feminine place. Probably the way Sawyer loved Emma so much that he was more than happy to live there temporarily among the ruffled pink curtains and the overly floral furniture.

Emma patted my bare knee. "I'm sorry I wasn't the one to check him in. I didn't know he had arrived."

I set down the tea in front of me on the coffee table, happy it was only Emma and me. Sawyer was out in the stables with Mr. Carrington monitoring one of the mares who was about ready to give birth. "Goodness, it's not your fault that liar bypassed you."

Emma raised her brow. "Listen to you being fiery."

"I know. I should watch my manners."

Emma laughed. "You're going to have to do better than that to be considered ill mannered. Why don't you yell or throw that glass in the fireplace?"

"Gracious, I could never break anything of yours."

"We're going to have to work on that." Emma smirked.

I gave her a small smile.

"So, you saw him. Then what happened?"

"Well, after I insulted him by using his God-given name—"

"Which is what, again?"

"Carroll."

Emma stifled her laugh. "As tragic as that name is for a man, we are going to come up with some better insults for you."

I put my face in my hands. "I know. I'm pathetic. At the very least I should have punched him, but I just had my nails done yesterday and he isn't worth ruining my manicure."

Emma shook her head at me. She was more of a tomboy. "You're not pathetic, but a swift kick to the groin would have been appropriate. I've seen your moves when you and the girls are working out. Which, by the way," she groaned and slumped, "do you think I could join you?"

I leaned away from her. She'd never wanted to join our cardio dance workouts even though I'd asked her several times. She was more of a runner and obstacle course kind of girl. I used to teach a couple of classes at the fitness center in the hospital I worked for. It was something I still enjoyed doing, so several nights a week I did a class for just Macey and Marlowe at home. Mr. Carrington had asked if I'd be interested in doing a group class once a week during the summer for the guests. I'd said yes before I knew who all the guests would be. He'd even offered to pay me, but there was no way I could take that sweet man's money. He'd already done so much for me, letting me live rent free in his home. The Carringtons had become like family to me.

"Of course you can join us. What brought this on?" I asked.

"I went to the doctor," she snarled, "because I'm still not pregnant."

"It's not unusual for it to take several months."

"That's what he said, but he also suggested that losing a few pounds might help. Fine, I get that. Maybe I've gained a few extra pounds on top of my already extra pounds since I've been married. Sue me for being happy and loving food. But, get this, he wants me to quit drinking Dr. Pepper. I'm not even sure I can go back to him now."

I had to laugh at her.

She leaned back against the couch. "I know it's not good for me. But I'm not certain my body would know how to function without it."

"If you would like, I can help you do a sugar detox."

"That's sounds awful and unnatural."

"Well . . . it will be hard at first, but I promise after a while you won't crave sugar at all."

She squinted. "That sounds like some kind of voodoo."

"If I knew any voodoo, I wouldn't be using it on you, Miss Emma."

"Ooh, that's good. Let's work with that line of thinking. What would you do to Ryder if you could? And what I mean by that is, I'm totally willing to make it happen. I know Jenna and Aspen will be too. Jenna has already promised me she would be the first one there with a shovel if ever I needed to bury a body."

I took a moment to think. What type of revenge would I seek against Ryder? Memaw always taught me that a Hobbs woman never sought revenge; instead, we never looked back. She said to give someone who has hurt us a second glance allows them to injure us twice.

With that thought in mind, I let out a deep breath. "I would want him to know that I've never looked back." That was a lie, but he didn't have to know that.

Emma took my hand and tilted her head as if she knew I was not being honest, but her smile said she understood. "Jenna will be disappointed that her services won't be needed," she teased. She patted my hand. "I would say the only thing you can do, then, is to use this summer to show him that you've moved on."

I wished changing addresses counted.

By the time I left Emma's, the sun was starting to set. I used to think there wasn't anything prettier than a Georgia sunset, but there was something magnificent about how a Colorado sunset set the world around it on fire. From the way the pine trees appeared ablaze to the way the snowy mountain peaks looked as if they were dancing in flames. I took a minute to take it all in while I listened to Grady's band play in the distance. It was the first performance of the summer season and from the sounds of the cheering crowd, it was well received. I could picture the swing dancing around the bonfire now.

I hoped a certain someone wasn't partaking since I had to walk past the barn to get to the main house. Was he with *her*? I wasn't even sure if the *her* was here. There I was looking back again. I wrapped my arms around myself trying to stay warm in the cool mountain air as well as lend myself some comfort. Seeing them together live in living color would only plunge the knife deeper into my heart. Was he really that cruel? How had I missed that?

I picked up my pace the closer I got to the barn on the dirt road. I should have changed my clothes before going to Emma's. At the very least my heels. All I needed was a twisted ankle, or worse. I tried not to look in the direction of the large crowd as I scurried past the barn. My peripheral vision caught the firelight from the bonfire and swift movement from the dancing guests. It was all I was hoping to catch. The main house was in sight and the path had evened out, allowing me to walk faster.

"Shelby! Girl, are you trying to sneak away?"

Blast that Bobby Jay. I slowed down but still moved forward, refusing to turn around. For all I knew, he had his cheating cousin and *her* with him. Before I knew it, though, I was being picked up and swung around.

"Come on, girl, I thought we were friends." Bobby Jay stopped spinning us around. His sincere blue eyes touched my own.

It took all I had not to get emotional. I swallowed the lump in my throat down. He was right; we *were* friends and I had missed him and the entire rowdy Prescott crew, minus one. I would keep telling myself that lie until it was true.

"I only want to catch up." He flashed me a smile that played between disarming and I dare you.

It was probably a bad idea but . . . "All right, fine, but put me down first."

He gave me one more good squeeze before setting me down. "Do you want to talk and dance?"

I braved looking in the direction of the bonfire. That was a mistake. It was as if I had caught a case of tunnel vision, including the nausea that accompanied it. All I could see was Marlowe and Macey cozying up to Ryder. Even from the distance, I could see him smile as those beautiful creatures pawed and played with him as if he were their new pet.

Where were their dates? While holding my midsection, I caught a glimpse of Macey's poor date, Jaime, standing nearby watching with the same kind of kick-in-the-gut reaction as me. Jaime was sizing up Ryder, and by the way his head hung, he'd decided he'd lose if he had to go head-to-head with Ryder.

I made the mistake of looking too long. Ryder looked up through the narrow passage between Marlowe and Macey and zeroed in on me. Our eyes connected and his held me hostage where I stood. I waited for him to smirk, gloating over his catches for the evening. Instead, his face pinched as if he was angry. What did he have to be angry about?

"I think someone else misses you too. Though the darned fool won't admit it," Bobby Jay stated to my side.

I whipped my head toward the big oaf. "That is a lie if ever I heard one." I marched off toward the house.

Bobby Jay followed. "I guess you don't want to dance?"

"What are you even doing here, Bobby Jay?" I shook while I walked and not from the chill in the air.

"I told you I wanted to talk."

"That's not what I meant." I began my ascent up the porch steps.

Bobby Jay's large hand engulfed my slender one. "Shelby, slow down. Give a man a chance to explain himself."

I closed my eyes, took a deep breath, and let it out. I did want some answers. "I suppose this calls for some sweet tea."

"I hope you have a pitcher full, darlin'. I think we have a lot to talk about."

Chapter Four

BOBBY JAY SMILED at the glass in front of him on the breakfast bar. "You remembered the lemons. Thank you."

"My pleasure." I took a sip of my own tea across from him, standing in the kitchen.

Bobby Jay looked around the grand home that was reminiscent of a ski chalet with exposed wood beams and majestic stone fireplaces. I particularly loved this kitchen that was in the heart of the home. Large and functional with enough counter space to feed an army, yet its rustic charm with a hearth and spiral staircase at the back that led to the upstairs made it feel cozy.

Bobby Jay took a large gulp of his tea. "Ahh. No one makes a finer glass of the house wine of the South than you, Miss Shelby Duchane."

"That sounds an awful lot like you trying to sweet talk me into something. Besides, I know you think no one makes better sweet tea than your Leigh Anne. Where is she by the way?" I hadn't asked in front of the café how his wife was as their appearance had made me forget my manners.

Bobby Jay slammed his drink on the counter, making it splash over. I quickly grabbed a kitchen towel and wiped up the mess on the granite.

"Sorry," he apologized with a bloodred face.

"Not to worry." I pressed my lips together and studied him. Particularly his wedding finger, which was missing a gold band. "Did something happen between the two of you?"

He clenched his fists before taking several deep breaths in and out. With the last big breath out, his hands relaxed and his face returned to its normal tan color. He patted the high back stool next to him. "Come sit next to me for a spell. I told you we had a lot to talk about."

I grabbed my glass, more than worried. He and his wife had been high school sweethearts. The epitome of a Southern romance. Bobby Jay was the high school quarterback and Leigh Anne was head cheerleader and prom queen. The entire town of Eatonton had showed up to their wedding—on the football field, no less. I'd seen the pictures. The reception was held in the high school gym decorated in streamers with a large balloon arch in their high school colors of green and yellow. It was tacky but cute. The kind of reception Ryder would have preferred and would probably have one day. The thought didn't sit well with me, especially knowing he was outside right now wooing Marlowe and Macey. As their friend, I would have to warn them that he was a liar and a cheat.

I took my seat, unable to relax next to my old friend. I missed the easiness that once existed between us. He must have felt my hesitancy too since he pulled my stool closer to him with a stupid grin on his face. "You know I'd never bite you. Ryder would kill me."

My left brow raised, questioning his statement.

He shook his head at me and took another drink of his tea, not bothering to try to convince me.

"What happened between you and Leigh Anne?"

He stared straight out into the kitchen. "She moved on to greener pastures."

"I can't believe it."

He grabbed his glass and emptied it. With a loud sigh he slammed it on the counter. "Well it's true. She said it wasn't fair that she never dated anyone else. Said we got married too young. And she started to resent that we could never have children of our own."

Bobby Jay had an unfortunate condition where he didn't produce any sperm. They'd been foster parents from time to time, but it never resulted in them being able to adopt.

"She never even gave me a chance before she went running off with Eugene Farnsworth."

I shook my head. "Old Eugene Farnsworth, the widower who owned the barbershop?"

"That would be him." Bobby Jay's lip twitched a bit. "Can you believe she was having an affair with him?"

I thought about that old leather face with hardly a hair to comb and his missing back teeth. "Why?" I asked in disgust.

"She said he appreciated her for the woman she is now, not the girl she used to be," he growled. "I did love that girl who captured my fifteen-year-old heart, but not as much as I loved the woman who made me into a man." His voice cracked.

I touched his arm that was about ready to bulge out of the sleeve. Not from muscle, mind you. Bobby Jay had never come to terms with the fact that he wasn't as fit as he used to be. He was still buying the same shirt size from his glory days. "I'm sorry, Bobby Jay, I know how difficult it is when the person you love betrays you."

Bobby Jay's eyes widened. "Point me in the loser's direction and I'll kick his a—." He gave me a crooked grin. "Pardon me, I forgot who I was talking to, Miss Shelby." He and Ryder always teased me because I didn't like it when they swore. At least at first. After a while, I found it endearing and realized it was a part of who they were.

But who cared about proper language at the moment? I leaned away from him, more than confused. Didn't he realize it was his cousin who would be the recipient of his retribution?

Bobby Jay gave me the once-over with his eyes. "Any man who would cheat on you is a fool. Does he live around here?"

"As a matter of a fact he does."

"Like I said, point me in his direction. Though I gotta say, you moved on mighty fast after Ryder. You women." He shook his head.

Us women? Now my ire was up. I pulled my shoulders back. "Did Ryder tell you why I left?"

"Well of course he did. Not that it was a surprise. I mean, no offense, Shelby, but we all told Ryder your worlds would never mix, especially the way your momma and daddy hated him. You probably did both of you a favor leaving the way you did. Ryder's still mad as hell about it, though."

He was mad? The nerve. I stood and started pacing. The anger was accentuated with each click and clack of my heel against the hardwood floor. I had a mind to go right outside and slap Ryder's face. Not only was he blaming me, but he didn't even have the decency to have anything more than a fling with the woman in the pictures. Surely Bobby Jay would have mentioned her already. Ryder was big on his girlfriends meeting his family. Ryder really did want to have his cake and eat it too. Which brought me to . . . I stopped abruptly and whipped my head toward Bobby. "Why did he come here?"

Bobby Jay's eyes lit up. "You're a smart woman. I would have thought it was crystal clear why."

"Enlighten me."

"Isn't it obvious, darlin'? He wants to prove to you he's as good as you are."

"I never thought I was better than him." Until he cheated on me, that is.

"The problem is, I don't think he ever thought he was good enough for you."

"That would be the first thing he was ever right about."

Bobby's brows hit his hairline.

"What makes him so sure now that he's better than me?" I asked, still pacing.

"I never said better, only equal." His smile said this conversation and my reactions amused him.

"Fine. Equal, then."

"Not sure he'll ever be equal to you—you are too fine of a lady— but I think he'll settle for as rich as you. Girl, he's come into a lot of money."

"So he came to taunt me? Well, you can tell him I never cared about how little or much money he made, and for his information," I smoothed out my skirt while staring him down, "my parents have cut me off."

Bobby Jay whistled low. "What did you do this time? Did you get yourself engaged to another commoner?"

I hated when he said things like that. I never thought of him or Ryder as commoners. I bit my lip thinking about how to put it into words. "I decided to become my own person, which is far worse to them. But that's neither here nor there. Tell me about this business you're both involved in."

Bobby Jay rubbed his large hands together. "Ryder is a genius of a man. Do you remember that app idea he had a few years back?"

I shook my head. Ryder didn't like to talk about his work when we were together. He said he'd rather be doing other things, including listening to me ramble on about mommas and their babies. I didn't even know he was thinking about going out on his own. The small company he worked for back in Georgia, which provided cloud-based construction management software, was the perfect fit for him—not too demanding with decent pay and hours.

Bobby Jay narrowed his eyes, surprised that Ryder had kept it from me. I wasn't surprised at all. He had kept a lot from me. And apparently from his own flesh and blood. How dare he let them think our breakup was all because of me. Because I couldn't handle the differences in our circumstances. I was willing to walk away from the money to be with him. I had willingly given him all that I had because I loved him and thought he was giving his all to me. But he threw everything away for some exotic looking hussy.

"Well," Bobby Jay continued, "it's an app that hooks up people with like-minded interests."

I rolled my eyes. "He created a dating app. Why am I not surprised?" Maybe that's how he met his fling.

Bobby Jay laughed. "It's no dating app. It's more like a friendship app. It pairs people or groups of people to go on adventures together, like skiing, rock climbing, or even scuba diving, depending on where you live or are vacationing. We have over five hundred resorts and companies so far that advertise with us and give discounts to those who book their adventure with them through the app." Bobby Jay sat up straight, pleased with himself. "I've brought in several of those companies, but it's Ryder who brought in the initial investment."

"I didn't know he had those kinds of connections."

Bobby Jay shrugged. "Don't think any of us did, but man alive was his investor happy to throw money at him. Ryder's done his part and given him a good return so far."

I held onto the kitchen table chair closest to me and swallowed. "Well, I'm happy for you. I wish you all the best."

Bobby Jay tilted his head with a thoughtful gaze. "Miss Shelby, don't you think for one second any of this has made him happy. In fact, I think he's more miserable than when you left without a trace. More than anything, I think he misses that he can't share this with you. Hell, he wouldn't admit it, but I think that's the real reason he came here."

I shook my head. "I don't think so. He left me, not the other way around."

Bobby Jay's eyes popped. "What are you talking about?"

"Never mind. Just answer me this. How did he know where to find me?"

"That is a good question. It's one he's never given me an answer to."

Chapter Five

IT DIDN'T SURPRISE me to see Momma's name on my phone the next morning while I finished getting ready for the day. I knew if my second cousin Arlene, who had sent me the article about Prescott Technologies, knew about it, Momma was sure to get an earful. Arlene had a devious streak, so she probably saved it for Sunday brunch this morning. She loved to stir trouble and she'd want to get the maximum effect. Momma called her the black sheep of the family.

I envied Arlene. She never let anyone tell her how to live her life. She had tried her best to teach me her ways. When I was seventeen, she gave me my first and last shot of whiskey and dared me to smoke a cigarette. I threw up all night and never touched either again. Momma had her banned from brunch for an entire year.

Her yearlong banishment only fueled her desire to be shocking, so when she returned, so did her boyfriends—who were all around my age, though Arlene was fifteen years my senior. She loved to bring her college aged flavors of the month to brunch just to hear my momma gasp and her momma, my great aunt Camila, drown herself in champagne. Though I was pretty sure Aunt Camila would drink her weight in champagne anyway.

I always appreciated Arlene's *special friends* since it took some of the attention off Ryder's presence. He was always good to endure Sunday brunch even though my parents ignored him unless they were looking down their noses at him. He didn't let it bother him. He, like Arlene, made sure he caught their attention by pouring on the physical affection. Kisses that probably should have been private, a brush of my hair, stroking my cheek. We did have a hard time keeping our hands off each other. Who knew he had that issue with other women? I held my stomach, still sick over it.

I stared into the vanity mirror at my red-rimmed, tired blue eyes then down at my phone, debating whether I should answer Momma's call. She may have cut off my funds, but she was holding on tight to the umbilical cord that had never properly been severed since my birth. Heaven forbid she give up any say in my life. Her last breath would probably be used to tell me what to wear to her funeral. I sighed. I hadn't gotten enough sleep last night after my talk with Bobby Jay to deal with her, but with the final swipe of peach lip gloss, I decided I'd better answer; she would keep calling if I didn't.

"Hello, Momma." I put her on speaker.

"Hello, darling, are you getting ready for church?" She never went right in for the kill. Pleasantries always came before the lecture.

"Yes, Momma." I smoothed out my white sundress, realizing I should have probably gotten some more sun before attempting white, but I'd been missing white since Labor Day.

"That's a good girl." She was ramping up. I could hear it in the pitch of her voice.

"I'm running a little late and I want to get a good seat," I said, trying to play to her sense of order and decorum. According to Honey Duchane, you must arrive at least twenty minutes early to church. This way God, and most importantly, the pastor and the congregation, knew what a good Christian you were. You must also make a sizable and *noticeable* donation to the plate.

For the past several months, when I did go to church, I was usually five minutes late, sat in the back, and gave what little I could. But I made it a point today to get up early enough to go. If ever I needed Jesus, today was the day.

"A few more minutes, darling; we rarely get a chance to speak anymore."

Whose fault was that? She had me on a yo-yo. When I did what she liked, she made the time to talk to me, otherwise I was of little consequence to her unless, like today, she needed to assert her all-knowing wisdom.

I sat on the edge of my four-poster bed waiting, holding in my desire to fidget. Why? Why did I always have to worry about appearances, even when I was by myself? I let my legs swing, releasing some of the tension.

"How are you and Daddy?" I tried my best to delay the coming assault.

"We're beautiful." I heard the lie in there, but she had to keep up appearances. "Daddy wanted to say hello, but he had a tee time he couldn't miss."

Montgomery Duchane always had something he couldn't miss that was more important than me. Another reason I was so attracted to Ryder—he wasn't obsessed with work, until the end. Perhaps even now he was. The thought pricked my heart, though it shouldn't. I was more furious with him now than when I left last year. That liar needed to get himself some Jesus.

"Lovely. I should—"

"You know, your daddy is playing golf with Barrett Chapel today. You remember him, right?"

How could I forget? The man my parents had decided should be my intended. It was a match made in heaven—more like the stock market. Barrett's family owned one of the most lucrative contact lens companies in the world. "Yes, of course. How is he?"

"Perfect, as always. He asks about you all the time. You two were such a gorgeous couple."

"Momma, we only went out on a few dates." That was all it took for me to see that the handsome older man was exactly like my father. Business would always be his first love. I would have only been an easy-in to an exclusive contract with Hobbs Inc., and someone to look good on his arm while we attended society functions together.

"You never really gave him a chance before that . . . *boy* came around." The disgust was apparent in her tone.

"He isn't a boy." Ryder was five years older than me, and believe me, he was all man.

"Speaking of that boy," she spat out, refusing to concede a thing, "I heard some ugly rumors about him starting a company and moving to Colorado."

"Did you, now?"

"Don't be smart with me. Arlene already told me that she sent you the same information."

"What does it matter, Momma? We're over. Ryder can do whatever he wants."

"You don't think his moving there has anything to do with you?"

"Why would it? He obviously didn't want me," I choked out. That was the worst thing I could have done.

"Don't tell me you still have feelings for the boy after what he did to you?"

"Whether I do or not, it doesn't matter. We're over."

"I'm happy to hear you say that, but be on guard, young lady. You're a fool if you don't think that boy didn't come there for you. Have you seen him?"

I lay back on my bed, telling myself to lie. I bet she didn't know he was living here at the Ranch. That wasn't in the paper. Surely they didn't have a private investigator following him now. It still didn't sit right with me that they had before. Obviously, it was good to know he was cheating on me, but to think my parents would hire a PI to spy on my fiancé bothered me on so many levels.

"Well, Shelby Katherine?"

"Yes, I've seen him. Not by choice. He's here with Bobby Jay."

"That overgrown oaf."

I sat up and took a deep breath and let it out. "Bobby Jay is one of the kindest people I know. And for your information, they've both made a lot of money over the last year." Money made people, in Momma's opinion.

"You can't buy class, darling."

"You're right. Good thing it doesn't cost a dime."

"What are you implying?" Her voice was telling me to proceed with caution.

Well, I was past living under her rules. "Only that some of the classiest people I've known have had little to no wealth."

"What a charming thought. Just remember you used to think that way about the boy."

"Will you please stop calling him that? He has a name. A name that no longer means anything to me, and I would rather not discuss him further."

"Yes," she responded curtly, "best not to ever talk about him again, or see him."

"I have no intention of seeing him again."

"Then I suppose my work is done. By the way, darling, Barrett would love a chance to catch up with you. I believe he has a business trip to Colorado scheduled. Be a good girl and say yes when he calls you."

There was no doubt who passed along my number. I had to take several breaths to hold myself together. How dare she continue to treat me like a child. "I don't believe I will have the time. Goodbye, Momma." I hung up.

I'd never hung up on anyone before. It was liberating. I let out a huge sigh of relief and stood, ready to face the day, my life. *My* life.

I faced myself in the mirror. I touched my pulled-up blond hair, making sure the tendrils fell just right. "You got this, Shelby Duchane," I said to myself out loud.

I headed downstairs via the back spiral staircase that led to the kitchen. It was closest to the part of the house I was living in. I was staying in Emma's old room. It had a full private bath and sitting area. It was smaller accommodations than I was used to, but I'd never felt so at home. That wasn't exactly true, but life with Ryder felt like make-believe now.

I entered the kitchen to find Mr. Carrington helping himself to the spread that Frankie, the Ranch's head cook, always prepared for us on Sunday. I could smell her blueberry muffins from upstairs.

"Good morning, Mr. Carrington."

He turned from the counter, holding a large muffin topped with streusel, smiling. "Good morning, Shelby. Are you ever going to call me Dane?"

I returned his smile. "No, sir."

"Then maybe you can teach my youngest daughters some of those manners."

I walked toward the refrigerator to get a bottle of water. "They do just fine at the boutique. They are the best sales associates I have."

"Glad to hear that. Make sure you help yourself to a muffin."

"I will, but it will have to be to go. I'm headed to church before I open the boutique."

"Are you going with Marlowe and those new guests? I believe they're from your neck of the woods."

I froze, staring into the contents of the refrigerator, forgetting what I was looking for. "Umm . . . No . . ." I stuttered.

"They seem like good men." He was half right. "I met them last night."

"Did Dolly's foal arrive?" I blurted, changing the subject.

"Yes, and she's a beauty. You should go have a look at her later."

I remembered I was in search of water and finally grabbed a bottle before shutting the refrigerator door. "I'm happy to hear that. I will after work. I should probably get going. Have a great day." I hustled out of the kitchen.

"What about your muffin, honey?"

I waved at him. "I'm not really that hungry."

"Have a good day," he shouted out. "Don't forget about the family barbecue tonight. Frankie's making your favorite, pecan peach cobbler, for dessert."

I stopped, touched that he always made me feel so included. I turned and faced the handsome older man. He had thick gray hair and soulful brown eyes like someone else I knew. "Mr. Carrington, if I haven't said it lately, thank you. I've treasured my time here."

The tips of his ears turned pink. "You've been good for this place and all three of my girls. You've brought back some of the sweetness that my wife used to breathe into this home, so thank you."

I reached up and wiped the tears before they fell down my cheeks. To be compared to his late wife, Shannon, was the highest compliment I could be paid. By all accounts she was a saintly woman, revered by all.

"Now you've made me cry and late for church," I teased. "Good-bye, Mr. Carrington." I had to get out of there before any unwelcome guests showed up. I prayed they were all attending a different church from the one I was currently calling home—the sweet little church made of stone near my future residence on Downing Street.

I opened the door to find I was, indeed, too late. Two men dressed in their Sunday finest, meaning jeans and a button-up shirt, were coming up the steps of the wraparound porch. I kept ahold of the door. Ryder in jeans, oh heavens. It was like they were made for each other. And I couldn't get over his new haircut. Had I known he could look so good with short hair, I would have suggested a haircut a long time ago.

He's a liar and cheat, I had to remind myself. My eyes drifted from the beautiful, deceitful man to the mischievous one looking awfully pleased with himself this morning.

"Miss Shelby, look at you, so beautiful on the Lord's day." He nudged his cousin, who was staring at me with eyes that waffled between admiration and anger. Mostly anger, judging by his taut jawline that was pulsating. "I told Ryder you can take the girl out of Georgia, but you can't take Georgia out of the girl. I knew you'd be headed to church and could tell us where we could find a place to worship."

"There are a few options," I stuttered. "I believe the Carringtons prefer the nondenominational church on Pine Street. Enjoy." My plan was to scoot right on past them, making as little eye contact as possible. However my eyes were begging me to inhale Ryder, if for nothing else than for old times' sake. Thankfully, my brain was still functioning and reminded my eyes what he had done to my heart.

Bobby Jay laughed at me while taking me gently by the arm. "Girl, which church do you go to?"

I looked up into his dancing wicked eyes. "Well, it's a small church; you probably wouldn't like it."

Bobby Jay smirked. "You've been to Eatonton; that's all we have, so fess up, girl."

Marlowe came strolling through the front door looking like a

Victoria's Secret Angel dressed in a sheer cream dress that only covered her lady parts. She certainly knew how to draw attention. For that I was thankful. Bobby Jay let go of me with his tongue a wagging. Unfortunately, I naturally glanced at Ryder. His eyes were wide with wonder too. He did love dark-haired beauties after all. I was sounding so bitter in my head. That was my cue to escape. I would warn Marlowe later about Ryder. By the way she laser beamed in on him, there was no doubt it was him she had her sights set on.

I was barely down the steps when I heard Marlowe say, "You never told me last night how you know Shelby."

"We are old acquaintances," Ryder quickly growled as if he didn't even want to admit to it.

Acquaintances? Acquaintances? I seethed. We were about as acquainted as two people could get. Now more than ever I was grateful I had never mentioned Ryder to Marlowe or Macey. Though we were friends, they were also my employees, and perhaps a tad on the self-centered side. It didn't make for the kind of relationship where you should or could confide your secrets.

"That's nice," Marlowe replied before moving right along. "I'm not really a church girl. We could go to breakfast instead. I just have to be to work by ten."

It had surprised me when Mr. Carrington said that Marlowe was going to church. I didn't think any of the Carringtons went that often unless it was on Christmas or Easter.

"Sorry, darlin'," I heard Bobby Jay reply, "our mommas would tan our hides if we didn't go to church."

That was true, especially Momma Jo, Ryder's momma.

Focus, Shelby, your heels were made for walking so make some double time. I followed the concrete path that led to the garage next to the house where Mr. Carrington had been so kind to make a space for my Audi. It was my graduation present from seven years ago when I received my undergrad. It was the first gift I believe Daddy ever picked out for me. Graduating from his alma mater, Emory University, was the one day I'd felt truly loved by him. I treasured the picture of me in my cap and gown hugging him in front of the expensive gift. It was probably the first and last time I had done something that my father was proud of.

With that depressing thought, I entered the code to access the four-car garage.

"Miss Shelby, where do you think you're going?" Bobby Jay hollered.

I ignored him and ducked under the raising garage door.

Dang that man's long legs, he was to me in no time, smiling like a cat who had cornered a mouse. "I see you are still driving your fancy little coupe. You know, me and Ryder got us some sweet new rides. Do you wanna take a spin in my new truck, or maybe Ryder's new Camaro?" He wagged his eyebrows.

Camaro? My nose wrinkled. That didn't sit well with me. Ryder drove old trucks and motorcycles, not expensive sports cars. "No, thank you. I'll be heading to work after church. Have a good day." I opened my car door.

"Shelby," he paused, "you're going to have to stop running one of these days and face him. He deserves at least that."

I couldn't meet Bobby Jay's eyes for fear I might not only cry, but tear into him. How dare he tell me what that man deserved. He had no idea what Ryder had done to me, to us. "He doesn't deserve the honor, not after what he did. I won't look back."

"Girl, what are you talking about?"

I stood tall and faced him. "Why don't you ask him?"

Chapter Six

I PARKED DOWN the street from the church in front of *my* house. For a few minutes, I took the liberty to stare out the car window at my little dream home. I tried to take comfort in it, knowing I had something to look forward to and reminding myself how far I had come.

I pictured all the things I was going to do to my home. For starters, I was going to put a swing in the big oak tree out front and plant purple coneflowers, columbines, and oxeye daisies around the house. Then I was going to adopt a puppy and a baby. I'd told Ryder I'd wanted a baby before I was thirty. Once upon a time he was happy to accommodate. I would be thirty next year on Valentine's Day. If only I could change the date, since that was the day that louse proposed to me.

I'd better get myself into church before I started having even more sinful thoughts of running him over with my car like I wanted to do this morning when I saw him walking with Marlowe toward the cabins.

It was a beautiful day with abundant sunshine, though the air still had a slight chill in it, but that would be gone by the time church was over. The street was sleepy except for a couple of runners who had passed by, and the grinning idiot who parked his too big truck in front of the sidewalk right in front of me. How had they found me? This was getting out of control.

I didn't wait for Bobby Jay or the other occupants in his truck to get out. Not that it mattered. Bobby Jay hopped out faster than a jackrabbit and met me on the sidewalk. He put his arm around my bare shoulders as if he was escorting me.

I looked up at him, put out by the whole business. "What are you doing here?"

"Worshipping, same as you."

"There are other churches in town."

"But you go to this one and I've missed your pretty singing voice."

I elbowed him. He only laughed.

I could feel the presence of Ryder and Marlowe behind us without them saying a word. Was this a date for them? Was Ryder so classless he would rub my face in it? The thought had me taking comfort in Bobby Jay's arms. There was nothing romantic about it at all—it honestly felt no different than Emma hugging me, except she was shorter than me and didn't loom as large as Bobby Jay. Bobby Jay did the kind thing and pulled me a little tighter.

"Why'd you park so far away? Don't tell me you're trying to lose weight, sticks and bones."

"It has nothing to do with that. I'm hoping to buy the house I parked in front of. I've been saving up for the down payment."

Bobby Jay craned his head back. "That little yellow thing?"

"It's darling and it has charm."

"If you say so, darlin'."

"Well, I do."

He chuckled. "It just seems a little beneath what you're used to."

I glared up at him. "What is that supposed to mean?"

"Don't get fussy with me. I've seen the mansion where you grew up."

I pulled away from him and walked on my own. "That's not who I am."

Bobby Jay turned around and gave Ryder a pointed look. Not sure what all that was about, but I was too chicken to look at Ryder. Instead, I stepped on a rock and faltered a bit.

Bobby Jay was quick to hold me steady. "Lands, girl, are you still wearing heels everywhere?" He stared down at my leather wedges and laughed. "This reminds me of when we tried to teach you how to mow a lawn and you wore shoes just like those"

I thought back to that day and had to smile. I had never done anything like mow a lawn. I was awful at it at first, but thankfully Ryder's parents had a huge lawn, so by the end—and after a twisted ankle—I could mow straight lines. Ryder and Bobby Jay told me I would have been better off doing it barefoot, but I was out to prove to them I could be stylish doing yardwork. I was ridiculous.

I nudged Bobby Jay. "I'll have you know I go camping now. *Real* camping. And no, I don't bring my heels. I can even pee in the woods."

Bobby Jay stopped and bent over to laugh. "You're yanking my chain."

"I am not."

Bobby Jay turned around. "Do you hear this, cousin? Our Shelby is peeing in the woods now."

I wasn't anyone's Shelby anymore, but I didn't voice my dissent. I did find some courage to face Ryder. That was a mistake. Immediately I was caught up in his eyes. They pulled me in like a tractor beam. My heart cried, yearning for him. My soul was so lost it didn't know what was good for it. It had been for a long time, yet here I was getting lost in those brown eyes that were so unsure of me. We both shook our heads at the same time to break the connection. I spun away from him and headed toward the church, seriously needing some Jesus in my life.

Marlowe, from behind, said, "I thought you said you barely knew her?"

A look passed between me and Bobby Jay that said we wondered how he'd explain that one. Bobby Jay couldn't help himself, though, and answered, "Oh, he *knew* her, all right."

Ryder cleared his throat telling Bobby Jay to shut up. "Does she really camp?" he asked Marlowe instead of answering her.

Marlowe took a second to process that she wasn't going to get an answer. "Shelby goes camping all the time with my older sister and brother-in-law and their friends. I'm not really into that sort of thing."

43

She was trying to impress Ryder. I had news for her: that wouldn't work. Or maybe it would. Sometimes it still amazed me how we got on so well being so different, but from the beginning it was as if this bridge existed, built by love and respect that connected us. Our differences only made us closer. Like how he taught me how to mow a lawn and I taught him how to follow the stock market and properly wash delicates. While he taught me how to fish, I taught him how to speak Latin. Latin never sounded so Southern and charming. And those fishing trips were always multicultural affairs. After Latin lessons I would get a lesson in French. French kissing, that was. Mylanta, was that man well-versed.

I had to stop thinking about those nights on the river bank, sweat dripping off us . . . Stop, Shelby. I needed Jesus. Or maybe a man. I rushed toward the church. Jesus was always the safest choice. He, at least, always kept His word.

The new associate pastor was greeting people by the door. He'd only been here for the past few weeks, fresh out of school and off a service mission in Africa. "Good morning, Shelby." He shook my hand, holding it a bit longer than I expected.

"Good morning. How are you?"

"Very well." His cheeks tinted red. "I was wondering if perhaps—"

Bobby Jay rudely cut off the poor man by taking my hand and pulling me toward the chapel. "Moving on. That associate pastor was acting like he wanted to do some private association with you."

Why did Bobby Jay care if he did? I knew Bobby Jay didn't have those kinds of feelings for me. He used to tell Ryder I was a beauty but he would stick to Leigh Anne, a woman who had a little more meat on her bones. And if he was pulling me away for his cousin's benefit, he was misguided. Ryder had made his choice. By the way Marlowe was looking at him with her come hither eyes, he would have another choice to make. That was, until I told her he was a cheat.

"All the men around here do," Marlowe exaggerated. "But she never gives them the time of day." That part was true. I always tried to be kind about it when I turned down any advance. It's not like I would never try again, but until I had full custody of my heart, it didn't seem fair to the other person. I wanted to make sure I was dating for all the right reasons, not just because I wanted to feel wanted.

Bobby Jay's brows raised to the sky. "I thought you said last night that—"

"It's almost time for the service to start. We better find a seat." This time I pulled Bobby Jay along with me.

I snuck into the second to last row. That dang Bobby Jay moved past me and sat on my left, leaving my right side wide open, and wouldn't you know it, but that louse sat next to me instead of taking the end of the pew and letting Marlowe sit by me. I scooted as close to Bobby Jay as I could. It wasn't helping. I could feel the same electricity crackle between Ryder and me. My body didn't know whether to sit on his lap or slap him Scarlett O'Hara style.

Ryder looked just as uncomfortable as me. He was sitting unnaturally still, though I had to say his eyes were fixed on my bare legs. The ones his hands used to rest on and caress. He could eat his heart out. Except next to him on his other side were a pair even longer and shapelier. The twins were known for those legs.

"I thought you told me last night that some idiot around here broke your heart," Bobby Jay tried to whisper, but he was awful at it.

There was sudden movement to my right. I could feel Ryder's gaze shift from my legs to my face.

Since we were in God's house, I decided it was best not to lie, and perhaps Ryder needed a come to Jesus moment. He could confess his sins right here.

"You asked if he lived here." I turned my head and faced the perpetrator. Ryder was waiting for me. Anger and confusion stirred like a chocolate vortex in his eyes. The only person he should be angry at is himself. I didn't let it deter me. "He lives here now."

Ryder's eyes went wide before narrowing. He leaned in and whispered close to my ear, making me shiver and catch my breath. "You and I are going to talk later."

I tried to act unaffected, but my hands were shaking so bad I had to hold them together. "Fine, Carroll."

He smirked before facing forward.

"I hope I get to watch the show," Bobby Jay laughed.

There was only going to be one private performance. I was going to have my say and then never look back.

Why did Marlowe have to invite them to the boutique? The better question was, why did they agree to come? Surely they had better things to do on Sunday, like drink beer and watch sports. I guess football season was a ways away, but I bet the Braves were playing. Or fishing. They both loved to fish, and rumor had it that Colorado had some of the finest fishing in the country.

I didn't like the way Ryder was studying me like he didn't know me. Like his slow hands hadn't memorized all my curves. Oh, I had to stop thinking about it.

I was so grateful when Miss Kate came in with her two daughters to distract me.

"Shelby!" Olivia, Miss Kate's oldest daughter, ran toward me. She was a pretty little thing all of fourteen years old.

I wrapped her in my arms. "Hey, sugar, how was the dance?" She had been in two weeks ago to pick out a dress for continuation. It was a dance they held for the eighth graders around here before they headed off to high school.

She squeezed me tighter. "It was so fun. I have some pictures to show you." While she reached for her phone, her momma and baby sister, Libby, made it to us. Libby in her momma's arms reached out for me. I happily took the redheaded cuddle bug. Libby snuggled right into me.

"She's getting so big." I smiled at Miss Kate.

"Ten months old today." Miss Kate beamed at her baby.

I kissed Libby's head and breathed in her baby fresh smell. My biological clock skipped a few minutes. It didn't help that Ryder was in my line of sight standing over by the accessories and handbags. He tilted his head and, for a fraction of a second, I saw the warm smile he used to flash me. It was almost as if I could see him remembering the dozen times I'd told him that my life would be complete if we had a curly redhead like the one I had in my arms now. But just like that, his smile was gone and he was back to staring at me as if I was a stranger to him. I flashed him my own look that said the feeling was mutual.

Olivia pulled up the pictures on her phone that she wanted to show me. "I think this one is my favorite." She blushed.

A gangly, nervous boy had his arm around her in front of the school. She was smiling up at him as if this was the greatest night of her young life.

"You are gorgeous. Going with the mint green was the perfect choice with that updo." I smiled up at Kate. "You did good, Momma, with her hair."

"That's what Pinterest is for," she replied.

I laughed and nodded.

"Nate said I had the prettiest dress there." Olivia bit her lip.

"Of course you did, darlin'."

"We've been telling everyone this is the best place to shop for clothing in the Cove," Kate commented.

"I appreciate that." I smiled down at Libby, who now had my tendrils wrapped in her chubby hands.

"We better let you get back to work." Miss Kate reached for Libby.

"Make sure you check out the sales rack in the back. We just marked down what was left of our spring line. You should check out the summer line too. I know you're getting ready for your cruise, and there are some lovely maxi dresses up front that would be perfect for you."

Kate wagged her brows. "You twisted my arm."

I gave Libby one more kiss and Olivia a squeeze before I said goodbye to them all.

Bobby Jay was quick to find me in the crowded boutique. He was holding up a neon pink tankini. "Do you think this would make my butt look too big?"

I laughed and swiped the swimsuit from him. "Give me that. Don't you have something better to do today?"

He flashed a sly smile at Ryder, who had moved closer to one of the mannequins in the store, before focusing right back on me. "No, ma'am, we're enjoying watching you run your hoity toity little store."

I rolled my eyes at him. "It's only a tad hoity. Definitely not toity."

His booming laugh filled the boutique. "We did miss you, girl."

I don't think *we* missed me. I placed the swimsuit back where it belonged.

Bobby Jay and Ryder followed, though Ryder kept his distance. Marlowe took that as her opportunity to chat him up. She needed to be helping customers, but I let it slide. My other sales associates, Talia and Holly, were also in working today. Macey had the day off and was supposed to be going with Jaime on his inaugural backpacking excursion for the Ranch.

"I saw you with that baby in your arms. Why aren't you working at the hospital?" Bobby Jay asked.

I tucked some hair behind my ear and without thinking began rearranging the swimsuits according to style and size. "I wanted something new."

"Uh-huh, you little liar. You loved your job as a midwife and whenever you were around you always had someone's baby in your arms."

That was just it—I wanted my own baby. Ryder's baby. "The licensing here is different," I gave him a poor excuse, "but I did act as an unofficial doula for one of my friends."

Jenna, Emma's best friend since forever, had a baby last November and she was determined to go natural. I told her I could help, so I worked with her before and in the delivery room. She did beautifully and her baby boy, Elliot, arrived safe and sound. Unfortunately, her husband, Brad, didn't do so hot. He spent most of the time puking and apologizing for being so lame. To this day he had to wear a mask to change his son's diaper. Emma and Jenna teased him about it whenever they could. At least he did it, so he got credit in my book. And the way he held his little guy was precious.

"So, the question is, Miss Shelby," he placed his large hand over mine on the rack, "are you happy here?"

I glanced at Ryder deep in conversation with Marlowe before meeting Bobby Jay's gaze. I gave him a small smile. "I am happy here."

Chapter Seven

"HE SAID HE hardly recognized her."

Emma raised her brows. We were eavesdropping on her sisters. I knew it wasn't polite, but Emma and I, and even Sawyer, were curious to see what Macey and Marlowe had to say about the new guests at the Ranch. We were sitting on the deck eating while they lay nearby on lounge chairs soaking in the evening sun. I did love them, but they were so self-absorbed. I don't think they even thought to check that I might be nearby listening to them talk about me.

Before I could stop myself, my jaw dropped in a very un-ladylike manner. "How dare he say that about me," I whispered. "Do I look different to you?" I asked Emma and Sawyer.

Sawyer looked to Emma to answer. He was a good husband and that was an unfair question for me to ask him considering I threw myself at him last summer. Goodness, I was still so embarrassed by that. Moving on. I had other issues at hand.

Emma pecked Sawyer before addressing me. "If anything, you look better. Really, how do you do it?" She grabbed her second bottle of Dr. Pepper and downed half of it. She gave us a cat-like grin when she set the bottle down. "I know. I know. I'm giving it up tomorrow."

Tomorrow started our sugar detox. I had to admit, I was reveling in my last glass of sweet tea before we embarked on our sugarless

49

journey. Poor Emma already had the shakes about it. I was shaking, but for other reasons.

"I think Shelby likes him," Marlowe snarled. "She totally tried to warn me off him. She said she heard that he cheated on his last girlfriend. I think she's just jealous because he was paying attention to me and not her."

She couldn't have been more wrong. I had never gotten annoyed with Marlowe, but she was testing my limits.

Macey turned her head toward her sister and lowered her shades. "Maybe you should listen to her. Shelby's the sweetest, and, well, remember last year?"

"Don't say his name," Marlowe warned.

Emma, Sawyer, and I all looked between ourselves with tentative expressions. We knew they were talking about Ashton, Sawyer's on-the-run-from-the-law brother. Emma rubbed Sawyer's back. "Sorry," she whispered.

He stood hastily and kissed his wife's head. "I'm going to get some dessert. I'll bring you both out some." He walked away without another word.

I bit my lip. "I feel bad."

Emma waved her hand. "Don't worry about it. It's not your fault my brother-in-law slash ex-stepbrother is a felon and a gigolo."

Emma made me smile.

"I can tell Ryder's not like you-know-who," Marlowe continued.

"How?" Macey was smart enough to sound skeptical.

"You know how country boys are. They go to church and open doors. He was a total gentleman. Did I mention that he can sing? You should have heard him at church. It was weird, though, because Shelby can sing too, and they sounded amazing together, like their voices were meant for each other."

I used to think so. I had to quit singing the hymns today because the reminders of us singing to the radio or out on the beach at night by a bonfire while he played his guitar got to be too much. Not to mention the way he looked over at me perplexed as if he had missed us, too.

Emma reached over the patio table and squeezed my hand.

I fanned my face. Acting unaffected was much harder than I thought.

"I wish I could have been there," Macey whined. "I'm so sore from hiking all day."

Emma rolled her eyes.

"I told you not to go out with Jaime." Marlowe sat up and patted Macey's head. "Good thing for you, I invited Ryder and Bobby Jay over. You and Bobby Jay would be cute together," she said condescendingly. "At least he's taller than you."

"Uh," Macey said, affronted, "what if Ryder likes me?"

I couldn't see it from my angle, but I could imagine Marlowe rolling her eyes.

"I thought you just said I should listen to Shelby about him," she taunted her sister. "Besides, I already called dibs on him," Marlowe stated firmly.

Macey sat up and challenged her with her stiff stance. "I don't remember that."

"We already went out. Sorry." Marlowe shrugged and lay back down.

Macey folded her arms and pouted. "You went to church. I would hardly call that a date."

I sat there stunned into silence. My employees were fighting over my ex-fiancé and he was coming here tonight. Not only that, but the only man I had ever truly trusted continued his betrayal of me. How could he say that to Marlowe about me? If anyone was unrecognizable, it was him. I wasn't talking about his new haircut and wardrobe, either. The man I thought I knew would have done anything to protect my heart and feelings.

"Shelby, are you okay?" Emma waved her hand in front of my face.

It took me a second to register she was trying to get my attention. "I'm fine. I'm not looking back. I can't," my voice cracked.

"Why don't you go inside? I'm going to talk to my sisters," she raised her voice.

Macey and Marlowe both turned our way, surprised to see us on the deck. Macey's face tinged pink, but Marlowe, ever defiant, shrugged her shoulders, though she refused to make eye contact with me.

I stood. "I think I'm going to go for a walk."

"Do you want me to come with you?" Emma asked.

"You are the sweetest, but I think I need some time alone."

Emma tilted her head, trying to decide what was the right thing to do. "Okay, but . . . I'm here for you."

"I know you are." I mustered up a smile for her. "Enjoy your Dr. Pepper; tomorrow we begin."

She grimaced before adoringly looking at her bottle of Dr. Pepper with doe eyes. "I better get pregnant after all this or someone is going to die. Starting with my doctor."

She could always make me laugh. "If you're going to kill someone, can I make a suggestion?"

Emma's eyes widened. "Very good, Shelby. Jenna will be so excited she can finally put her shovel to good use."

"I'm going to go. If you see Frankie, tell her dinner was divine."

"I'll make sure we save you some cobbler."

I nodded my appreciation and set off toward the lake first, praying I didn't run into any other native Georgians on my way. Macey and Marlowe weren't even their type. I wasn't Ryder's type either, but that was beside the point. If Marlowe wanted Ryder, she could have him. I had warned her what kind of man he was. And if he wanted a woman who only thought about herself, so be it. It would probably work out since he cared more about himself than he ever had about me.

I breathed the mountain air in deeply, trying not to think about him. The air was filled with the smells of campfires and Frankie's special barbecue sauce. One of the Ranch's perks was a full dinner served every night in either the large pavilion if the weather was amenable, or in the indoor dining hall that was also used like a community center. Guests could go there during the day and do crafts, or sometimes speakers would come in and teach participants about the history of Carrington Cove. They even had instructors teach about fly fishing or wildlife and plants. Very soon, guests could take an exercise class there from yours truly. According to Mr. Carrington and Emma, several people had already signed up for my first class, which would be held on Tuesday night.

I shoved my hands in the pockets of my favorite white shorts, thankful for the warm evening air. I didn't see anyone while I walked down the well-worn path to the lake. Most people were probably eating, and the lake was still too cold this time of year to swim in it unless you were adventurous. It did make for a beautiful walk, though, any time of year. However, I preferred this time of year when I didn't have to dress in layers. In my opinion, the lake was prettier unfrozen. I loved watching the ripples reflect the sun and the way the lapping water hit the rocky shoreline. The water was so blue and clear here. The lakes back home were murkier due to the red clay, albeit warmer.

There were a few couples and a family enjoying the scenery once I arrived. A dad was teaching his daughter and son how to skip rocks across the lake while the mom hunted for the smooth flat stones that were ideal for skipping. Emma had tried to show me how to last year, but I could only get two skips. She and Sawyer could make them skip for days. The little boy had the same problem as me and settled for just throwing in large rocks to see if he could splash his family.

I smiled at the scene as I walked past, trying not to be envious. I wanted my own little mischievous creatures to splash me unexpectedly with water cold enough to make you squeal like the mother of the two just did, to the little boy's delight. Oh, did he have a rascally laugh. It reminded me of someone's. Someone I was trying not to think about.

The cute couples holding hands and giving each other longing glances didn't help. Maybe a walk around the lake wasn't the best idea. It was then I remembered there was a foal to be seen. I headed toward the stables, my favorite part of the ranch. It was not a secret that Mr. Carrington was a passionate horseman. The stable he had built for the dozen or so horses he owned was one of the finest I had seen. My parents went to the Kentucky Derby every year and were acquainted with several of the breeders and owners, so I had seen my fair share of horse stables and silly hats. I'd even owned a few—hats, that is. The British had nothing on Kentucky Derby hats.

The Ranch's stable had more of a western flair to it, with a stone foundation and pine logs to finish it out. Not only that, it was the largest structure on the property. The upper level was where Mr. Carrington's office was. I believed it was his sanctuary. He had a large picture window in his office where he could look out into the corral and pasture to see his beloved horses. It also gave him a pristine view of the nearby mountain range. The stalls themselves were roomy and well equipped to handle any kind of weather Colorado was known for.

The large sliding barn doors to the stable were open when I arrived, allowing me to peek in before I entered. Most of the horses, it looked like, were out on trail rides or in the pasture. The only human in sight was Mr. Orton, Mr. Carrington's right-hand man and head wrangler. He was at the far end near the birthing stall where I assumed Dolly and her foal were.

I tiptoed in. "Hello, Mr. Orton."

The old wrangler in dusty boots and a large cowboy hat looked up from the bucket of water he was filling and laughed. "Honey, I'm a ranch hand, not a city slicker. You should call me Ray."

I bit my lip. "I'll think about it."

He grinned before setting down the bucket of water and stretching his back. "I'm guessing you came to see our new little one."

I nodded, eager.

"Come on over," he waved.

I practically skipped like a schoolgirl I was so giddy.

Dolly poked her beautiful Palomino head out to greet me. I could see in her brown eyes that she was tired, like any new mother would be. I rubbed her muzzle. "Hey there, girl." I peeked in the stall to see her chestnut foal curled up in the hay not far from Dolly. "You did good."

"Another filly," Mr. Orton informed me.

"She's beautiful. Does she have a name yet?"

"Madison."

"I like it."

"Dane picked it out."

Dolly nudged me to make sure I didn't miss any of her spots. She and I were well acquainted. I'd spent my fair share of time out in the stables talking to her. Not sure why I chose her to tell all my cares to. Maybe it was her understanding eyes or her docile manner. I moved my hand up to rub her forehead and then her neck. "How's the momma doing?" I asked Mr. Orton.

"She came through it like a champ." He patted her neck. "I have to head out. We have a group coming back from a trail ride. As always, you are welcome to stay as long as you like. You know where we keep the apples and carrots. Dolly probably wouldn't mind a treat or two." He gave me a wink.

"Thank you, Mr. Orton."

He shook his head at me. "You're too polite to live here."

"Have a good evening," I called to his retreating figure.

I sighed and kissed Dolly's muzzle. "It's just you and me. Sweet girl, these last few days have been something. Remember my ex-fiancé I told you about?"

I swore Dolly nodded her head.

"Well, he's here. I recommend that you stay away from him. He can charm just about anyone. It's the eyes and the accent. Don't fall for it." I walked toward the refrigerator near Dolly's stall that was made to look like a cabinet to grab her an apple or two. Her favorite was the pink lady variety.

Dolly eagerly gobbled up the first apple, always careful not to nip.

"You know," I rubbed Dolly's head while she chewed, "he said he hardly recognized me. Can you believe that? I have half a mind to go find him and tell him off. What do you think?"

"I think he'd be interested to hear what you had to say."

I dropped the extra apple, hoping by some miracle Dolly had learned to talk, but that voice was unmistakable. I slowly turned in the direction of the voice that could charm anybody into about anything. I'd had firsthand experience.

He stood at the entry with the sun behind him showing off everything God had given him, including his cocky smirk.

"What are you doing here?" I stuttered.

"It's time, Shelby."

Chapter Eight

I WANTED TO crawl in Dolly's stall with her despite the less than appetizing smell and the pile of manure in the corner. It was surely better than the pile sauntering toward me.

Dolly nudged me as if to say *stand tall, girl.* I did my best. "How did you know I was out here?"

Ryder let Dolly smell him before he patted her. The traitor Dolly acted as if she enjoyed it. She even closed her eyes like I used to when he stroked me.

"I heard there was a new foal and wherever there's a baby of any kind, you're sure to be around," Ryder spoke more to Dolly than me.

My heart pounded so hard I was finding it difficult to form a reply.

Ryder picked up the apple I had dropped and started tossing it in the air and catching it with one hand. His troubled eyes made contact with mine. "Why, Shelby?" Anger surrounded my name.

I shook my head—my own anger welling up inside. "You know why I left."

"I heard that bull you told Bobby Jay about me leaving you. It was called a business trip and you knew I was coming back. Hell, I came back early. You want to know why?" His voice raised.

I said nothing.

"I'll tell you why. Because my fiancée's phone number no longer worked and none of my relations could get ahold of her. I drove all night to make sure you were okay, and guess what I found?" His eyes seared into mine. "A moving truck in front of your place." He shook his head in disgust. "My momma got a note that day saying you left and weren't coming back." He stepped closer, heat and anger rolling off him in waves. "How could you? No decent person would do what you did."

I got right in his face. "How could I?" I cried, reaching into my pocket to get my phone, fumbling from shaking so bad. I was trying to pull up those god-awful pictures I had been refusing to look at since the first time Momma sent them to me. I don't even know why I saved them. Maybe for this very moment. It took me a few tries, but I was finally able to pull them up.

Sick. I felt sick even seeing a glimpse of another woman in his arms.

I shoved the phone in his face. "You want to talk about decency? Let's talk about your supposed business trip. Looks a lot more like pleasure to me!"

His eyes widened before he grabbed my phone and began swiping through the pictures at a furious pace. With each swipe his face turned a deeper shade of red.

"How. Could. You?" Tears poured down my cheeks. "I loved you. I believed in you even though you had been *working* longer hours and putting me off more and more. Mine wasn't the only phone that didn't seem to work anymore. At least I didn't give you the pathetic excuse that I was busy."

That lit a fire in him. He threw Dolly's apple, making me jump as it splattered against the wall. "Who in the hell took these pictures?"

"Why does it matter?"

He gave me a look that said it was a matter of life and death.

"A private investigator," came spilling out of my mouth before I could stop myself.

"Did you hire the PI?" he spit out.

"No. I trusted you."

"If that were true, Shelby, we wouldn't be here right now."

"Why, because I wouldn't know the truth? Wouldn't know that you took that hussy to *our* place?"

Ryder's jaw tightened before he held up my phone. "Think about that Shelby, and look at these damn pictures again."

I closed my eyes. I couldn't stomach it.

"Look!" Ryder yelled.

My eyes flew open but landed on him. "I've had my fill of them."

He lowered the phone, seething. "Maybe Bobby Jay was right; you did me a favor leaving like you did. I was wrong today to think maybe you had changed, that you no longer let your momma and daddy rule your world, but they're still calling all the shots. I loved you, Shelby." His eyes welled with tears. "This last year has about killed me, but I would never want a wife who wouldn't have at least given me the chance to explain. Who wouldn't have given some thought before she up and left and wrecked my world. Did I mean so little to you?"

His words and tears pierced not only my heart but made me begin to question all I knew. "You meant everything to me," I whispered.

He shoved my phone in my hand. "No darlin', like I said, we wouldn't be here if that were true. Goodbye, Shelby." He turned and strode off.

"Wait," I begged.

He stopped but didn't turn around.

"Who was that woman?"

His shoulders dropped. "I don't know her anymore." His boots echoed heavily against the concrete floor making me feel hollow and more alone than I had ever felt.

I stared down at my phone—at Ryder and the woman tangled up with one another at *our* beach, Rosemary Beach. Her long, dark hair was draped around them. Her leg wrapped around his just like . . . Oh . . . I looked closer. I noticed the red flag in the distance that warned beach goers not to enter the water. It was the same flag that was up the last time we visited. We found other things to do that day on the beach, much like the . . . or maybe exactly like the couple in the picture. I tilted my head, my heart beating out of control. My hair was eerily similar to the woman's in the photo, except for the color. Our hair curled the exact way in the sea air.

No. No. No. I would never wear a neon green cover up. I swiped to the next picture, trying to tell myself I hadn't misjudged or been swindled. That I hadn't thrown away the best thing that had ever happened to me.

The next photo was of Ryder and that woman eating at our favorite restaurant by the beach, Cowgirl Kitchen. They sat at the same table with the red umbrella just like we had. She was feeding him with her own fork, just like I loved to do. But she was wearing something I didn't own. And that tacky floral hat she was wearing was atrocious. Her face was hidden, but her hair. . . *Her hair?*

I leaned against the stall door. Dolly nudged me with her cold nose.

"Oh, Dolly, I think I made a horrible mistake."

"These are really well done. It would be hard to tell they had been photoshopped unless you knew what you were looking for." Jenna was trying to make me feel better while I lay in Emma's lap. Emma stroked my hair while Aspen sat on the floor near me trying to feed me dark chocolate, to no avail. I thought I might vomit. When I refused them, she shoved them in her own mouth.

"The one on the beach is most obvious. Every aspect is too in focus. Multiple pictures were used to produce this." She set down my phone on Emma's coffee table. "I'm sorry, Shelby."

I had no words, only tears. Lots and lots of tears.

Aspen leaned over and peeked at my phone. "Wow." She tilted her head several times, getting in every angle. "That beach picture. I hope it was a private beach."

I groaned. It was mostly private, but like I'd said before, we had a hard time keeping our hands off each other.

"Those pictures are pretty hot," Jenna added. "That PI must have enjoyed his job."

I curled into myself, sick thinking that my flesh and blood—my so-called parents—had paid someone to not only spy on me, but to doctor pictures to make me think the love of my life had cheated on me. The worst thing was that I had believed them. I hurt the man I loved—love. The man who now hated me and had every right to.

Aspen picked up the phone and swiped through the pictures. "You two were obviously in love."

"I know," I blubbered. It was the most I had articulated since I arrived at Emma's, fell into her arms, and regurgitated what had happened in the stable. She'd called Jenna and Aspen for backup while Sawyer did the smart thing and left.

Emma began blotting my cheeks with tissues. She put one up to my nose. "Blow." That was a good friend, there.

I obediently blew.

Emma tossed the tissue to the side and went back to stroking my hair. "What are you going to do?"

"What can I do? He made it clear he doesn't want anything to do with me, and I can't blame him. I should have known my parents might do something like this."

"They must really hate him," Aspen commented.

"You have no idea. They offered him money to walk away from me. I didn't think they could get lower than that."

"Dang!" Jenna exclaimed. "Your life is like a soap opera."

It really was.

"This could be good, though," Jenna continued. "In soap operas all the hot couples get back together. It's good for ratings. The guy here is probably not even Ryder. It could be his evil twin who's locked up the real Ryder and the real Ryder is screaming from his prison right now, 'Just hold on Shelby, I love you! I'll find a way out of this hell hole if it's the last thing I do!'"

We all busted out laughing while Jenna dramatically acted out the scene.

When the laughter died down, I went back to sniffling. "If only that were true."

Aspen unwrapped another piece of dark chocolate. "You're better off without him. Eventually he would have screwed you over. They all do."

"Aspen." Emma threw a wadded-up tissue at her. "Not all men are like your ex."

Aspen rolled her eyes. "You're in the honeymoon phase. I had one of those too. Then the d-bag left me and our baby for a woman he met at a bar."

"I stand by my comment; not all men are like your ex." Emma was fiercely loyal and in love with Sawyer. As she should be. He really was a good guy. He reminded me a lot of . . . well . . . thinking about him only made me tear up more.

Aspen shrugged her shoulders. "Be that as it may, I don't ever plan on finding out."

"Whatever." Jenna ruffled Aspen's hair. "All it would take is one sexy Brit to walk through the door and you'd be eating those words."

Aspen had a bit of an obsession with the BBC. She said she loved their humor, but we all really knew she fancied the men and their accents.

Aspen pressed her lips together trying not to smile. "Since there are no sexy Brits around here, I think I'm safe."

"You never know," Emma sing-songed. "We get a lot of tourists who come through our town."

Aspen popped another piece of chocolate in her mouth. "Fine. If a tall, dark Brit with aqua eyes comes around, call me. After you've made sure he's single and done a background check," she teased. "But enough about me." Aspen swiped my brow as she would Chloe's, her twelve-year-old daughter. "Is he really worth all these tears?"

I closed my eyes and a thousand reasons flooded my memory. Everything from the way he loved his momma to the many times he showed up after work, even in the middle of the night when those babies seemed to love to come, just so he could kiss me good night and make sure I made it home safely. One time I caught an awful stomach virus and he stayed with me, holding back my hair each time I vomited. It was so bad I fell asleep on the bathroom floor. When I came to, he was right there beside me, holding my hand. That summed up our relationship until the end; he was always right there beside me, holding my hand through the good and the bad.

He was right. After all we had been through, I shouldn't have left without speaking to him, no matter how damning the evidence appeared.

I opened my flooded eyes and nodded. "He is."

Chapter Nine

"I CAN'T TAKE it." Emma grabbed onto my arms and gave me a gentle shake. "I. Need. Sugar."

"Darlin'," I took her hands and held them firmly in my own. "The first couple of days are the hardest. You're almost through day two."

"I can't do it. Today I begged Sawyer to drink some Dr. Pepper so I could kiss him right after, just to get a little hit."

I tried to suppress my laugh. "Did he?"

"NO! He said he wouldn't be my dealer."

I squeezed her hands. "After our exercise class, we are going to go back to the house and split a 100 percent dark chocolate bar dipped in almond butter. It will help curb your craving."

She squinted. "That sounds awful."

"We could broil a grapefruit," I suggested as an alternative.

She shook her head. "This is what hell must be like."

I laughed. "You got this. I promise you, in a week, you won't give Dr. Pepper a second glance."

"Shelby, I love you, but you might be the person I end up killing at the end of this."

"Just make it painless." To be pain free at the moment would be a godsend. I wasn't sure which hurt worse, the guilt or the all-consuming loss.

Emma pulled me to her and hugged the air out of me. "I'm sorry. I shouldn't have said that to you right now. Have you seen him?" she whispered in my ear.

I shook my head against her. "I think he'll be doing his best to stay away from me for the remainder of his stay, and probably the rest of his life," I choked out.

She patted my back. "You never know. I mean, Sawyer married me even though my dad divorced his mom and I want to stab something every time I hear her name. Not to mention I accused his brother of stealing and adultery in front of a large audience."

A small laugh escaped me. "True, but you didn't skip town without a trace. Or accuse him of cheating on you with . . . yourself."

"Well . . . okay, that's definitely worse, but—"

"No buts." I pulled away from her with the fakest of smiles. "I made my choice and now I must find a way to come to terms with what a horrible, awful person I am."

"Shelby, you are one of the sweetest people I know. I mean, heck, I couldn't even hate you when I thought you were trying to steal my man."

I cringed and bit my lip. Another reminder of how clueless I could be, or maybe blind was a better word. I saw the signs between Emma and Sawyer, but because of their unusual connection at the time, I ignored it because I was hurting and hoping Sawyer could help me heal.

With Ryder, I was so hurt and infuriated about those pictures I didn't stop to think about how uncharacteristically kind my parents were behaving. Or how they had everything lined up for me so I could start over here in Colorado. Pain had blinded me. I'd desperately wanted a quick fix. I should have known my love for Ryder wasn't going to go away easily, or perhaps ever. I should have been brave enough to confront him. Running from problems never solved them. I knew that. Now I was paying the price for it.

"Emma, I deserve to think ill of myself."

She placed her hand on my arm. "That should be directed toward your parents."

Oh, believe me, I had directed some feelings toward them. I had left them some very unladylike messages. They hadn't had the decency to answer when I called the first time, or even respond to my message. Like they somehow knew this was all going to come out. It made me wonder what else they lied about over the years.

"I have enough feelings on the subject to loathe all of us," I responded.

Emma rubbed my arm. "I promise it will be okay. My mom used to say just because you can't see how it will work out, doesn't mean it won't."

I sighed. "Maybe Ryder was right—I did him a favor."

Emma shook her head. "I can't believe that. I saw those pictures." She wagged her brows.

I bit my lip, embarrassed. "We always had . . . chemistry."

"That's a word for it." She laughed.

"It's not the only reason we *loved* each other," I cried. He loved me, as in past tense.

"Aww, Shelby."

I stood up tall, though I was anything but proud of what I had done. "Let's go do some cardio." I reached for her hand and pulled her into the dining hall. The place reminded me of a lodge, with all the stone and the large fireplace in the center. There were already several women there in varying types of workout apparel ready to burn some calories. Emma knew a few of them so she left me to set up while she spoke to them.

Emma carried the title of Lady of Carrington Ranch and she took her duties seriously. She followed in her mother's footsteps and tried to make every guest feel as if they were family. It's why so many people came back year after year. I think at times Emma missed her job as a metallurgist but watching her smile and easily converse with the guests as if she saw them every day made it seem as if she was born for this life and job. I knew as soon as their eye center opened next week that she would bring that same warmth and feeling. There was no doubt it would be successful. Both she and Sawyer knew how to treat people right.

I thought I did, but goodness was I wrong. I breathed out, trying to put it out of my mind if only for a few minutes. I plugged my phone into the speaker and pulled up my playlist for the night. In the background, I could hear people filing in. One voice was unmistakable.

"SH-EL-BY!"

I turned to find Bobby Jay heading my way looking ridiculous in a T-shirt he'd ripped the sleeves off that announced to the world that he was too sexy for his shirt. If that wasn't enough, he wore a thick cotton headband pushing his dark hair up, making him look crazed.

"What are you doing here?"

He looked around at all the women and then back at me. "Girl, what do you think I'm doing here?"

"I hope you aren't trying to pick up women."

He pulled me in for a bear hug. "Honey, I can't help if the women just flock to me."

I laughed against him. Once upon a time that might have been true.

"Look at you, laughing at me and here I came to see you."

His thoughtful tone caught me off guard. I leaned away from him.

He tapped my nose. "I've been meaning to see how you're doing but getting a new office up and running is time consuming. After a month, I think we are almost there."

I stepped farther away from him. "How long have y'all been in town?"

A mischievous grin erupted on his five o'clock shadowed face. "Girl, we've been going back and forth for the last few months. You don't think you can just up and move a company and open a new office?"

"Well, no . . . I just . . ."

"Yeah, Shelby, we've been around for a while."

"So why stay here now?"

He let out a heavy breath and scrubbed his hand over his face. "I think Ryder was holding out some hope . . . until . . ."

"He found out how awful I was?" Tears popped up in my eyes.

He pulled me to him. "Don't cry, girl."

I pushed away from him. "I'm fine. I'm fine. I have a class to teach."

He looked me over in my sports bra and tight leggings. "You are most certainly *fine*. Too skinny for my taste." He gave me a wink. "But there's not a man around who wouldn't be attracted to you."

"I can think of one."

"That's where you are wrong, Shelby. Why do you think he's so angry?"

"Because he hates me."

He shook his head. "No, ma'am. I think he'd like to. It would be easier on him. Don't worry about him right now." He gave me a little push. "I came here to sweat, girl."

"Uh-huh. I think you came to see some women sweat."

He wagged his brows. "What kind of man do you think I am?" His laugh filled the large space. "Come find me afterward."

I waved him away. The crazy man. He found a spot right in the middle surrounded by a few younger women who giggled at him. He ate it right up and charmed them with his Southern accent.

Marlowe and Macey hustled in with the crowd. Macey gave me a wave and a smile, but Marlowe avoided any eye contact. She had been since Sunday. I had a sinking feeling why. Today she only worked a half day. I overheard her tell Macey that she was heading up to Edenvale to meet someone for lunch. A certain ex's company just happened to be in Edenvale. I rubbed my stomach and took deep breaths to stave off how nauseous that made me feel.

Meanwhile, Bobby Jay was hollering, "It's the M&M twins! You girls come on over here and show me how it's done."

Marlowe rolled her eyes while Macey smiled on their walk over to him.

It was time to get things started. I turned on the wireless mic I had attached to myself. "Welcome ladies and *gentleman*." I flashed Bobby Jay a grin. "I hope y'all are ready to have some fun dancing while we burn some calories."

"Yeah, girl!" Bobby Jay yelled, making everyone laugh except

Marlowe, who raised her brow at him. I wanted to shake her and tell her she would be so lucky to have a man like Bobby Jay, but I had a feeling she was getting the best man I knew.

Chapter Ten

"Great class."

"That squat song was amazing. I'm going to have buns of steel after this vacation."

I was pleased with how many women came up after class and thanked me. But no one was as enthusiastic about it as Bobby Jay. During class he was everyone's cheerleader. I don't think he had ever met a stranger. He ran up afterward, dripping in sweat, and picked me right up and swung me around. "Dang, girl, I forgot how much you could swing those tiny hips of yours."

I had forgotten how ripe a Southern boy could get in the summer. I tried not to take deep breaths. "Thanks, Bobby Jay."

He set me down. "You want to take a walk or maybe go get a beer? Or your fancy little umbrella drinks you always used to get?"

I peeked around him at Emma, who was walking our way wiping sweat off her brow. "I'd like to, but Miss Emma and I have a date with some pure chocolate and almond butter."

Bobby's face contorted. "That sounds god awful."

"Doesn't it, though?" Emma agreed.

"Hello, Mrs. King." Bobby Jay tipped his head. "How are you this evening?"

She stretched her back. "Sore," she groaned. "Shelby, I think I'm going to take a rain check on us gagging together."

I shook my head and laughed. "It's not that bad."

"I'll take your word for it. Good class, by the way. Now I know why you look like you do. I'm not sure it's worth it."

"You're gorgeous just the way you are."

Bobby Jay gave her a once over. "I'd say Mr. King is a lucky man."

Emma actually blushed. It was cute. "Speaking of my husband, I'm off to find him. I think he may need to carry me home. I thought I was flexible, but I was wrong. So, so wrong." She pulled up her leg to stretch her hamstring.

"Do you want me to walk you to your cabin?" I offered.

She shook her head. "I got it. Why don't you go have a drink, and I will too. A deep, dark one," she sighed.

I placed my hands on her shoulders. "You got this. Drink some lemon water—it will help."

"Shelby, please don't make me hurt you," she teased. I hoped.

Bobby Jay laughed at Emma before holding out his hand to me. "Looks like we have a date."

We said our goodbyes after I gave Emma the peppiest of pep talks about how denying herself now would make it that much easier to do it the next time. I'm pretty sure she didn't appreciate it by the way she growled at me. She left muttering that if she didn't get pregnant after all this she was suing her doctor for malpractice.

I agreed to a walk around the lake with Bobby. I figured with him I wouldn't feel so lonely this time. I did have to ask him, though, as we made our way down the well-worn path, "Why are you being so nice to me?" He and Ryder were more than cousins—they were best friends. What you did to one was like doing it to the other.

He tilted his head and squinted as if I'd spoken to him in a foreign language. "You were always good to us. Generous to a fault. Whenever one of us was sick, you were the first one there with a meal and words of comfort. And we all know it was you who paid for little William's surgery."

I bit my lip and stared out into the distance. I never wanted anyone to know that. William was Bobby Jay's younger half-brother. He'd fallen out of a tree and broken his arm. His family didn't have insurance at the time. I worked out the surgery and payments with one of the surgeons I knew at the hospital I was employed at.

He gave me a crooked grin and nudged me. "You became family, Shelby. You don't stop loving family, even when they do stupid things."

I wrapped my arms around myself. "Stupid is one word for it."

Bobby Jay put his arm around me too. "Why didn't you talk to him?"

I thought about what I should say as we walked in companionable silence all the way to the lake. I didn't want it to sound like I was blaming Ryder. I knew full well our breakup was all mine to bear, well, and my parents, but ultimately, I made the wrong choice. I let out a deep breath when we hit the shoreline. Cold water ran up over my tennis shoes. It felt welcome after the intense workout.

"Bobby Jay, he changed. I could tell he was hiding something from me. He wasn't making time for me like he used to, and the business trips he never used to take were getting longer and more frequent. I didn't want to be like my Momma—always lowest on my husband's priority list and maybe not the only woman."

Bobby Jay raised his brows and gave me a questioning look.

I had my suspicions about Daddy. His eyes often roved in public and Momma drank more than she should—in private, of course. I didn't elaborate any more on that subject, not having any hard evidence to support my suspicions.

"Bobby Jay, all I ever wanted was a man who was going to come home to me every night. I didn't care that it wasn't going to be in a mansion. I wanted the life Ryder promised to give me. A simple, happy one with a small house and babies and maybe a dog or two," I choked out.

Bobby Jay pulled me tighter against his side, not saying a word, just letting me have my say.

"I tried to talk to him about it, but he kept putting me off. Then he left for Florida on another spur-of-the-moment trip without even coming to say goodbye to me. The next day I got those pictures and it all made sense. Or at least I thought it did." I stared down at my feet.

Bobby whistled low. "If he ever gets over being angry, he's probably going to kick himself. Shelby," he stopped and peered down at me, "that entire time he was working on getting investors for Worlds Collide. He wasn't sure it would happen, so he didn't want to get your hopes up."

"Those weren't my hopes."

He let out a heavy breath. "I'm not taking sides here, but he knew what you were giving up by marrying him. It didn't sit well with him. He wanted to give you the kind of life you deserved."

"I just wanted him," my voice hitched. "He was more than I thought I deserved." I began walking again, trying not to cry.

"Well dang, girl, you're making me want to go knock some sense into my cousin."

I shook my head. "I know we're over. I should have been brave enough to confront him. I should have at the very least said goodbye to y'all."

"Yeah, you should have, especially Aunt Jo."

A chill that had nothing to do with the weather went through me. I rubbed my arms. "I know. How is she?"

Bobby Jay took my hand. "Why don't you call her and ask her yourself?"

My heart thudded before stopping. "I couldn't . . . I mean, she must hate me."

"Like I said, you're family."

Family didn't up and leave the way I did or lie to you the way my own had.

"Think about it, Shelby."

"I will," I whispered. "Now, why don't you tell me what you boys created." I'd been wondering about Worlds Collide, but had been too chicken to look them up. I knew that sounded silly, but I had been doing anything to keep the pain away. I had a feeling, though, that if I was ever going to get over it, I had to go through it, as unpleasant as it was going to be.

A smile engulfed his face. "Girl, it's amazing." He reached into his pocket and pulled out his phone. We both stopped to look at it. He tapped an app icon that looked like a map with a pinned location. "Every user creates a profile, which includes an interest-based survey as well as a psychological questionnaire that they must complete. Then our app will suggest adventures or activities in their geo location. The businesses that we partnered with can add schedules and events to the system. Most of them are group-based discounts. Our program will also send out invites using the information in the user-profiles to those we feel would be interested in certain activities."

"Impressive. Do you give out personal information to those who join the group?"

"No way. Ryder is serious about security. You can message other users through the app, but it's up to you if you want to share any personal information. Most people like to chat through the app to get to know each other a bit before they meet up. Once you get to know the other users you can even make your own groups and send out invites."

"Hmm."

"What do you mean, hmm?" He faked being offended.

"I'm not sure I would want to meet up with a bunch of strangers I don't know to go sky diving."

"I can't see you sky diving with people you do know."

"How do you know I haven't been, Bobby Jay Prescott?"

His left brow arched, making his smirk more pronounced. "Have you been, Shelby Duchane?"

I tried not to smile but utterly failed. "No . . . not yet."

"Yet? I'd pay money to see that."

"I'm not going anytime soon."

He busted out laughing.

"Hey, I'm saving all my money to buy my house. Sky diving is expensive."

He put his phone back in his pocket. "I never thought there would be a day when the tables would turn."

I shrugged. "I meant what I said. I had my fill of fancy things. I wanted something real and lasting. Still do."

"You got your eye on someone?"

"Goodness no." I gazed out over the lake. The gentle ripples had a soothing effect. "It wouldn't be fair to anyone I dated or myself."

"You still love him." He wasn't asking.

I let out a long, slow breath. "I should get back home." I ran my hands through my damp hair. "I'm sure I look a fright."

Bobby Jay put his arms around me. "That's not possible."

I sank against his chest even though he didn't smell all that pleasant. The comfort he offered was worth the offense to my olfactory system.

"Thank you for being my family, Bobby Jay." My eyes filled with tears.

He kissed the top of my head. "Don't forget, families fight for each other."

I leaned back to catch a glimpse of his sneaky eyes. "What does that mean?"

"You'll see."

Chapter Eleven

I SAT IN the middle of my bed, showered, dressed in a night shirt, with a towel on my head, holding my phone as if it carried the weight of the world, yet I couldn't let it go. I knew I had to bear it. I needed to call Momma Jo to try to make amends if I could, but it was too late to call since they were two hours ahead of us.

Another task called me tonight. It was time to delete Ryder's emails once and for all. To carry the evidence of his love was torturing me. Why hadn't I believed in his words? In him? Us? Why didn't he share with me what he was doing? Didn't he trust me enough to know that whether it succeeded or not, I was proud of him? Did he believe I was that shallow and snobbish? Did he not believe in me enough?

He was mistaken if he thought I wanted who he was becoming. Bobby Jay had invited me back to their cabin for a drink. I declined even though he assured me Ryder was still at the office. That bit of information broke my heart. My Ryder didn't work late.

I clicked the file folder on my phone. Rows and rows of emails appeared. For the first two years we were together, he sent me one every day. They became less frequent and almost non-existent toward the end. I missed them. They were treasures to me. I imagined one day telling my children's children about how romantic their grandfather was, sending me all sorts of love letters, making me fall deeper and deeper in love with him. I was going to tell them why he called me

Chief instead of by my name. I was going to tell them how, under a blanket of stars, he slipped a ring on my finger while I lay in his arms and said, "All I'm asking you for is forever, but I'll take more if you'll give it to me."

I promised him all that I had. Not once did I think about what I was giving up. He was worth more than any inheritance. I wanted to tell our babies and grandbabies that if they found our kind of love, to never let it go no matter the cost. Tears dripped down my nose and splashed on my phone's screen. *I had let go.*

I wiped the moisture off my screen, making it accidentally open an email. The words, *Dear Chief, After you left last night I started writing my vows*, hit me like a hurricane. *I hope it's not bad luck to share them with you, but I can't wait any longer.* My head said to stop reading right there, but my heart had already memorized each word.

Shelby Katherine Duchane, I haven't been the same since the day our worlds collided. You brought out the man in me. You made me think more of someone else than I did about myself. Your happiness became my own. I live to see you smile. When you take my hand, I never want to let go. Today you take my name. There is no greater honor I could receive. Today our two worlds more than collide, they become one, as it was always meant to be.

I was crying so hard I could no longer see the screen. The weight of what I had done crushed me. I fell onto the bed and curled up into a ball. "I'm so sorry, Ryder," I whispered to no one but myself. I hoped someday I would be brave enough to tell him in person. He deserved that. For now, though, he deserved for me to let him go. I pulled my phone up and, through bleary eyes, I made out the trashcan icon. My thumb hovered over it. *Let him go. It's the least you can do.*

I love you, Ryder. Thank you for showing me a different kind of world, the one where I really belonged. With all my might, I made my thumb drop. To add insult to injury, a warning popped up. Are you sure? No, I wasn't, but I had made my choice. I clicked yes and the world Ryder and I had created disappeared.

Ryder seemed to have disappeared in real life as well. I didn't see him at all the rest of the week. Bobby Jay came around because he claimed I was the only one within fifteen hundred miles who could make sweet tea, and he loved getting a rise out of Marlowe and Macey. He regaled them with crazy tales from his youth, like how he and his buddy shaved the eyebrows off almost all the football players during a football camp, or when they made a corn maze in their neighbor's field—unbeknownst to said neighbor—and actually charged admission. They made about five hundred dollars before the neighbor caught them. Macey giggled and asked for more while Marlowe rolled her eyes and challenged him on the truthfulness of his stories. That only lit a fire under Bobby Jay; he rose to the occasion by spinning grandiose tales with such detail about peeing in water balloons and tossing them at people. While this grossed Macey and Marlowe out, they never did leave.

I had a feeling Macey might have a crush on him even though Jaime was still interested in her. He had a bouquet of daisies delivered to the boutique. Macey said not a word about them, which made me wonder how much she liked him. Marlowe, on the other hand, was going to Edenvale whenever she could for lunch. I didn't have the heart to ask Bobby Jay if he'd seen Marlowe and Ryder together. He was smart enough to know not to bring it up.

While I was still reeling from the revelation of how utterly deceived I had been, I threw myself into helping Emma and Sawyer get their eye clinic up and running in my spare time. I did know a thing or two about that business, whether I wanted to or not. Managing one of my so-called parents' eye centers in Edenvale last year gave me hands-on knowledge I could pass on to Emma since she would technically be running the behind-the-scenes at their new optometry practice.

Monday evening I was helping Emma familiarize herself with the appointment and inventory software I'd recommended while Macey and Marlowe closed up the boutique for the night.

Emma's hands were shaking while she typed in the business information to get started.

I grabbed her hands. "Are you okay?"

She looked straight at me with wide eyes. "I can't take it anymore. I. Need. Sugar. If I eat eggs and spinach one more time for breakfast, I may vomit."

I pressed my lips together and squeezed her hands. "You're doing great. I have a yummy mint chip smoothie or chia pudding recipe you can try for breakfast."

"Shelby, this isn't natural and no offense, but you can take your chia seeds and shove them where the sun don't shine," she growled. "I don't care that I've lost three pounds. I want to die happy with a full stomach."

"Darlin', I'm not saying this is easy. Believe me, I'm missing my sweet tea, but this I know, sometimes just a five-pound weight loss can make all the difference in the world when it comes to getting pregnant."

She let out a heavy breath. "That's what my stupid doctor said."

"You're almost there."

"I just want my eggs to get fertilized! Is that too much to ask?"

"I'm trying my best," Sawyer shouted from one of the exam rooms he was working in.

"You're doing a great job, babe," Emma shouted back.

I dropped her hands and laughed. "It will happen. I promise."

"How about you? How are you doing?" Emma asked.

"I'm not trying to get my eggs fertilized right now but thank you for asking."

She smacked my arm and laughed. "That's not what I meant, but I give you props for the smart aleck reply. I fear Jenna and Aspen are rubbing off on you."

"That wouldn't be so bad."

"Not at all." She started typing. "But really, how are you? Have you seen . . . you know?"

"Ryder? No." I bit my lip. "I actually think he might be seeing Marlowe."

"What?" Emma whipped her head my way.

I shrugged my shoulders. "They would make a handsome couple."

79

"They are both beautiful."

"Hey, your husband heard that," Sawyer complained.

"Honey, you know I only have eyes for you," she responded to her husband before leaning toward me and whispering, "I just have to say this—Ryder, dang, he reminds me of Chris Hemsworth in the new Thor movie. The one where he has short hair. I can see why you chose him to uh, fertilize your eggs. You would have the prettiest babies."

I tucked some hair behind my ear. "I thought so too." I managed not to cry.

"Do you think there is any hope?"

I shook my head.

"Are you sure about Marlowe?"

I nodded. "Pretty sure."

"I'll talk to her if you want."

"You're the sweetest, but no thank you. It wouldn't be fair to either one of them. Besides, I already inserted myself where I didn't belong there. Worse, I turned out to be wrong. So wrong." Not only that, I wasn't sure Macey and Marlowe knew that Ryder and I had been engaged. That was, unless Ryder told her. I had a feeling he hadn't. I was sure Marlowe would have said something by now. Tact wasn't her strong suit. Unless he had told her and that's why they hadn't been seen together. Except I don't think either one of them would care about sparing my feelings. Regardless, I had to brace myself for seeing them together one of these days. In my heart, I knew why she was going to Edenvale whenever she could.

"Shelby, you're going to have to forgive yourself. Honestly, I could see myself doing the same thing as you if I ever got pictures of Sawyer with another woman. I mean, *after* I poisoned all the food in our refrigerator before I left."

"Em, baby," Sawyer peeked his head out, "I can hear you."

"Then let this be a warning," she flashed him a playful grin.

He, in return, gave her a warm smile. "Em, you've ruined me for all other women."

"That's what I like to hear." Emma winked.

Sawyer darted back into exam room one.

I focused on the computer screen. "I'm glad you are both so happy."

Emma rubbed my back. "Aw, Shelby, you're going to find the right guy."

I already had. "Let's get you up and running. Opening day will be here before you know it."

"I can't believe it." Emma looked around their practice in awe.

It was beautiful. I loved the soothing blue they had chosen for the wall color. It played beautifully against the dark wood floors.

"Our dream is coming true." Emma sighed.

I couldn't think of better people for it to happen to.

A knock interrupted us. Both our heads popped up to see who was at the door. A big, burly Southern man with a grin as wide as the Mississippi was waving at us. Two beautiful identical sisters flanked him.

"Ladies, open up, I just closed a big deal and I'm taking y'all to dinner."

Emma gave me a look that asked if he was for real. The answer was a resounding yes. There was hardly a soul around that was more genuine than Bobby Jay Prescott. Sawyer walked out with a hammer in his hands looking as if he meant to use it for more than hanging pictures. "No man is taking my wife to dinner unless I can come."

"Of course, you have to come." Emma batted her eyes. "Who else would I share my food with?"

They were probably the cutest couple in the history of couples. Sawyer always ordered something Emma liked so they could share. Ryder and I never shared food like Emma and Sawyer, but I was known for making him try my "fancy city food," as he called it. He would never admit to liking any of it, but he never turned any of it down, especially when I fed it to him or bribed him with kisses.

"Are you in?" Emma interrupted my thoughts.

"Sure." Anything was better than going home alone to think more about the man who I made disappear.

Chapter Twelve

I searched my menu at the Cove Café for something that stayed within the no sugar guidelines while I listened to the chatter around me. Mostly I was focused in on Emma lamenting over the fact that she had ordered water with lemon instead of her usual Dr. Pepper.

"Who have I become?" she groaned.

Sawyer kissed her head. "You're doing great."

Macey and Marlowe sat on either side of Bobby Jay. Marlowe scrolled on her phone while Macey asked Bobby Jay about the deal he had closed. That piqued my interest. My eyes drifted over the top of my menu to across the table.

Bobby rubbed his hands together with his eyes all alight. "This is the one I've been waiting for, Diamond Brothers' Extreme Sports. Have you heard of them?"

Sawyer's head popped up. "We did one of their caving tours last year while we were on our honeymoon in Australia. They're all over the world."

Bobby's grin grew wider. "Yes, sir. They do everything from caving and rappelling to mountaineering."

"Their setup and tour was amazing." Sawyer put his arm around Emma, smiling. It was as if I could see him reliving some of their honeymoon memories in his mind. They must have been good judging by how sultry his smile was becoming. I had seen some of the pictures, and Emma had mentioned how risqué they had gotten down under.

"We had to agree to some customizations, and due to their security audit they are requiring some enhancements for this next software release."

"When does your next release come out?" Emma asked.

"Why don't you ask the man himself?" Bobby Jay looked past me, but not before flashing me a hold-onto-your-hat grin.

Everyone directed their attention to the man behind me—except me. It became all too clear now why Bobby Jay made sure I sat where I had near the empty seat. Bobby Jay made it out like he was being a gentleman, pulling out my chair and telling me it was the best seat at the table because it wasn't under the air vent and he knew how cold I could get. I was anything but cold. Heat crept up my cheeks and I swore there was a drummer in my chest doing an epic solo.

"Ryder," Marlowe and Macey purred at the same time.

Emma caught my eye with empathy pouring out of hers. Even Sawyer looked pensive on my behalf.

Bobby Jay stood up. "You finally made it, brother. We saved a seat for you."

Macey looked pleased and hopeful, as she sat on the other side of the empty chair. Marlowe wore a look of contempt, which wasn't surprising; she wore that look often.

I knew without looking up that Ryder was staring down at me.

I rubbed my neck, thinking of ways to gracefully excuse myself. As soon as I left, I would be thinking of ways to kill Bobby Jay.

"Sit down," Bobby Jay commanded Ryder. His hard stare said he wasn't playing around.

Within seconds I heard the chair next to me scrape against the tile floor. I leaned as far as I could toward Emma, trying not to look too ridiculous or obvious. The extra distance didn't help, not even a little. My entire body sensed him from his sandalwood scent to the way our pheromones danced between us. My body begged for his.

Bobby Jay smirked between Ryder and me. "Just like old times."

"Old times?" Macey asked.

Thankfully our waitress—who looked all of eighteen in her dark ponytail and who had been inattentive up until now—rushed to our table. From the corner of my eye, I could see her leaning in. "What can I get *you*?" she asked in her I-wouldn't-mind-a-sugar-daddy voice as if the rest of us didn't exist.

"A beer. Do you need my ID?" Ryder asked.

"No." She winked. "I'll be right back." She flashed him a seductive smile.

Marlowe tsked. "Wow, Evie got full of herself all of a sudden. Didn't Andy just dump her?" she asked Macey.

"Yes. I heard he asked her if she wanted to borrow his guide to being a better kisser."

Marlowe smiled evilly. "Figures. Her lips do look thin."

"Girls," Emma interjected, "be nice."

"Fine, *Mom*." Macey turned her attention back to Ryder and me. She pointed between us. "How do you two know each other?"

The drummer in my chest decided to obnoxiously beat on the crash cymbal.

I felt Ryder turn and look at me. My body, of its own accord, did the same before I could stop it. It was a conditioned reaction.

Anger swirled in his chocolate eyes while they bore into me.

I wanted to tell him how sorry I was. I ached for him to look at me like he used to. Like that's all he ever wanted to do. I wanted him to tell me it was okay. Instead, he added to the hurt of it all.

"Miss Duchane and I . . ." he paused to make sure the knife cut as deep as he meant it to. His eyes also dared me to call him Carroll.

I refused the bait. My lip quivered, but I bit my lower lip to stop the trembling while my eyes welled up with tears.

For half a second his eyes softened, but then he shook his head and turned from me as if he was disappointed he couldn't bring himself to further hurt me. "We met at a concert," he said barely above a whisper.

Bobby Jay glared at him.

"Did you two date?" Marlowe asked, annoyed at the thought.

Sawyer jumped in and played superhero. "You were telling us when your next release comes out?"

Ryder looked relieved not to have to answer Marlowe. He sat up straight and looked past me right on to Sawyer. "My team and I have a July 31st release date."

"Do you do the programming?" Sawyer asked.

"I coded most of the original application, but I'm more of the architect now. Though I'm still heavily involved in testing."

In his voice I heard not only the pride of what he had created, but the man who wanted to make his father's dream for him come true. The father who took a second job on top of running the dairy farm to buy his son a computer. He wanted more for his son than back-breaking work. There wasn't a prouder father than Boone Prescott. He loved telling people his son got a job in the city, and those community college courses Ryder had taken had really paid off. Boone and Jolene must be overjoyed with his success. I really should call them, but . . . I was a coward.

"That's a lot to take on," Sawyer responded, "considering you're running the company too."

"Some *things* are hard to let go of." He flashed me an aggrieved look. Every clenched muscle in his face said how much he resented me.

I thought nothing could be worse than thinking he had been unfaithful to me. I was so wrong.

Evie returned with Ryder's beer, wearing the face of utter adoration. "Can I get you anything else?" she breathed out.

"We'd all like to order," Marlowe said, annoyed.

Evie bit her lip, keeping her sights on Ryder. "I'll start with you, handsome."

Ryder looked down at the menu in front of him that hadn't been opened. He tapped it with his fingers. "You know, I'm not all that hungry anymore."

He hated me so much I made him lose his appetite? A disgruntled Evie looked at me like, *well, I guess I'll help you.*

I stood, not feeling all that hungry myself. In fact, I felt quite ill. I found Bobby Jay's friendly but concerned face. "Bobby Jay, I'm real,

real proud of you. Congratulations." Before Bobby Jay could respond, I braved looking at Ryder, who was already staring intently at me. "Congratulations to you too," my voice cracked, though I meant every word. From the bottom of my heart I did. I took a quick deep breath to steady myself. "I'm going to go now. I forgot I need to set up some social media ads."

Bobby Jay stood and went to say something.

I waved for him to sit down. "I'm just fine. Good night, everyone." I spun on my heels and click-clacked my way out of there, but not fast enough. I heard Bobby Jay growl, "You damn fool."

That only lent fuel to Marlowe's and Macey's suspicions. I made out Macey asking why I was so upset and Marlowe replying, "Isn't it obvious?" Emma told them to drop it before she came running after me.

I'd made a scene. A properly bred Southern woman was never supposed to make a scene. We were supposed to grin and bear it. Never let them see past the perfect faux exterior. Now it made sense why Momma came home and drank herself into oblivion. When you had to pretend your life was an endless fairytale, it got exhausting and lonely. It was one of the reasons I fell in love with Ryder. I didn't have to pretend. If I had a bad day at work, I could vent with no judgment. Once I had to deliver a stillborn—one of the worst experiences of my life. He let me cry all night in his arms.

I hit the sidewalk before Emma made it out. "Shelby."

"I'm fine. I'm fine. I'm fine," I desperately tried to keep my voice steady while I walked away.

Emma wasn't having it. She took my hand to stop me before embracing me. "You're not fine," she whispered. "And that's okay."

That was all the permission I needed. I collapsed into her arms, for once not caring that I was making a scene in the middle of the busy sidewalk where onlookers were passing by, trying not to look but unable to help themselves. My tears bathed her shirt. "I love you, Emma."

She squeezed tighter. "Shelby, a year ago I never thought I'd say this, but I love you too. You are one of my best friends."

"I told you we would become the best of friends," I laughed through my tears.

"Who would have ever thought?" She laughed along with me.

"Emma," I clung to her like a child, "what am I going to do?"

"I've got a few ideas. For starters, I'm going to let Jenna know to get her shovel ready."

Chapter Thirteen

ASPEN SET DOWN a platter of veggies and hummus on her kitchen table, looking happier than I'd ever seen her. "This is going to be sooo good!" She sat and put her arm around me. She hadn't told me yet what we were doing, but she promised she had the solution to what ailed me. I was desperate to get over Ryder, so I came. Besides, a Saturday afternoon with girlfriends was always a good thing.

Aspen had us all sitting in a row facing her laptop that was perched on her small table in her cramped apartment.

I looked from left to right at the women who had become not only my friends but my family over the last year. Jenna sat at the end nursing Elliot. Was there anything more beautiful than seeing a mother feed her child? Whether by breast or bottle, I always felt it was like observing pure love. I wanted that so much for myself.

Emma sat next to me grimacing at the healthy snack platter. "It's been almost two weeks; can we please take a break? Betty has been calling to me, and the Doughboy is butt hurt over our long separation. Don't even get me going about the Doctor. He's about ready to make our breakup Facebook official. And I'm not talking about my husband."

We all laughed.

I rubbed her back. "But don't you feel better now that you've detoxed from sugar?"

She scrunched her face. "You want to know how I feel? I feel hungry."

"Well, you look great. Your skin is glowing."

"Ugh," she snarled. "Sawyer made that same comment today."

Aspen jumped up from her seat next to me. "Ooh. It's almost time."

"Time for what?" I asked.

Aspen wagged her perfectly shaped brows. They were so perfect they looked micro bladed, but they were all natural. Honestly, she was one of the most naturally beautiful women I knew, with long wavy golden-brown hair and the most stunning emerald eyes. Her daughter Chloe was her mini me. Chloe was at her grandparents' house because Aspen said whatever it was we were going to watch wasn't for her tween's eyes. That made me nervous. Surely she knew I wasn't that kind of girl.

"This is going to be amazing." Aspen logged into her computer.

I looked over at Emma and Jenna. "Do you know what we're watching?"

Their grins both said yes.

"We thought you needed a little help getting over that d-bag, Ryder," Jenna growled.

"Technically, I was in the wrong." That's what made it so much worse.

Emma rolled her eyes. "Perhaps, but after the way he treated you at the café, we all hate him now."

He had hurt my feelings, but honestly, I couldn't blame the man. Thankfully we hadn't had any more run-ins. Even Bobby Jay had known to stay away from me. Why he thought inviting us both to dinner was going to turn out well, I had no idea. And thanks to him, Macey and Marlowe knew we had been engaged. I wasn't sure who told them, but I overheard them talking about it at home. Macey had commented that since I was the one who broke up with him, I probably wouldn't mind if she asked him out. Marlowe proceeded to smack her, which only confirmed that Marlowe was already seeing him. I went and hid in my room for the rest of the night after that. If my heart wasn't so set on my little yellow house, I would be looking for a place to move.

"Let's not talk about him," I suggested. "How are things going at the eye center?" I asked Emma instead. They'd had their grand opening on Wednesday. I'd popped over for the ribbon cutting. I swore half the town showed up for it. There was even a big front-page write-up about it in the paper. I guess when your dad owned half the town anything you did was a big deal. Not to say it wasn't or they didn't deserve all the attention. They truly did.

Emma beamed. "So good. Sawyer loves having his own practice. Several of his old patients from . . . Oops." Emma cringed.

"It's fine. I'm happy his patients followed him. He's an excellent optometrist. I don't feel any loyalty to Hobbs Eye Care Centers. I never have. Besides, look what my own flesh and blood did to me."

"Speaking of flesh and blood, it's time." Aspen clicked on one more screen before sitting down, excited like a child on Christmas.

I was getting more and more worried. "When you say flesh and blood, you aren't talking about naked men are you?"

They all laughed at me.

"This is better," Jenna commented before holding baby Elliot against her chest to burp him. I couldn't wait to get my hands on the chubby little guy. "Though if we want to put on *Magic Mike* or something afterward, I'm down."

Emma smacked her.

"Shh," Aspen hushed us. "It's time."

Suddenly the screen was filled with a giant cockroach resting in someone's hand, the likes of which I'd never seen, and that was saying something considering I grew up in the South. I shivered just from the thought of holding the nasty creature. To make it worse, it hissed.

"This guy here is named Leland," the woman on what looked like a live feed of some sort announced.

"Yes!" Aspen shouted.

I was very confused. I looked at Aspen to clarify, but she was glued to the screen.

"He was named by a viewer in Colorado who goes by the name of

Aspen. She wants to wish Leland a painful death and hopes his soul goes to hell."

"What in the world is this?"

Emma and Jenna were giggling so hard they couldn't answer me.

I tuned back to the screen to see the woman holding the cockroach approach an enclosure filled with meerkats. "Where is this person?"

"It's a zoo," Emma said through her fits of laughter. "During Valentine's Day they allowed people to pay to have a cockroach named after their ex fed to a meerkat. It was so popular they do it every Saturday now. All the money goes to help the animals at the zoo."

The woman knelt and several meerkats came to the edge of the enclosure and stood on their hind legs, begging. Some of them even bared their teeth. The cute things began to look vicious. The hissing cockroach was then dangled in front of the littlest meerkat. He snatched it quick-like and began devouring it.

"Oh my goodness, that is disgusting." I turned my head.

"It's freaking brilliant," Aspen shouted. "Die, Leland! Die!" She stood up and cheered on the meerkat with all her heart.

It was then I remembered her ex-husband who'd abandoned her and her daughter was named Leland. It suddenly all made sense.

Once the meerkat had devoured its prey, she fell into her seat next to me and blissfully sighed. "That was the best thing ever." She smiled over at me. "Now it's your turn."

"My turn?"

"Yes," she smiled, "look who's up next."

With a churning stomach I faced the screen one more time. A new large and hissing cockroach was in the woman's hand. "This fella here is named Ryder."

All my friends cheered. I wasn't sure how I should behave. I was more of the cockroach in this scenario, though he had called me Miss Duchane and he knew how much that hurt me. I only hurt him because I thought he cheated on me. So, I should have probably made sure those pictures were real or at the very least told him off in person about it before I left.

"Y'all, I'm the awful one in this situation."

Aspen shook her head vehemently.

"Don't think of this in terms of who is right and who is wrong," Emma suggested. "Think of this as a way of letting go."

"Yeah," Jenna agreed.

Aspen grabbed my hand. "Watch him die."

She was beginning to frighten me.

"This guy's sacrifice was requested by Shelby, also from Colorado. She wishes for Ryder to kiss her tight, perky butt and die."

"Who came up with that?"

Aspen raised her hand. "Me. You really do have a great butt."

Jenna and Emma nodded in agreement.

"Y'all are crazy. I can't watch this."

Emma placed her hand on my head and held it steady, focused on the screen. "Yes, you can. Say goodbye to Ryder, right here and now."

"What if I don't want to?" I whispered.

They all whipped their heads my way with mouths agape.

I bit my lip. "I know it's over, but," my voice cracked, "I loved him. I still do."

"Whoa, whoa, this guy is trying to get away," the cockroach wrangler's voice caught our attention. Sure enough, that cockroach was putting up a fight. It took a dive off her hand and landed on the ground in a thud, which spoke to how big and gross it was. It scrambled to get away. A few people jumped in to try and catch it, but it managed to evade them and wriggled under a wall. That was going to give me nightmares.

The woman came back on the screen. "Sorry, Shelby, looks like Ryder is coming for you."

I sank into my chair and whimpered.

Aspen jumped up to turn off her laptop. "I want my money back. I paid to see two cockroaches get mutilated."

Jenna stood and placed Elliot in my arms. "No one can be sad when they're holding this ball of cuteness." There was never a truer statement.

I sat up straight and cuddled the little cottontop. That was Southern for blondie, or towhead like I heard them use out here. Elliot was a cuddly little bug and he snuggled right into me, but not before I caught his punch-drunk smile. Breast milk was intoxicating to little tykes.

All three of my friends were staring at me with concern.

Emma spoke first. "Maybe that was a sign."

Aspen tsked. "It was an unfortunate mishap."

Jenna surprised us all when she sighed. "I just finished reading this book, *How to Get Over Your Ex in Ninety Days.*"

Emma scrunched her face. "Why are you reading a self-help book about getting over your ex? Is everything okay between you and Brad?"

Jenna rolled her eyes. "Of course, we're good. Even if we weren't, I pushed his baby out of my insides, so he's stuck with me for life."

We all giggled.

"It's a romantic comedy," Jenna cleared up. "Freaking hilarious," she added. "It totally should be made into a movie. But anyway, the guy in the book does something really stupid. Kind of like Shelby here." She pointed at me.

I kissed Elliot's head before responding, "I hope you aren't trying to make me feel better."

"Just wait." Jenna grinned wickedly. "Like you, the hero was, let's say, coerced into breaking up with the love of his life. When he figures that out, like you have, he spends the rest of the book trying to get her back, all while she's doing everything she can to get over him. Honestly, it's comedy gold. You should read her journal entries."

I bit my lip. "Does she take him back?"

Aspen, exasperated with the direction of the conversation, threw herself in the chair next to me. "Shelby, do you really want him back?"

I stared down at baby Elliot resting so peacefully against me. I ached so bad to have a little one of my own. A little Ryder and Shelby. "Well . . . yes. But I know it's impossible."

"I don't know," Emma said, albeit reluctantly.

I turned toward her. "What do you mean?"

She squirmed a bit in her seat. "At dinner on Monday night, I couldn't help but notice the way he looked at you between the anger."

"Explain."

She shrugged. "It's just, I know that look. It's the same way I looked at Sawyer. It's this impossible frustration of being so in love with someone but not being able to see how it would work out."

"Do you think he still loves me?"

Emma gave me a close-lipped smile and nodded. "I do. He almost came after you."

"He did?"

"He stopped himself. I couldn't tell if he was angrier that he wanted to go after you or that he wouldn't."

"But what about Marlowe?"

Emma shook her head. "I don't know if there is anything there. I mean, she and Macey obviously both have eyes for him, but to be honest, I don't want to see either of them dating an older guy like him after you know who. Besides, he left almost as soon as I came back in and smacked the back of his head."

"You did?"

She patted my leg. "That's what we do for friends."

I grinned before letting out a gigantic breath. "What should I do?"

"Work it, girl." Jenna snapped her fingers.

"I can't watch this." Aspen jumped up. "Men are evil."

I paid her no mind and focused on Jenna and Emma. "Work what?"

Emma rolled her eyes. "Come on Shelby, you ooze sexual fantasy."

I waved them off and giggled.

"We aren't joking." Jenna took Aspen's vacated seat next to me. "But you're going to have to liven back up. You need to be perky Shelby who showed up last summer. Not sullen Shelby."

"Yes, and use your leaning skills on him," Emma said, half annoyed.

"Leaning skills?"

"You know what I'm talking about. That flirty way you lean into men and touch them and laugh at all the right moments. You're a master at that."

"But you're going to have to be subtle," Jenna cautioned. "You can't just come right at him after everything that's gone on between you."

My head ping-ponged between the two.

"True," Emma agreed. "I think it would be better for now if you only reminded him exactly what he's missing. Be flirty and fun, like the real you, but project that onto the people around him."

I had been kind of a downer lately, but when you find out you ruined the best thing in your life, it kind of does something to you. "Okay. I think I can do that. What if that doesn't work?"

They collectively sighed.

Emma shrugged. "Shelby, I've seen you in action, and if you can't convince him then . . . well . . . we'll order another cockroach and make sure he dies this time. You'll have to say goodbye and move on."

I snuggled Elliot closer and nodded. Emma was right, but I wasn't going down without a fight.

Chapter Fourteen

I TOOK EMMA'S and Jenna's advice to heart. Sunday morning, I woke up perky with a plan. There was no better way to a Southern boy's heart than through his stomach. Not Ryder's, per se, but Bobby Jay's. I got up extra early and made homemade biscuits. Bobby Jay could eat an entire dozen by himself. Not only that, but I broke out one of the jars of homemade peach jam I had made last year using Ryder's momma's recipe. Who knew Edenvale was known for their peach orchards? The peaches were nothing like back home, but they were tasty, and they made incredible jam. My heart pricked thinking about Momma Jo.

One of these days I really did need to call her. I needed to apologize to Ryder first. Then his momma. But Emma and Jenna were right, I needed to finesse the situation. I'm not sure how much my apology would mean to him right now. Though I wanted nothing more than to tell him how sorry I was.

After I made two dozen biscuits, I dressed in Ryder's favorite red sundress. It was sleeveless and short, his favorite combination when it came to clothing. I wore my long hair down in waterfall curls. Ryder loved when I let my hair fall loose. It always ended up that way regardless. Oh, man, did I miss his hands running through my hair and over all my curves. I fanned myself. Goodness, did I need some Jesus this morning. I would go to church after I made my delivery.

While I was filling my basket with biscuits and jam, Mr. Carrington joined me in the kitchen. "Good morning, Shelby."

"Good morning." I placed a plate of biscuits in front of him on the breakfast bar, including a jar of jam. "I know Frankie will be bringing you breakfast, but I hope you like these."

"They smell wonderful."

"Thanks." I finished rearranging my basket. I wanted everything to look perfect against the red checkered background.

"You're chipper today."

I smiled up at him. "I'm trying to be."

He tilted his head. "I've heard some rumblings about an old beau. I'm assuming the biscuits are for him."

I swallowed hard. "Not exactly, but hopefully." I knew that made no sense, but the twinkle in Mr. Carrington's eyes said he understood.

"Oh, the games we play." He grinned.

"I'm not playing . . . I mean . . ."

"Honey," he stopped my rambling, "you don't have to explain yourself to me. I've been there a time or two, especially with my Shannon." Longing filled his words. "I hope the man you're going to all the trouble for is worth it."

"He is."

He took a bite of a biscuit and childlike wonder filled his eyes. "Don't tell Frankie, but these are the best biscuits I've ever had. Your beau is a lucky man."

I lifted the basket off the counter. "He's not mine anymore, but I'm going to see what I can do about changing that."

"Good luck." He held up his biscuit as if toasting me.

"Thank you. Have a good day, Mr. Carrington."

He shook his head with a smile at my still formal way of address-ing him. "If I need to talk to the man, let me know."

"Will do," I called back to him.

My nerves were singing like a Baptist choir once I walked out the door, but I knew I had to act as if they were strung out on smooth jazz. I headed in the direction of the lake. Per Emma, their cabin was near that end of the property. They were staying in Buckhorn. All the cabins here had names based on Colorado wildlife or vegetation.

I gingerly walked the gravel path lined with pine trees, telling myself I had to do this no matter how uncomfortable it would be. I was determined to tell our future grandbabies that I hadn't let go of our love. That ours was a love worth fighting for.

All too soon their cabin was in sight. Out front was Bobby Jay's big country boy truck. Next to it was a sleek black Camaro. That gave me some pause. I reasoned it was just a car; Ryder was still Ryder. It was silly to think we both hadn't changed some over the past year. I knew I had. For the first time, I was calling my own shots, despite what Ryder thought. I was going to show him he was wrong about me.

I breathed deeply, in and out and in and out before approaching the small, one-level cabin with a covered porch. The fresh mountain air invigorated me and gave me a bit more courage to walk up the porch steps. I stood on the porch, letting the sun warm my back while I waited for the bravery I'd felt last night resettle into my heart and mind. Ryder's sultry smile popped into my head. I wished so badly to be on the receiving end of it once again. It was all the encouragement I needed. I knocked on the pine door, hoping they were awake.

I heard some rustling and then the doorknob turned. I put on my perky smile, showcasing thousands of dollars' worth of orthodontics. It did not prepare me for what waited on the other side of the door. Shirtless Ryder in blue jeans with the top button undone.

Oh, Mylanta.

Sinful thoughts surged through me as I took him in from his mussed hair to every single taut muscle down his defined smooth chest and abs. I counted each ripple and had to hold back my desire to drop the basket and glide my fingers across his washboard stomach. But it all had nothing on the name he still wore across his heart in the prettiest red script. My name. That had to mean something, right? I stayed fixed on it longer than I should, wishing my fingers could dance across it. I longed to see his skin raise and feel his heart race because of my touch. His pectorals flexed and twitched, sending me a signal to look elsewhere.

My eyes darted up to meet the pools of chocolate I wanted to get lost in, but they weren't exactly inviting, though they were less menacing than the last time I saw him. Those eyes began to rove over me from head to toe. I felt their touch course down my body. His eyes lingered longer on his favorite spots. Did he wish to kiss the hollow of my neck like he used to, or brush his lips across my ear as he whispered things I would never repeat out loud? Did his fingers ache to glide across my shoulders? Could he hear in his memories the intake of my breath and the pleasurable sighs his touches induced? He drew closer as if he did remember and wished, as I did, to relive every touch, but he abruptly stopped and shook his head.

"What are you doing here, Shelby?"

I had to remind myself not to be hurt by his callous tone, or at least not to show it. I took a deep breath and plastered on a smile. "I'm here to see Bobby Jay." I held up my basket. "I didn't get to properly congratulate him the other night, so I baked him some biscuits."

Ryder narrowed his eyes but said not a word.

"Do my senses deceive me or is the prettiest girl from Georgia standing at my door with fresh baked biscuits?" Bobby Jay came rushing over to me from the back hall where the bedrooms were, dressed in dinosaur pajama pants, no less, and a holey T-shirt. Both men looked as if they had barely woken up. I wondered if they'd had a late night out and if they had been with anyone. It was unusual for them not to be up and ready for church. Who was I to judge, though?

I held up my basket and smiled widely at Bobby Jay. "I also brought some homemade peach jam."

Bobby Jay pushed Ryder out of the way and picked me up, allowing me entrance into their home for the summer. "Girl, if you weren't so skinny, I'd marry you," he teased.

Ryder cleared his throat and glared at Bobby Jay while he slammed the door. I kept on playing my part and giggled. "Bobby Jay, you're all talk."

He set me down and drooled over the basket. "I don't know, if those biscuits taste half as good as they smell, I might have to haul you down to the courthouse."

I used my leaning powers that Emma said I had and sidled right up to the burly man. "Get ready to get hitched, because these are the finest biscuits you'll ever have." I peeked at Ryder, whose brows were raised, not sure what to make of it all. I did note his unshaven jaw pulsing, telling me he wasn't all that fond of this conversation.

Bobby Jay swiped a biscuit from the basket and devoured it in one bite. A look of pure, unadulterated pleasure filled his features. He shook his head, chewed, and sighed. "Mmm, girl, I forgot what a good cook you are. Meet me at the courthouse first thing in the morning."

I playfully smacked his arm. "Sorry, darlin', but I'm all booked up tomorrow." I handed him the basket. "I just wanted to say congratulations again and tell you how proud I am of you."

Bobby Jay cocked his head to the side. "Thank you, Miss Shelby." A mischievous glint appeared in his eye when he looked between me and the basket. "I imagine you're just as proud of Ryder, seeing as you made what looks like his momma's peach jam."

Ryder's and my eyes locked. Electrical currents danced between us briefly. In that moment I saw a flicker of hope—a tiny tug at the corner of his mouth—but it was extinguished before anything could spark. He ran his hands through his thick, dark blond hair and breathed out heavily as if he couldn't believe this was happening.

I knew I had to play my cards right. "There's no better recipe than your momma's."

He threw his hands up in the air, frustrated, showing off more of the body God had blessed him with. I wanted to shout amen watching those sinewy arms go up with the barbed wire tattoos around his biceps that I always found enticing. He kept looking at me and shaking his head. Confusion was good, or at least better than outright contempt. It was time to make my exit.

"I don't want to keep you boys. I'm off to worship the good Lord. Make sure you do the same." I smiled at a flabbergasted Ryder before winking at Bobby Jay.

"Miss Shelby, I think I better escort you." Bobby Jay wagged his brows. "I don't want anyone making eyes at my girl," he teased.

Ryder clenched his fists as if he wanted to throw a punch.

I couldn't help but smile. "That would be lovely. I'll meet you there." I waved demurely at Ryder. "Bye."

I felt him watch me walk out the door. Once I closed it and was securely on the other side, I rested against it while holding my stomach. *I did it.*

I heard Bobby Jay hoot and whistle. "Don't tell me you don't have feelings for that woman."

"Just keep your hands off her," Ryder warned.

I pushed off the door, pleased with myself, but I knew this was just the beginning. Ryder was a proud man and I had cut him deep. I would do everything in my power to heal that wound. Only then would my own hurts be bound.

Bobby Jay slid into the pew all smiles with his hair still wet and unshaven after the service had started.

"You're late," I whispered.

"I had a hot date last night."

I leaned away from him, surprised. "With who?"

"I don't kiss and tell."

"You're lying in church." At least, I suspected he was. I only knew him as a married man, but I had a feeling he wasn't one for decorum.

Case in point, he laughed too loud and drew attention to himself. He didn't mind in the least. He waved at everyone who looked his way. I rolled my eyes and smiled, trying to pay attention to the sermon. The pastor was speaking about grace. Did I ever need some in my life.

Bobby Jay wasn't making it easy for me to listen. He whispered in my ear, "It's about time you showed up."

"At your place?"

"Girl, I'm not talking about the cabin. I'm talking about *you*. This morning was the first time I've seen Shelby since you left Georgia."

I looked down into my lap at my folded hands. "Y'all coming to town hasn't exactly been easy on me."

Bobby Jay put his arm around me. "It's not easy on him either, especially after your appearance this morning."

I pressed my lips together as to not show how pleased I was to hear that. "I was only there to say congratulations to *you*."

"Now who's lying in the Lord's house?" He chuckled. "We need to talk after church."

I closed my eyes to focus on the sermon.

"We should extend grace to all, even ourselves," the pastor's words rang in my head. I was working on it.

After the services, Bobby Jay was quick to lead me out of the small church into the bright sunshine-filled day. He swore the associate pastor was ready to make his move and ask me out and he couldn't have that. I took Bobby Jay's arm as we strolled through the neighborhood toward what I hoped would be my home.

"You really aren't going to tell me who you went on a date with?"

"Maybe someday," he laughed. "Right now we're focused on getting you and my pigheaded cousin back together."

"And who says that's what I want?"

"Please, girl, don't play coy with me. I know you didn't show up this morning looking like a man's last meal for my benefit. Nice touch with his momma's jam and those biscuits you used to bring to Sunday dinner that everyone loved."

I leaned into him. "So maybe I had ulterior motives."

"They worked like a charm. The man had to take a cold shower after you left. He's still mad as hell at you, though. More now that you keep reminding him of what he's been missing."

"I miss him too, but should I back off?"

"Hell no, girl. Like I said, families fight for each other."

"I have to ask. Is he seeing someone?"

Bobby Jay got awfully quiet. The kind that made your stomach wriggle. We both slowed our pace.

"Bobby Jay?"

"Listen, honey, I don't know for sure. I know he dated a few women back home after you left. Nothing serious, but since you left, he's not one to talk about those types of things. And I'm not his babysitter. I don't know how and where he spends all his nights. That's his business."

Was he sleeping with Marlowe? That wriggle in my stomach turned into roiling.

He patted my hand on his arm. "Hey, now, that's no reason for you to stop bringing me biscuits." He gave me a wink.

"If he's with someone else, it's not fair for me to—"

Bobby Jay stopped, turned, and rested his strong hands on my bare shoulders. "Listen to me now, Shelby. None of this has been fair to either one of you. I don't know a lot of things, but this I do know, that stubborn fool has never gotten over you. I don't know if it's possible. So as far as I see it, you would be doing a service to the other woman."

My brows raised.

"If there is one, mind you." Bobby Jay smirked.

"Will you help me?"

A broad smile filled his face. "There's not much I wouldn't do to see the two of you back together."

That warmed my heart. "We have to be subtle."

He barked out a laugh. "Like you were this morning, flaunting your feminine wiles?"

I tucked some hair behind my ear. "Should I be doing something different?"

He shook his head. "No, darlin'. You keep being subtle like a jackhammer and I'll figure out the rest."

Chapter Fifteen

THE NIGHTLY FESTIVITIES had to be brought indoors. The beautiful sunny day had turned into a stormy Sunday evening. That being the case, Grady's band moved into the barn. Which meant no bonfire, but the twinkle lights made up for it. And there was something romantic about the sound of rain dancing on the roof of a barn. Especially when you were in the loft wrapped up in the arms of the man you love. There was no hope of that happening tonight, but I did have a glimmer of hope it could be in my future.

Bobby Jay promised me he would make sure Ryder came tonight—all I had to do was be me. I loved a good excuse to dance, so I agreed. Besides, I would take any excuse to see Ryder. My heart longed for his. I needed him to forgive me for what I had done so I could forgive myself.

When I arrived, there were already several Ranch guests in attendance. I even recognized some people from town who frequently came out whenever Grady's band was playing. Ryder and Bobby Jay hadn't made an appearance yet. I did wonder if Bobby Jay could convince him to come. Ryder loved music but dancing wasn't really his thing unless it was in his momma's kitchen to the old clock radio she kept on the counter. We always cleaned the kitchen together Sunday nights after dinner just to listen to that radio play songs accompanied by static. For some reason, the static added to the charm of it all. Ryder and I would slow dance barefoot on the aged linoleum floor for hours, sometimes not saying a word, other times we couldn't stop talking. I missed those long talks about our pasts and especially our future. We envisioned a much different one than we were leading now. I prayed we could see a way forward to salvage some of it. Mostly the part where we were together until the end of time.

Emma and Sawyer showed up hand-in-hand to support me and to dance the night away. It was here in this very barn while dancing under the twinkle lights that Sawyer had popped the question. Both of their smiles when they entered said they remembered that night. I was lucky enough to have been invited for their special evening. As romantic and beautiful as it was, though, I would have never traded the private proposal I'd received—and managed to throw away. I could kick myself, but I was determined to get it back. To wear his ring again that I had hidden in my nightstand drawer.

Emma hugged me, all smiles. "You look very Shelby tonight."

For the occasion, I wore my turquoise embroidered cowboy boots with snug jeans. "Ryder bought me these boots," I confessed. He said every girl from Georgia needed a pair, and it was a shame I didn't have any. It wasn't a pair I would have picked out, but I loved them because he loved them and they'd come from his heart.

"Nice touch," Emma responded.

Sawyer brushed Emma's lips. "Looks like there will be a good crowd tonight."

"Music to my ears." Emma took Sawyer's hand. "I like to see happy guests."

I looked around and everyone seemed to be in a good mood so far. It was hard not to be with the spread on the serving tables. There was everything from Frankie's famous lemon-raspberry-filled cupcakes to homemade apple pie. Throw in some punch and a keg of beer, and it was a party.

Grady's band began warming up, making the crowd gravitate toward the raised stage at the back of the barn. I looked around, but still no Bobby Jay or Ryder.

"Shelby," a familiar voice called.

I turned to see Jaime, the man who was running backpack excursions for the Ranch this summer, coming toward me. He gave me a warm smile. He seemed like such a nice guy. I hoped Macey was giving him some serious consideration, even if he was shorter than her. In my opinion, he was handsome. He had a baby face, though I knew he was older than me, but it exuded goodness, which made him all the more attractive.

"Hey, Jaime. How are you?"

He did a scan of the barn before answering. "I'm great. Have you seen Macey?"

"I haven't, but if I see her, I'll send her your way."

"Thanks." He ran his hands through his coarse brown hair.

I turned to look for my own somebody, but then Jaime asked, "Do you want to dance?"

I faced him, surprised by his invitation. It was cute how red his face burned. "I'd love to."

He took my hand and pulled me out onto the makeshift dance floor. "Try and keep up."

Grady's band was playing a lively country tune. Several couples joined us on the dance floor, including Mr. and Mrs. King, who decided to make this a slow dance. They swayed close together on the edge of the crowd.

Jaime plunged us right into the middle and before I knew it, he was twirling me around like this was some sort of dance contest. When he pulled me back to him, he wore the biggest grin. "You're a dancer, Shelby."

"I was on the dance team in high school, and in college I was part of their dance company."

"In that case, let's show off. Do you know the Lindy Hop?"

"Yes, sir."

He didn't waste a beat and we went right into the rock step, triple step. He was a pro and even threw in some more advanced moves. He had perfect timing and made the most of swinging me out and in with a flair all his own. I had forgotten how much fun the Lindy Hop was. Several other couples joined in, following our lead.

By the end of the dance I was smiling and breathing harder than normal. Several in the crowd cheered for us. Jaime raised our clasped hands up. It was then I realized Bobby Jay had made good on his word. Ryder stood on the edge of the floor, eyes focused on me. More like eyes focused on the hand that was holding mine up in the air. I couldn't get a good read on his emotions, but whoa, did he look good in his tight jeans and white T-shirt that spoke of how defined his body was.

I didn't get a chance to really gauge his emotions, good or bad, or admire him. Before I knew it, I had several men lined up asking me to dance. I could hardly say no, so I accepted an invitation from Ray's son, Morgan, who was also a ranch hand. He was probably all of twenty, but his too sweet smile made it easy for me to accept. He hardly said a word to me as we danced a slow song, except when he apologized for stepping on my feet.

At the end of the dance, with wide eyes, he breathed out, "You're so beautiful," before he walked away embarrassed. I had to say I was flattered.

I was hoping to find Bobby Jay and Ryder after Morgan walked away, but there were more men waiting to dance with me. I accepted a few more invitations, not knowing any of them. They were guests who all belonged to the same group up here, enjoying a bachelor party weekend. A couple of them asked for my number, but I declined, citing I was unavailable. That was true. My heart belonged to someone else. During each dance I kept trying to catch glimpses of him, but he'd either left or he was being elusive. I decided to decline any future invitations when Bobby Jay cut in, irritating the chemical engineer I was dancing with.

"Dang, girl," Bobby Jay pulled me close, "are you trying to cause a fight tonight?"

I breathed in that muscadine wine scent of his and took comfort for a moment in his embrace. "What are you talking about?"

"Oh, I don't know. Only that you have about every man here in heat. Not to mention you've got Ryder all fired up. He's about ready to leave. I told you to be flirty, not incite a riot. You Southern girls don't know the power you wield, especially you, Miss Shelby."

I smacked his chest. "You're being silly."

"No, ma'am. Now get over to that refreshment table and work your charm on my cousin."

I bit my lip. "I don't know. Maybe you should come with me."

"Girl, I've got to get my game on out on the dance floor. You've got this." He gave me a gentle nudge. "Now get out of here. I'll clear a path for you to keep all these idiots away from you."

He acted like a steamroller, pushing people out of the way. I followed right behind him until we made it to the edge of the dance floor. It gave me a clear shot of Ryder helping himself to a cupcake. Bobby Jay pushed me in the right direction. "Get out of here, girl."

With a deep breath, I scooted my boots over to Ryder. I hadn't felt this nervous around him since our first date when he'd picked me up on his motorcycle. I had been warned what dangerous vehicles they were, but his bike had nothing on the way he looked at me that night. I knew my life would never be the same.

I smoothed out my eyelet tank before I braved approaching him. Nonchalantly, I grabbed a bottle of water next to him. He was eyeing another cupcake. They were a piece of heaven on earth; unfortunately, I was still abstaining from sugar.

"Hi." I tucked some hair behind my ear with my free hand.

He hardly glanced at me. "Hey there." At least he acknowledged me.

I twisted the cap off my water. "Are you enjoying yourself?"

He narrowed his gorgeous eyes at me, taking note that I was wearing the boots he had bought me. "Not really." He went right back to staring at the cupcakes, refusing to make this easy on me.

I thought about what I might say if I hadn't wrecked his world and I was trying to get his attention for the first time. "I downloaded the Worlds Collide app today."

That piqued his interest. He set down the cupcake he had just picked up, but he didn't look at me. "What did you think?" There was an eagerness to his tone.

Ooh. This was good. "I'm impressed. I thought the questionnaire was comprehensive and insightful."

"You created a profile?"

"Yes." I smiled. "GeorgiaBelle214."

His lip twitched. "You should change that. For security purposes, it's not a good idea to use your birthday."

I wanted to say, what about the day you made me the happiest woman in the world? Was that secure? "Oh. Okay. Any suggestions?"

He faced me, looking intent, not sure what to do with me. "You could drop the numbers or use something generic like 123," he suggested, albeit begrudgingly.

"I'll go with 123." I smiled, trying to disarm him.

It didn't work. The cupcake won out.

I stepped closer, leaning my arm on the table, making it hard for him to ignore me. "I was thinking you should talk to Mr. Carrington about signing on as one of your partners."

He turned toward me, still unsure. His tortured eyes searched my own. I wanted desperately to ease the pain I had caused him. He said not a word, only continued to peer into my eyes.

"You don't have to be a guest here to take advantage of their backpacking excursions or trail rides," I continued with my idea. "I think it would be a good fit for your company."

"You think so?" A half smile played on his handsome face.

"I do." I leaned closer.

His half smile faded, replaced with pressed lips, but in his eyes, I saw the longing. I felt it too as he drew closer. I deeply breathed in his sandalwood scent. My body was hungry for him.

"Ryder," I breathed out, "I'm so sor—"

"There you are," Macey interrupted us.

Ryder backed away from me, running his hands through his hair while letting out a heavy breath of *why was I letting this woman affect me this way.*

Marlowe was with Macey, looking between Ryder and me as if she was deciding what to think about it and what her next move should be.

"Do you want to dance?" Macey asked Ryder, doing her best not to make eye contact with me.

Marlowe smacked her arm. That was some next move.

Ryder cleared his throat while staring at the beauties dressed to break hearts in short skirts and halter tops. Ryder didn't get the chance to answer. Jaime was upon us, standing up as tall as he could and puffing out his chest. "Macey, you made it."

Macey's shoulders sagged. It was the first time I ever wanted to smack her. Jaime, while not beautiful like Ryder, was adventurous, well-spoken, and kind. He was obviously thoughtful too, since he'd sent her flowers and his face lit up whenever he saw her. She would be a fool not to pursue him. Don't get me wrong, I could see the appeal of Ryder. He possessed the same qualities as Jaime wrapped up in a gorgeous package. But he was mine! Okay, I was working on it.

Bobby Jay, sweaty from dancing, entered the mix and tried to save the day. "The M&M twins have arrived. Who's dancing with me first?" He wagged his eyebrows at both sisters.

Macey and Marlowe both eyed him carefully. I could see them comparing all three men in their midst and their options. I was about ready to take Bobby Jay's hand and dance with him myself but then Jaime said, "Macey, I wanted to see if you could come on our backpacking trip next weekend. It's the first overnighter we're doing up at Falling Lake."

Falling Lake, I'd heard, was amazing—crystal blue waters with several waterfalls cascading into it.

Macey rubbed her lips together and swallowed hard, stalling to answer. She looked to Ryder as if he would save her somehow from having to commit one way or the other. He was uncharacteristically interested in the cupcake in his hand.

It was getting so uncomfortable I had to speak. "Can anyone go? I'd love to."

All heads turned toward me, but I was only interested in one. The one who was asking *who is this woman I used to know?* I wanted to say she's the same woman who loves you.

Jaime too wore a look of surprise when he addressed me. "It's a ten-mile hike and we sleep outdoors in hammocks." I think he was trying to scare me off.

"Sounds lovely."

"Lovely?" Bobby Jay laughed. "Well, hell, now I have to go. I would pay good money to see Miss Shelby hike and pee in the woods."

I nudged him with my hip. "Those are fighting words, Bobby Jay Prescott. But you should come. I won't mind showing you up one bit." I grinned.

"It's a date, girl." Bobby Jay wrapped his arm around me. "You in, cousin?" he dared Ryder.

That perked Macey and Marlowe up. I knew they would agree to come if Ryder said yes. But one of them would have to stay behind. During the summer, at least three people needed to work at the boutique at all times. Which meant if I wasn't working, either Macey or Marlowe would have to.

Ryder's eyes were lasered in on Bobby's arm around me. His tight, unshaven jawline said he wasn't all that fond of it. Nor did he like being put on the spot. His gaze shifted toward me. So much angst and confusion bounced between us.

"Everyone's welcome," Jaime said begrudgingly. "I just need numbers before Wednesday."

Ryder broke his connection with me, leaving me feeling empty. "I'll let you know," he addressed Jaime. "I have a lot going on at the office right now."

I looked up at Bobby Jay, disappointed. "Do you want to dance?"

Bobby Jay threw Ryder an ugly look before squeezing me. "Sure, darlin'."

Ryder stepped forward with fury written all over his face like he had something to say about it, but it never came to fruition. A frantic man ran into the barn yelling. At first I couldn't make out what he was saying. He yelled again, waving his hands. The barn started to quiet, and the band stopped playing.

"Please, someone help! My wife is having a baby."

Chapter Sixteen

I SPRINTED OUT into the rain, almost slipping in the mud while I followed the panicked man to his luxury SUV. Several people joined us, including Ryder.

"Her water broke. She's in the back." He was practically in tears.

"It's going to be okay," I tried to assure him. Just because her water broke didn't mean that the baby was on its way anytime soon. It could be hours.

The back hatch to the SUV was open and I heard her before I saw her. I either had a screamer on my hands, which was fine, or she was close. When we arrived, the woman was lying in the back on the reclined seats breathing hard between grunts and screams, surrounded by Carrington Ranch towels.

"I'm Shelby." I crawled into the back of the car and knelt in front of the woman's bent legs, wiping the water off my face.

"Are you a doctor?"

"Midwife."

"I don't want a natural birth!" she yelled. "I want drugs."

"Well, let's see what's going on. Do you mind if I check you, uh . . ." I realized I didn't know her name.

"Jerri."

"Nice to meet you, Jerri. I'm going to need you to remove your pants."

"Don't do that," her husband stuck his wet head in. "The baby will come out."

I tried not to laugh. I turned back to see who was out there. Sawyer and Emma came into view. My eyes asked them to please help. They both took the man by the arms, trying to calm him down. I heard Ryder tell him, "Shelby knows what's she's doing."

I focused back on Jerri and began helping her remove her yoga pants and underwear, using my body to block anyone's view of her. Immediately, I knew they weren't making it to the hospital. The baby was about to crown.

"Someone please call 911. I need more towels," I shouted, "and some latex gloves if anyone has them. Also, some shoelaces and a pair of scissors." I heard a flurry of activity behind me. I hoped that meant I would get what I needed, but my main focus was the momma in front of me.

"What's wrong?" Jerri asked.

"Nothing at all. You are about to become a mommy." I smiled, doing my best to reassure.

"Here?"

"Yes, ma'am. Have you given birth before?"

She shook her head, tears streaming down her face.

"It's okay," I tried to soothe her. "How far along are you?"

"Almost thirty-eight weeks."

"That's perfect. Do you know if it's a boy or girl?"

"Girl."

"Well, this baby girl is anxious to meet her momma." I smiled again, locking eyes with Jerri.

"We were up here on a babymoon," she cried. "My doctor said it was fine. I wasn't even dilated two days ago."

She was a ten now and one hundred percent effaced.

"Have you had any complications during your pregnancy I should be aware of?"

She shook her head before screaming, "I need to push!"

"Jerri, I know you want to, but I need to you to pant for me."

"Like a dog?"

"Kind of. Fast, shallow breaths." I turned my head and shouted out of the car. "Hurry with the gloves and towels." I didn't want to touch her or the baby with my bare hands without washing them. And I knew that if she pushed, her baby would be on her way out.

"We have a first aid kit in the car," her husband seemed to have suddenly remembered. "There are gloves in there."

"Great. Will someone please get those for me?" I quickly asked.

"I will," Ryder's unmistakable voice hit me. Before I knew it, he was opening the passenger side door and retrieving the ever-important gloves. He reached over the seat and handed them to me with a genuine smile. The one I had been missing.

I reached up and took them. "Thank you. Is someone getting me towels?"

"Mr. Carrington is," he informed me.

I hastily put on the gloves and got her under the one clean towel she had left. "Jerri, this is going to sting a bit, but you've got this. The hard part is almost over."

Jerri screamed loudly.

"Is my wife okay?" Her husband rushed the car. "Baby, are you all right?"

"Do I look okay to you, Patrick? I'm having your baby in the back of the freaking car. I told you I didn't feel good earlier."

"I'm sorry, honey," Patrick apologized.

"Patrick, why don't you open the back-passenger door and hold Jerri's hand, but keep the rain away from her." I needed him out of my way.

Mr. Carrington arrived with towels, scissors, and a handful of shoe strings. He also threw a poncho over Patrick.

"It's time, Jerri. I need you to give me a good push."

Her grunt filled the car while she pushed. The baby's head crowned.

"Very good. This baby has some dark hair."

"She does? Oh, thank God. I didn't want her to be bald like Patrick."

Patrick looked highly affronted.

"I need you to pant again. We want to ease this baby out."

"Damn this hurts," she yelled.

"I know. I know. You're doing great. You're almost there." I placed my hand, ready to catch the baby's head. "Keep it up. Here comes the baby's head."

Within thirty seconds, a tiny little head landed in my hands. "I need you to stop." The umbilical cord was around the baby's neck, but thankfully not tightly. I slipped it over the baby's head. "Okay, one more big push."

Jerri screamed and pushed. Her little girl's body was delivered, allowing me to pull her the rest of the way out. I quickly wiped the mucous out of her nose and her cries pierced the rainy night, making my heart soar. There was no better sound.

"Hey there, sweet girl." I grabbed a clean towel and wrapped the bundle of joy up, gently but firmly wiping her before placing her on Jerri's chest. "Congratulations, Momma. Keep her close to you. It's important we keep her warm. I suggest unbuttoning your shirt so baby can rest on you, skin-to-skin."

Jerri nodded crying. "Thank you, Shelby. Thank you."

"It was my pleasure." I grabbed the shoestrings and tied off the umbilical cord in two places. "Dad, do you want to cut the umbilical cord?" I asked Patrick, who was helping his wife with her shirt.

Patrick shook his head. "No thanks," he stuttered. He focused back on his wife and baby in awe, kissing them both.

I reached back for the scissors but connected with a hand. *My hand,* I meant Ryder's, but I'd held it so many times if felt like my own. I had missed the feel of his strong hand. I turned to look at him, soaked from standing in the rain. He was the sexiest creature in the world.

He looked down at my hand resting on his then back up at me. "Shelby," there was an ache in his tone. I wanted to say something, but I still had work to do. I squeezed his hand before removing mine. He smiled while handing me the scissors as if we were in this together. I had a hard time maintaining my composure while I focused on cutting the umbilical cord between the ties.

Ambulance sirens filled the air and as soon as the paramedics arrived, I let them do their job including delivering the placenta. I ripped off the gloves and exited the vehicle in clothes that would need to be thrown away. Ryder was right there waiting for me with a look of adoration. The scent of the rain mixed with his sandalwood scent made me want to throw myself into his arms. Caught up in the moment he raised his hand ready to run his fingers through my drenched hair while he leaned down as if he were going to kiss me, but he stopped himself inches from my lips. His sweet breath was heavy and lingered between us. My heart pounded and ached for him to finish what he had started.

"Ryder." His name came out more like a sigh.

He shook his head and backed off. "I need to go." He ran away, making my heart feel like it needed the paramedics. It was then I noticed I had an audience. Several people, including Mr. Carrington, Emma, Sawyer, Bobby Jay, Macey, Marlowe, and Jaime were standing back looking at me as if I just returned from an arduous trip.

"You're amazing!" Emma squealed.

I looked up and let the rain wash over my face. In that moment, I felt anything but amazing. I silently asked God if Ryder would ever forgive me. I swore, hidden in the sound of the pitter-patter on my face, I heard the answer, "That is a good question."

Chapter Seventeen

"I FORGOT TO ask. Who was the enormous, beautiful bouquet from that came through the Ranch's front office for you today? They wouldn't be from a certain ex, would they?" Emma asked while we shopped for a backpack at the wilderness store in Pine Falls.

"No," I sighed. I hadn't seen Ryder since our moment after the delivery four days ago. Bobby Jay said he was head down at work. More like trying to avoid me at all costs. I had gone to their cabin every night after I got home from work, but he was never there. Bobby Jay and I had dinner a couple of nights together and watched reruns of *Chuck,* waiting for Ryder to come home. But Bobby Jay said I could only stay so long. Apparently, his mystery woman was suspicious of our platonic relationship. He was still refusing to tell me who she was. "It was from Jerri and Patrick, thanking me for delivering their baby girl, Cami," I clarified for Emma.

"Wow. What a night. Now I'm not the only baby who was born at the Ranch."

I looked up from the backpack I was buckling around me. "You were born at the Ranch?"

"Yep, during a blizzard by both my fathers. Weird, huh?"

"I think it's precious."

"Only you would call it that," she teased.

"What do you think about this backpack?" I turned in a circle so she could get a full view.

"I think you're sullen Shelby, not perky Shelby today. Talk to me."

I tightened the strap around my waist to see if it was comfortable. "Bobby Jay told me that Ryder thought it was best for him not to go on the backpacking trip. I think trying to win him back is a lost cause. I'm pretty sure he's dating Marlowe. She was quick to volunteer to work instead of Macey this weekend. Ryder must have told her he wasn't going."

Emma rubbed my arm. "Well . . ."

"It's okay. You don't have to say anything."

Emma started tugging on the pack I was wearing, assessing it. "I don't know. I see the way he is when he's around you. Half the time he looks like he wants to devour you. If my sister wants to compete with that, she's crazy."

"I think I'm the crazy one. Ryder isn't ever forgiving me."

"Then he doesn't deserve you." She handed me another backpack to try on.

I undid the one I was in and handed it to her. "Maybe we just weren't meant to be. We didn't exactly have the easiest go of it with my parents being so against us. It was one of the reasons he took so long to propose."

"What were some other reasons?"

"He hated seeing me torn between two worlds, as he called it. He worried that eventually I would resent giving up my fortune. That there would be a day that I really wanted something, and he wouldn't be able to provide it. I think that thought killed him more than anything."

"Then he's an idiot if he wants Marlowe. I love my sister, but you see how she and Macey live. Dad has never given them limits. I was surprised when he sold the boutique."

I latched the backpack belt and pulled it snug around my waist. "Ryder has money now, so they are all set." I held my stomach at the thought of them being together.

Emma tightened the straps for me. "Does his money bother you?"

I thought for a second. "I don't begrudge his success at all. I always thought he was super smart. It's just . . . the amount of time he spends at work and his fancy car—it's not him. I fell in love with him because he valued time over money. Something my family never did."

"Speaking of your family. Have you talked to them?"

"No," I snarled. "Not even my memaw has called me back, which is unusual. I hope my parents didn't poison her."

Emma's eyes widened. "Why would they do that?"

"I don't think they would, but you never know. Memaw still has a controlling number of shares in the company. And the board of directors listen to her, sometimes above Daddy. She loves to stir trouble."

"Did she like Ryder?"

"I think so. She thought he had a great body. She always told me she could see why I fancied him. But she used to needle him, saying he was only romancing me to get to my money. He didn't take it well, as you can imagine. See, she and granddaddy had a love for the ages and Hobbs Inc. was like a child to them. So, she was always cautious about anyone who was brought into the family. My daddy went through a grueling vetting process of doing everything from being granddaddy's caddy one summer to having to start out as a sales manager, even though Daddy came with his own wealth."

"So, could she make it so you inherited Hobbs Inc.?"

I shook my head. "My parents own the majority of controlling interest. When Daddy was made CEO, that was part of the package. And to my momma's irritation, Memaw is giving most of her money away to charity when she dies. She gives to all sorts of animal charities and she's determined that her alma mater name a building after her."

"She's sounds like a character."

"You have no idea. When I showed her the pictures of Ryder and well . . . *me* . . . she vowed to chop off his 'thing' and feed it to her Doberman Pinscher."

Emma giggled before cutting off with a frown. "You don't think she was in on it, do you?"

I shook my head. "I don't think so. If she was, that would shatter my heart. Memaw was the only person I felt like loved me growing up. She came to every dance recital and performance, even when I was in college. The same could not be said for my parents."

Emma smooshed my cheeks with her hands. "Know this. You have a family now who loves you, even while extremely jealous of your gorgeousness."

Tears welled up in my eyes. "Thank you, Emma. You're like the sister I never had."

She dropped her hands. "I feel the same way about you," she teased. "Now let's get you prepared for Saturday. Are you sure you still want to do this? It's more difficult than any of the trips we took last year."

"You don't think I can do it?" I had thoughts of not going because of the cost of the backpack and supplies, but I wanted to prove to myself and Ryder that I wasn't the same woman who left Georgia. The one who was so easily persuaded by my parents to betray the man I loved.

"Shelby, you never cease to surprise me. I have no doubt you're up for it."

❧

"I'm not sure I'm up for this," I whispered to Emma, who had come to see me off in the too early light. She and Sawyer couldn't come on the hike because of previous obligations to the Ranch, and Emma's soccer team had a game today.

She smiled sleepily. "You've got this. Stay hydrated and eat small snacks as you go to keep your energy up." She looked me over from head to toe. "By the way, you look too cute for this."

I ran my hand down my French braid and looked at my attire. I wasn't dressing to impress, that was for sure—plain shorts, a T-shirt, and a long-sleeve shirt tied around my waist for the cool morning hours in the mountains.

"Maybe I'll meet someone," I teased. We both knew even if I did, I wouldn't act on it. I was still too hung up on my ex. The man who had managed to disappear.

Emma looked around at the group of brave people congregating in front of the barn. She flicked her head to the right. "There are a couple of candidates over there," she whispered.

Nonchalantly, I glanced over at the two tall, handsome, well-built men talking to Jaime. I averted my eyes back to Emma. "Not bad."

She shook her head at me and grinned. "So, they aren't Ryder hot, but think about it."

Maybe it was time for me to really work on moving on.

Emma reached out suddenly and grabbed my arm. "Don't look now, but I think your trip just got a lot more interesting."

"What are you talking about?"

She didn't get to answer.

"Look at our Shelby, all dressed like a wilderness girl," Bobby Jay shouted. "Dang, woman, you're making me wish I decided not to give up my spot."

What? I turned around to find Bobby Jay walking toward me not dressed for hiking. He was wearing dress slacks and a button up. But the one who caught my attention loomed behind him looking unsure, dressed like all my already fulfilled fantasies and the ones I hoped to relive in the future.

I looked at Emma with wide eyes, biting my lip. The drummer was back in my chest wildly beating on my heart.

Bobby Jay was picking me up and squeezing the air out of me before I knew what hit me. "Good morning, Miss Shelby."

"Bobby Jay, why aren't you coming?"

He set me down with a wicked grin. "It's my Christian duty to be a good Samaritan." He wagged his brows. "That and my girl and I have plans."

"Your girl? Are you official now?"

"Working on it." He leaned in and whispered in my ear. "You have some work to do this weekend too." He nodded toward a pensive Ryder standing several feet away. Mylanta, did he look fine in his cargo shorts and tight T-shirt. I loved it when he didn't shave in the mornings.

Unfortunately, he wasn't alone for long. Macey bounded up to him looking more than good in her sports bra and shorts shorter than mine. "Ryder, I'm so happy you're coming." Did she know he was beforehand? Was it Macey, not Marlowe, he was interested in?

My already nervous stomach began to feel queasy. "Maybe I should stay."

"You aren't afraid of a little competition, are you?" Bobby Jay asked.

"Is she my competition?"

Bobby Jay shrugged.

"Why is he coming?" I whispered.

"One of us has to see you pee in the woods." He laughed.

I smacked his arm.

He snaked his arm around me, his tone changed from playful to thoughtful. "Shelby, you've got that boy so wound up and scared as hell. Go easy on him."

I looked into his sincere eyes. "What do you mean?"

"You put a world of hurt on him, and that's not easy to forget."

My eyes misted.

"Don't cry, girl." He reached up and wiped away a tear that had escaped. "You had your reasons. And honestly, he bears some of the blame, but he hasn't exactly come to terms with that. See how this weekend goes. Work your charm, but maybe more subtly." He chuckled.

Emma handed me my backpack, which she had carefully helped pack to make sure the weight distribution worked for me. "Give him hell."

Bobby Jay's eyes popped. "You have some spirit, Mrs. King."

"I'm team Shelby, and as far as I'm concerned, it's your boy who should be charming her."

Bobby Jay's right brow quirked. "I do like you, Mrs. King. And I might be inclined to agree with you."

That was all well and good, but what did that mean I should do?

Chapter Eighteen

I decided the only thing I could do was be myself. Which meant hanging out with Jaime, who was obviously a bit forlorn that Macey was throwing all her attention at Ryder. She was incessantly chatting behind us about how she wanted to create her own makeup and moisturizer line and how Mr. Carrington was going to fund her venture.

"Maybe I could sell my line at our store!" she yelled up to me.

Shamefully, I pretended like I didn't hear her. I had never been so irritated with someone in my life. Not only was she monopolizing Ryder, who wasn't exactly responsive to her ramblings, but she was being awful to Jaime. I did my best to listen to Jaime explain about the different plant and wildlife we were encountering, as well as soak in the sun and scenery.

My thighs were also demanding my attention. They had never burned so bad. Why I ever thought carrying a thirty-pound pack while I traipsed through the woods was a good idea was beyond me. You don't know how happy I was after the first hour when Jaime said we were taking a ten-minute break. I couldn't believe we had five to six more hours to go.

I eased out of my backpack and found a sturdy log to rest on before I pulled out my protein bar and water. A protein bar had never tasted so good. While I reveled in it, I glanced at Ryder, who kept close to me, but not too close. He landed nearby on a boulder. His faithful sidekick, who stuck to him like molasses, sat close to him, sexily pretending to wipe the sweat off her chest and down her sports bra. I had to admire her tactics, but as arduous as the hike had been, it was only in the sixties and no one was perspiring in the dry cool air. I wondered if she was more than a sidekick. I couldn't tell, because he obviously wasn't repulsed by the ebony-haired beauty, but he wasn't all that responsive to her either. And not that long ago, if I had been doing the same thing Macey was doing, he would have grabbed that bandana and offered to help me. Believe me, I would have let him. But the only communication I had with him today was a simple hello before we headed out.

I was perplexed by what I should do. I seemed to scare him off by trying to engage him in conversation or, you know, delivering a baby, but a glance here and there didn't seem to be working either. And I wasn't sure what Emma meant by give him hell, so I just decided to take a moment for me. I breathed in the fresh pine-scented air with a hint of campfire and enjoyed watching two chipmunks in the distance scurry around as if they were playing a game of tag.

My moment was interrupted by one of the handsome men Emma pointed out to me back at the barn.

"Do you mind if I share your log?" Mr. Tall Dark and Handsome asked.

"Not at all." I scooted away from the center to give him more space.

He set his large backpack on the ground before sitting next to me. "I'm Julian." His voice was quite pleasing. Mellow with deep undertones.

"Shelby. Nice to meet you."

"You come to this place often?" he teased, making me giggle.

"This is my first time. How about you?"

"Me? At least twice a week. I love this log." His bright green eyes shone.

He sure knew how to make a girl smile. "It's lovely. Firm and mostly bug free," I kept up the banter.

He flashed me a brilliant smile. "I'll call my people to make sure the pest situation is more under control for next time."

"You are a gentleman, thank you."

He leaned in closer. "And you sound like a fine Southern lady."

"I do try to be. I'm from Georgia. How about you?"

"I'm from—"

A figure towered above us, blocking the sun. "Jaime said it's time to get moving," Ryder informed us in a menacing tone.

Julian eyed him warily. "Thanks, man."

Ryder didn't respond to him. His eyes were zeroed in on me. What should I do? Put on the subtle charm or give him hell? I went with smiling, pushing myself off the log, and brushing my backside off with my hand. Who knew what I had picked up sitting on the log?

"Do you need some help with your pack, Shelby?" Julian asked.

"You are sweet, but I think I can manage just fine. Thank you." More than anything, I had a desire to prove to Ryder that I was my own woman.

Ryder remained still.

"Can I help you?" I spoke softly.

His eyes said yes but his head shook no.

"Ryder, can you help me?" Macey asked in her come-hither voice.

I was pleased to note the grimace on Ryder's face before he turned and left to help the not-so-distressed damsel.

"Friend of yours?" Julian asked.

"Not anymore."

The next part of the arduous journey had me between Julian and Jaime. I think their goal was to see who could tell the best story to make me laugh. This was good and bad. It partially took my mind off who was hiking right behind me, but I needed all the oxygen I could get and didn't have much to spare for things like laughing. This hike was no pleasure cruise. I wasn't sure I could even pee outside anymore, because that meant using my legs, and they felt like jelly.

"No joke," Julian, who worked for the police department in Denver, said. "Last year my partner and I were waiting in our uniforms to get coffee when this idiot pushes us out of the way to get to the front of line. He then proceeds to pull out a fake gun to rob the place. We arrested him, obviously."

"No way. Who would be that silly?" I responded through some labored breathing.

My side was hurting too. The strap around my waist wasn't doing me any favors. I noticed when we stopped for lunch, the skin on my right side was getting red and irritated, so I tried making adjustments. The guy at the store said it was the most comfortable pack he sold for women. I wasn't so sure. I decided to try and breathe through the pain.

Julian flashed me a sideways grin. "The way you say silly is absolutely charming."

"I have a silly tale for you then, Miss Shelby," Jaime jumped in, ready to one-up Julian.

"Do tell." I needed anything to distract me from the raw pain I was feeling. The next two hours couldn't go quickly enough.

"When I was flying home from Paraguay last year, two of the flight attendants, who were obviously lovers, got into a huge argument right before we were going to takeoff. The male attendant was so furious, he opened the emergency door and activated the emergency slide and slid down it. His girlfriend followed him, but she bounced off the slide and hit the tarmac."

"Oh my goodness. Was she okay?"

Jaime grinned. "She seemed to be, but they were both arrested."

"Yikes."

"That was also the flight I woke up to my shoes being completely stuck to the floor because the woman next to me had a jar of honey on the floor, and while she slept it spilled out."

"You're teasing me."

He held up his hand. "Scout's honor, I'm not. I loved those shoes, but I had to lose them because I would have missed my connecting flight. That honey was some sticky stuff. I arrived home barefoot."

I giggled while I adjusted the belt around my waist again and tried to stuff my long-sleeve shirt between the belt and my T-shirt.

"Well—" Julian started.

"Shelby." Ryder gently grabbed my arm, startling me.

We all stopped and looked at him, but he only paid me any attention.

"What's wrong with your side?" he asked.

"I'm fine," I lied, confused as to how he knew about it.

"You're not fine. I've been watching you fidget and grab your side for the last hour, and I just heard you whimper" He scowled at Jaime and Julian like they should have noticed.

I was quickly becoming the center of attention as most of the fifteen people in the group had now stopped, wondering what the hold-up was.

"Are you hurt?" Jaime asked concerned.

"Really, it's just some irritation. You know, new backpack and all," I tried to play it off.

"Let me see." Ryder started unbuckling my waist strap without warning.

"You want me to lift up my shirt for you?" I teased bordering on flirting.

He smirked.

I had missed that smirk. It felt like old times.

When the waist strap came undone, a loud breath of relief escaped me. Ryder proceeded to remove my pack completely off me.

"This is unnecessary, and we are causing a scene," I said under my breath.

He gave me a pressed-lipped smile. "All right." He pulled me and my pack to the side, making me feel all sorts of wonderful. I missed his touch like I missed sweet tea and nights under the Georgia stars with him.

"Why don't y'all go on," Ryder suggested to the group, "while I see to Miss Shelby."

Jaime and Julian protested, Jaime being the loudest. "I should be the one to stay with her since I'm liable for the group."

"I think the rest of these good folks would like to get to their destination," Ryder countered.

Several people in the group nodded. We were all tired.

Jaime debated while looking between me and the rest of the weary travelers and decided it was best to keep on moving.

127

"I have medical training," Julian offered.

Ryder grinned crookedly. "Shelby has a master's degree in nursing, so I think we will fare just fine."

Julian looked at me as if to ask if I was okay being left alone with a man who I had admitted was no longer my friend.

"I'll catch up soon," I promised Julian.

Ryder made a sweeping motion with his hand. "I got this. Shelby, here, is modest, and I know you wouldn't want her to feel uncomfortable." He was such a liar.

Julian scurried away. That left Macey, who suddenly became very sympathetic toward me. "Shelby, are you okay? I'll stay with you." She batted her piercing blue eyes at Ryder.

I stayed silent, not sure what to say. If he wanted Macey, how could I begrudge him?

Ryder cleared his throat. "Darlin', I won't be long."

Was he calling her *darlin'* as a term of endearment or was he just being himself? I couldn't tell. Either way, I didn't like it. "Why don't you both go, and I'll take care of this myself? I have a first aid kit if needed."

That turned Macey's pout into a wide smile.

"That wouldn't be prudent, now would it?" Ryder said smooth as silk. "I think the first rule of hiking is to never go by yourself." He gave Macey a heart-stopping grin. "We'll catch up."

She sighed before trudging off.

"Stay on the trail; it leads straight to the lake," Jaime called out as he led the rest of the group forward.

That left the two of us on the rocky trail standing under the shade of the pine and aspen trees. I bit my lip. "You're such a liar."

He knew exactly what I was talking about. "You were never one to go showing off your body for no reason. Not to say I didn't mind when you had reason to," he admitted under his breath.

My cheeks burned.

He got right to business, dropping my pack and taking off his own. "Let's see what's under that shirt."

My brow raised.

He grinned wickedly before gently lifting my shirt only enough to see the damage my backpack had inflicted. I noticed the way he swallowed hard staring at my bare skin. He hesitated to reach out and touch my body around the injured area, but when he did, his fingertips elicited raised skin and skipped heartbeats.

"This doesn't look good," he informed.

I winced and shifted before peeking at my raw skin that had started to bleed, leaving a nice stain on my T-shirt.

"Why didn't you say something?" He sounded angry.

"Why do you care?" I pleaded to know.

He slowly lifted his head and met my eyes. "Sometimes I wish I didn't." His response was delivered with honesty, not cruelty.

It ached my heart. "My first aid kit is in the side pouch."

"Keep your shirt up and I'll grab it."

"Thank you." I gazed deep into his eyes, wanting to do so much more, like kiss his lips and run my hand across his stubbled cheeks. Don't even get me going on how my fingers wanted to dive into his hair.

"You're welcome." He hastily went to retrieve the first aid kit.

"Ryder."

He looked up while bent down, unzipping my pack.

"I am sorry." I did my best to keep my emotions in check. I knew it probably wasn't the right time, but I needed to say it to him. Keeping it inside was killing me.

He breathed out a low growl. "I'm not ready for that discussion."

"Of course." My eyes hit my hiking boots. I contemplated hiking back to the Ranch by myself. I had a whistle, plus it would be mostly downhill. I could do it.

Ryder was back to me in no time with the first aid kit. I avoided making eye contact but reached for the kit. "I got this, thank you."

He wasn't letting go. "Shelby, let me help you."

I lifted my head to face him. "Why would you want to?"

He closed his eyes and shook his head, frustrated. "Because, God help me, I can't stand to see you hurt."

Chapter Nineteen

THE COOL WATER felt heavenly on my tired feet. The hike was the physically hardest thing I had ever done, but the view of the stunning crystal blue water and gently cascading waterfalls that fed right into Falling Lake made it all worth it. Even if I had to swallow my pride and allow Ryder to carry my pack the rest of the journey. Not like he gave me much of a choice. After he patched me up, he picked my pack right up and refused to let me have it until we arrived at our destination. Or as I liked to call it, heaven on earth. I had never seen anything like this place in my life. It was straight out of an enhanced movie scene. Everything in view was more vibrant and alive than it should have been. The foliage was greener, and I had never seen water so blue. Even the flowers were sharper hues of blue and purple.

The best scenery was in the lake—a certain someone who was under one of the waterfalls letting the water wash over his beautiful head and glorious bare chest. He'd been there for so long I wondered if he was hoping it would wash the memory of us away. I could see how torn he was. He didn't want to—or couldn't—forgive me, yet he couldn't stand to see me hurt. He'd hardly said a word to me as we walked alone on the path, trying to catch up to the group. His only communication was making sure I was all right.

I decided to give him his space, though I ogled him from afar between reading the book I had brought with me, *How to Get Over Your Ex in Ninety Days.* Jenna thought we should start a book club, and this was the first selection. Aspen only agreed to read the romantic, happily-ever-after comedy if we read a thriller of her choice next.

I took one more glance at the man I loved before focusing back on my book and how good the sun felt on me. The heroine kept a diary and wrote to Mr. Bingley from *Pride and Prejudice.* She paralleled her own life with his and compared him a lot to her ex in not only hilarious ways, but poignant ones. Unfortunately, they hit a little too close to home for me at times. Especially when she spoke of what a coward Mr. Bingley was for leaving Jane. She pointed out that he didn't even have the decency to tell her himself. Poor Jane had no idea what she had done to deserve his neglect. Just like Ryder hadn't deserved my cowardice or silence.

I dangled my feet in the water from the rock I was perched on and immersed myself in the world of Presley and Jackson. I laughed at the precarious situation Presley found herself in while trying to follow the rules of getting over her ex in ninety days, the overarching one being she was supposed to stay away from him. The problem was, they worked together, and like me, Jackson recognized the mistake he had made and did whatever he could to make sure he was present in her life. While that seemed to be working for him, it didn't feel like the best course for me to take. I had a feeling I was going to have to let Ryder come to me. Or, probably more likely, admit we were truly over and move on. A thought that killed me.

I didn't get much more reading in. Julian joined me, looking good in only a pair of shorts and some swim shoes. Like Ryder, he had a defined chest, though Julian's had more hair.

Julian smiled at the title of my book. "Finding any good tips in there?"

I closed my book and laid it in my lap. "I'm not looking for any." I didn't want to get over my ex. And I had already followed all the rules in the book, to no avail. Not even being away from Ryder for a year thinking he had cheated on me had helped me get over him.

Julian eyed me carefully before his gaze drifted over the lake. Several members of our group were swimming and playing in the water. My open wound precluded me from doing such. Julian's eyes fixed on Ryder before his attention landed back on me. "Are you in a relationship with Ryder?"

I rubbed my lips together and shook my head.

"Maybe a better question is, were you? I noticed the ink on his chest."

"Were you checking him out?" I giggled though I wanted to cry. My name across his heart was a beautiful reminder of what I had lost.

He nudged me with his muscular shoulder. "Your name was hard to miss."

"We were engaged a while back," I admitted with a sigh.

"Now he's with that woman, Macey?"

We both watched as Macey made her way to Ryder in her tiny silver bikini. I couldn't stomach watching it, so I turned away.

"I'm not sure. Maybe. Do you want to do that fishing thing Jaime talked about at the river?"

"Sure." He went with my abrupt change of subject.

I put my book and bottle of water in my knapsack and stood as hastily as I could. My side made that difficult.

Julian jumped up and helped me. His touch did nothing for me. But the sound of another man's voice sent shivers down my spine.

"Where are you headed off to?" Ryder said through heavy breaths.

Both Julian and I faced him with astonishment. That was quite the swim in such a short period of time. We are talking Olympic medal qualifying time.

Words escaped me as I internally panted. He never looked better than when he was in the water, droplets dripping down him with his hair slicked back, showing off why Macey was frantically swimming after him.

"We're headed over to the river to do some fishing," Julian informed him, but not before looking between me and Ryder with a sense of resignation.

"I'm in." Ryder walked out of the lake like the god Poseidon. He ran his hands through his hair before shaking his head to remove the excess water. Oh my. Even Ryder was more vibrant here in this unreal oasis. He headed over to the branch that had his T-shirt hanging from it. I'd had some thoughts earlier about clothes hanging from tree branches and warm, clear nights.

"Wait for me," Macey yelled, reminding me to come back to the present and face reality.

I did not, in fact, wait for her. I slipped on my shoes and began walking on the path through the willow bushes and sagebrush toward the river.

Julian was quick to follow. "Are you sure you're over?" he whispered.

"Very."

"I wouldn't be too sure if I were you."

I stopped and looked up at him with a question in my eyes.

He returned it with a half-smile. "I hate to say this, but I wouldn't count your ex out."

I let out a heavy breath and continued down the path. "You have no idea what I did."

"Must not be too bad."

"Oh, it was." I didn't elaborate. Ryder—and Macey—caught up with us.

Julian held out his hand to Ryder. "I don't think we were properly introduced. I'm Julian."

"Ryder." His voice sounded strained.

"I'm Macey."

Julian surprised me by not ogling her, only politely acknowledging her. Instead, he kept pace with me. "Do you like to fish, Shelby?"

"Um . . . yeah." I tucked some tendrils of hair behind my ear.

"Really?"

"That surprises you?"

"Most women I know would rather not."

"Well, it's all about who you're with when you do it." I swallowed.

He put his arm around me and gave me a quick squeeze. "I agree."

Ryder took my other side.

Julian dropped his arm and flashed Ryder a devious smile just like Bobby Jay would have done. "Would you agree, *Ryder*?"

I wasn't sure if he was taunting him or trying to help him out. Maybe Julian wasn't sure himself. Men. They confused me.

Ryder scowled at Julian. "Never had a woman complain about it."

I faced my ex-fiancé with a raised brow. "Do you take a lot of women fishing?"

"Only one." He gave me a wicked grin.

I tried to hide the zing that went through me. "Now that we've settled that," I said in a high-pitched voice, "does anyone know how we are going to fish without poles?"

"Jaime knows all sorts of ways how," Macey piped in.

I turned around and gave Macey a pointed look. "He's pretty amazing."

Macey hung her head without a word.

The river was in view.

"All right, boys, don't worry when I catch more fish than you," I declared.

Both men chuckled. I missed that sound coming out of Ryder.

We found Jaime giving demonstrations about how to fish using only fishline, a sinker, a hook, and bait. He looked absolutely adorable and in his element. He probably wouldn't appreciate that assessment, but the pure joy that radiated from him as he tossed his line out into the river's current was refreshing.

"Now," Jaime said, "since it's the heat of the day, it's best that you look for a deep pocket of water or a shady spot. Fish like to keep cool too." He pulled in his line and turned around to face his captive audience. "So, who wants to try?" He happened to lock eyes with Macey. Macey wearing hardly a thing. Jaime's jaw dropped while he turned multiple shades of red. "Man, it's warm out here," his voice squeaked. Poor man was smitten.

Macey, for her part, at least looked pleased that Jaime was so taken with her. Which made me even more confused. Were she and Ryder a thing? Would Macey try to start something with him if he was dating Marlowe? Was he dating Marlowe? Could he find a way to forgive me? My head hurt thinking about it all.

Everyone who had come to learn from Jaime stepped forward to try out this unusual way of fishing. Even some hikers not from our group joined in.

Jaime did his best to engage Macey and tried to get her to try it, but she was repulsed by the nightcrawlers he had dug up for bait. Macey batted her baby blues and asked Ryder if he would hook her worm. I watched and listened with interest to see how that would go.

"Darlin', if you can't hook the worm, you shouldn't be fishing."

I pressed my lips to hide my smirk. He had always baited my hooks for me. Not because I refused to, but because he loved me. A tiny shred of hope rose in my chest.

Jaime took that opportunity and offered to help Macey. Meanwhile, I unwillingly sacrificed the life of the slimy worm covered in dirt.

"Don't forget to cover the entire hook," Ryder whispered close to my ear, sending volts of electricity down my spine.

It took everything I had not to smile at him and ask him if he wanted to relive some of our "fishing" trips. Instead, I played it cool and baited the hook properly. "Watch and learn." I headed up river looking for a shallow, shaded bank.

Julian laughed and followed. Ryder's eyes said, *who is this woman?* He came along too. Thankfully Macey stayed put with Jaime.

Julian decided to make friends with Ryder on our walk, which was more like an obstacle course. We had to traverse rocks and walk under low lying branches. "What do you do for a living?" he asked Ryder.

"I own a software company."

"Cool. What sort of software do you sell?"

"We launched the Worlds Collide app."

"No way! My buddies and I use that all the time. We got a sweet deal on parasailing during spring break in Cali."

Ryder smiled, pleased. His demeanor toward Julian instantly warmed. "I can hook you up with some discount codes when we get back tomorrow."

While their bromance bloomed, I found a sweet spot where the river pooled near the bank. I plopped myself down on a moss-covered rock shaded by an aspen tree. Julian and Ryder both tried to join me.

"I don't think so, boys. You're going to have to find your own spot."

Julian chuckled and walked past me. Ryder, on the other hand, settled on a rock near me. Julian took note and gave me a wink as he headed farther up the river.

"What do you think you're doing?" I teased.

His eyes gripped me. "Hell, I don't know." He rubbed the back of his neck. "You have this pull on me."

I could tell this admission distressed him. "Well . . . why don't we act like two old friends fishing and see where it goes," I suggested, hoping that didn't scare him away.

He tilted his head, mulling over my invitation. He finally let out a heavy breath. "You've never ceased to surprise me." A faint smile crossed his lips.

I grinned and dropped my line in the dark water pooling beneath my dangling feet. *Play it cool,* I reminded myself. "How's work going?" That was friend-like.

Ryder dropped his own line and went with it. "Busy. We have a lot to do before our new release next month." He didn't elaborate further or ask me anything in return, so we sat in companionable silence for a bit, moving our lines here and there every minute or so.

After a few minutes, out of the blue he asked, "Why did you give up being a midwife? You loved it."

I focused on some of the leaves that had fallen in the river that danced among the light current. "I still love it. I just needed a change after . . ." This probably wasn't a good time for me to mention this all came about because I thought he was cheating on me and I left him. I faced him and was met with uncertain but soft eyes. I would take what I could get from him. "Anyway, I hope to get licensed here someday, but for now I'm enjoying running the boutique."

"It suits you." He grinned.

"I do love clothes."

"I remember." He moved his line farther out. "By the way, thank you for suggesting I talk to Mr. Carrington. Bobby Jay has a meeting with him this week to discuss a partnership."

"That's great. Mr. Carrington is a good man."

"Seems like good folk."

"Speaking of folks," I bit my lip, "can I ask how yours are?"

His ears tinged red and his jaw pulsed, but he took some deep breaths. "They're good, Shelby. They miss you," he was reluctant to admit. "Especially my momma."

"I miss them too."

He picked up a pebble near him and tossed it into the river. "They'd love to hear from you."

I had to choke back the tears. "I'll be sure to call them."

"You do that." His lip twitched. "How's your side feeling?"

I looked down at my side even though it was covered by my tank top and the dressing Ryder had placed over it. "I think I will survive."

"I'm glad to hear that."

I couldn't hide my grin. I was so pleased, I almost didn't notice the tug on my line. I jumped when I realized. "I think I might have a bite."

Ryder pulled his line out of the water and got right up next to me. "Gentle," he guided me.

I yanked a bit, and the fish or whatever it was fought back, almost making me lose my grip. "Goodness, it's lively."

Ryder laughed at me. "Darlin', this is no time to be proper." It wasn't the first time he had said that to me. "Don't give him any slack."

I used both hands to tug on the active line.

"Easy, easy." Ryder bent over to get a better look. "He looks like a big one. Start pulling him in slowly."

I did as he instructed. "He's putting up a fight."

"You're tougher than him. Show him who's boss, just like I taught you."

For a beautiful moment it felt like old times, but I reminded my heart not to get its hopes up.

I stood carefully, doing my best to keep ahold of the line.

Ryder stood too, all smiles. He was in his element.

I pulled the line up enough to see a bit of what I was dealing with. The fish was twisting and doing his best to get away.

"One good yank should do it," Ryder assessed.

"Okay." I pulled with all my might.

The fish came flying out, and before it hit me in the face, Ryder grabbed ahold of it. The thing wriggled fiercely in his hands. "Look what you caught." Ryder was as proud as could be.

I couldn't care less about the fish. My heart was hoping to catch something much bigger. I hoped this was a start.

Chapter Twenty

"I heard you cooked over a fire and ate trout off a stick." Bobby Jay nudged me. It was Sunday evening, and the two of us were leaning over the pasture fence like a couple of kids, hoping the horses would come our way.

"Trout that I caught." I nudged him back.

"Ryder mentioned you out-fished him."

"If you count me catching two and him none." I grinned wickedly. "I do have to give him some of the credit. He made sure they didn't get away, and he gutted them." For that I could have kissed him. I hated that part. I would have kissed him anyway, but he was still wary of me.

"I'm glad y'all had a good time."

"I think we did for the most part, but he sure hightailed it away from me when we got back this afternoon."

"You can't exactly blame him, darlin'. You ripped the man's heart out."

"I know," I whispered, "but I swear it wasn't on purpose."

"I know that."

"Does he?"

Bobby Jay turned around and leaned his back against the fence. "I don't think he knows what to think." He grinned. "He's got a battle going on inside of him something fierce."

"For that I'm sorry, along with a whole lot of other things. By the way, where is he tonight?"

"Working."

"On a Sunday night?"

"Girl, we have a business to run, and he was off gallivanting through the woods with you for two days."

"Yeah, but he never worked on the weekends like this before."

"Times change, honey."

"I suppose so." I wasn't sure I liked that particular change.

We got lucky and the old paint, Paddington, moseyed on over to us. I loved on his head. "So how was your weekend?" I asked.

He wagged his brows. "Enjoyable."

I rolled my eyes. "I don't want to know."

"That's a good call. I'd hate to burn those pretty little ears of yours off."

"Are you serious with this mystery woman?"

"I'd like to be, but she's taking some convincing."

"What's her hold up?" I wasn't sure I liked the sound of this woman.

He shrugged. "Nothing that can't be overcome."

"I want to meet her to see if she's good enough for you."

He tapped my nose. "All in good time, darlin'. You have your own love life to worry about."

I let out a deep sigh. "I thought this weekend was a start. Even though he kept me at arm's length, he took good care of me."

Last night he made sure my hammock was properly tied to the tree, and he even slept close by. Today on our hike back he carried my backpack all the way home. But he mostly talked to Julian. They bonded over hunting stories and their favorite beer. They even talked about getting together in the future.

Jaime had stayed close to Macey. Last night, Macey had asked me if I liked Jaime. I think she was hoping I did so it would give her a clear path to Ryder, though I was pretty sure he wasn't into her. I told her I thought of Jaime as a friend, but that any woman would be lucky to have his attention and affection.

"He mentioned you hurt yourself, but like an idiot you kept on going," Bobby Jay said.

"Did he call me an idiot?"

"No. Worse." He grinned evilly. "He said you were too dang irresistible." Bobby Jay chuckled. "Apparently, independent wilderness Shelby is a real turn on. I'm still mad I didn't get to see you pee in the woods."

I rolled my eyes at him and rubbed Paddington's neck. "What do you think I should do now?"

"Just keep doing what you're doing, girl. I can't say for sure whether it will work out or not. But this I know, he'd be a fool to let you get away again."

I wrapped my arms around Bobby Jay's middle. "Thank you for convincing him to go."

He patted my back. "It did take some work. For the effort, I think you owe me at least a gallon of sweet tea."

"If this works out, I'll make you sweet tea for the rest of your life."

"I'm going to hold you to that, darlin'."

That night I decided I should start the process of making things right with Ryder's parents, if that was even possible. I sat on my bed and stared at my phone for several minutes trying to think of how to even start a conversation. "Hi, this is Shelby, your would-be daughter-in-law. Sorry I left your son because my parents are awful people, which you already knew but were always too kind to say." Or maybe I could go with, "Remember when you told me there was nothing I could do that would ever change your mind about me? Did that include me ripping your son's heart out? Your only son? Your pride and joy?"

Ryder wasn't the only child. He had an older sister who died when she was four from the flu. Ryder was two at the time, so he doesn't remember Ada, but there were pictures of the pretty little girl with corn silk hair all over his parents' small home. Momma Jo used to tell me that she thought Ada and I could have been twins. It made my guilt feel all the more acute. But I knew if I was going to get Ryder back, I had to start mending the fence with his parents. They were a tight-knit family bound by love and hard times, Momma Jo used to say.

Maybe that was part of my family's problem—we had it too easy. We never worried about paying the mortgage. I'm not even sure we had one. It seemed like Momma's and Daddy's biggest worry was where we should vacation, foreign or domestic?

Ryder's family knew what it was like not only to go without luxuries, but things like new clothes and cars that didn't break down at least once a month. Just about everything they owned was a hand-me-down or bought used. Their mismatched furniture had an eclectic charm. But despite not having much in worldly wealth, they were the richest people I knew. They loved each other and God. They loved me. I hoped that was still true.

I picked up my phone and said a silent prayer before dialing their house number. Momma Jo didn't believe in cell phones. With bated breath I waited for her to answer. After three rings she picked up. "Lord, someone better be dead, calling this late at night." Oops. I guess it was ten there and they were early risers.

"I'm sorry for the late call, Miss Jolene." I didn't feel worthy to call her Momma Jo at the moment.

"Goodness gracious, girl, is this who I think it is?"

"It's Shelby, ma'am."

"Don't use those fine manners with me. How are you, sugar?"

I sank into my pillows, relieved she even took my call. "I. Am. Sorry," I choked out.

"I figured you would be, baby girl. Ya done made a mess of things, didn't you?" She was never one to sugar coat things.

"Yes, I did."

"Well, I'm still hoping to call you mine, so whatta ya goin' do to fix it?"

Tears poured down my cheeks. After everything, she still wanted me. "I'm doing everything I can think of, even if it means backing off."

"You always were a smart girl. Most of the time," she added.

I deserved that one.

"Just don't back off too much," she continued. "The boy's been pining for you for over a year now. A lot of bellyaching that I'm tired of hearing."

A tiny laugh escaped me.

"I miss your laughter, sugar. Tell me how you've been faring this past year."

"I've done my fair share of bellyaching too, but I've been good. I've missed you and Boone."

"We've missed you too. Things haven't been the same since you left. I think I cried a river last September on your wedding day that didn't happen."

I had too. I thought back to the organza gown with real pearl buttons and a chapel train. The one Ryder convinced me to sneak him into the bridal boutique and try on for him. My momma would have killed me had she known we went there together. That was anything but proper. I justified it because it wasn't my dress; it was only the one I tried on. Mine was on order from the designer in London.

I'd never forgotten the way Ryder's eyes had welled up with tears when I came out of the dressing room. The way he begged me to elope right then. He said he would have sold everything he had to buy the dress in the store and marry me that day. I wished I would have. After that is when things started falling apart. I thought maybe the whole seeing-the-bride-in-her-dress-before-the-ceremony-is-bad-luck was possibly true. Ryder started spending more time working, and apparently my parents upped their scheming. I did my part by falling for it all.

"Miss Jolene, I am so sorry. I thought . . . well . . . maybe I didn't think, but you must know I wouldn't have left him or you and Boone for all the world had I known the truth. I assume Ryder told you about what my parents did."

"Uh-huh," she sounded none too pleased.

"Those pictures broke me. Regardless, I should have been adult enough to face him."

"Sugar, I'm not casting stones at you. Lord knows your momma and daddy were going to do what they could to stop that wedding. The pressure they put on you wasn't ever right. And I warned my son the time he was keeping away from you was going to lead to a bad end. I didn't think it would go this bad, but sometimes things have to come apart to go back together better and stronger than ever. That's what I'm hoping for the two of you."

I pulled up my sore legs and curled into myself. "I hope that too."

"You're going to have to do more than hope, baby girl. Promise me you'll do something for me."

"Anything."

"My boy has a birthday on Wednesday. It's the first year I won't be with him to make his favorite cake. Can you do that for me?"

"The Chantilly lace and berry cake?" It was a special cake only made on his birthday, as it was quite expensive to make. Ryder looked forward to it every year.

"That's the one. Get a pen and paper; it's time I shared my recipe with you."

"You said that recipe was only for his wife."

"Desperate times call for desperate measures."

I reached over and pulled open my nightstand drawer to get the paper and pen. The box my engagement ring was hidden in was a glaring reminder of what was at stake. I wanted Ryder to place the ring on my finger again. I swore if I wore it again, it would never come off. I grabbed the paper and pen and put her on speaker. "I'm ready when you are, Miss Jolene."

"Quit calling me Miss Jolene. I'm Momma Jo to you."

Chapter Twenty-One

"I THINK I should taste test that for you." Emma was already licking her lips, staring at the whipped cream frosting with mascarpone that clung to the beaters while she sat at the breakfast bar to keep me company.

I grinned and popped the beaters off the mixer. I held up both between us. "I mean, I do want this cake to be perfect."

I was not only nervous about making the famed Prescott Chantilly lace and berry cake, but about delivering it to Ryder. I had only seen him once since we got back from our backpacking trip and it was brief. He and Bobby Jay had showed up last night after I taught the dance exercise class that took everything out of me. My thighs were still on fire and my side was sensitive from the wilderness excursion.

I was looking like a holy mess when Bobby Jay and Ryder conveniently showed up to give me back my basket and the empty jar of peach jam, which was apparently well loved. Ryder asked about my side. The bandage was in plain sight since I was wearing a half tank top to teach in. All that really passed between us were some pleasantries before he excused himself to get some work done.

Emma grabbed one of the beaters from me and practically drooled over it. "It's not cheating if we both eat sugar, right?" She had been so good about our detox even though it was killing her.

"Right." I swiped a bit of frosting off the beater with my finger, debating whether I should lick it off or not. Being off sugar for several days could make it taste overly sweet. On the other hand, it could be like a gateway drug and have me falling off the detox wagon.

Emma dove right in and licked the frosting straight off the beater. She closed her eyes and looked as if she were having a moment when she sighed, "This is right up there with sex. Don't tell Sawyer I said that," she quickly added.

I giggled before joining her. I licked the sweet frosting off my finger. It tasted like home and happier days filled with promises and dreams. I wanted all those dreams back with Ryder. "What's the verdict?"

"You're a goddess." Emma took another lick. "If he doesn't take one bite of this and marry you, he's a bigger idiot than I thought."

"You think he's an idiot?"

"He's not here, so yes." She set her licked-clean beater on the counter. "Promise me something."

"All right." I set my own beater in the sink.

"Don't lose your dignity chasing after him. I get you made a mistake, but don't let him punish you for it. You need to quit punishing yourself for it while you're at it. You don't deserve it. I can understand him needing some time to come to terms with the circumstances, but he knows how you feel and that you're sorry. It's time for him to decide to forgive you or let you move on. That's the fair thing for both of you."

I nodded. "You're right. It's easier said than done, but you're right. Do you think taking this cake to him is a bad idea? I promised his momma I would."

Emma stole one of the strawberries I had washed and hulled for the cake. "I think it's sweet, and he better appreciate it."

I hoped he would too. It was a fussy cake to make, with raspberry and apricot jam, fruit, and frosting between the homemade almond cake layers. Then you had to make sure the frosting was just right and the berries on top had to be arranged in such a way that was pleasing to the eye.

Dressed in a light blue romper I knew Ryder would love, I walked the finished product over to his cabin with trepidation, hoping he would be there. I rehearsed what I would say to him. My plan was to keep it short and sweet but leave no doubt about my intentions. I wanted a second chance. If this cake didn't say that, I didn't know what would, other than me coming right out and telling him how much I loved him, which I was sure wasn't the right thing to do. But Emma was right. I couldn't and wouldn't keep chasing after him if it's not what he wanted.

I was happy to see his and Bobby Jay's vehicles were both there when I arrived. I would hope so—it was already past eight and it was Ryder's birthday, after all. Not like he ever made a big deal out of it. All he ever wanted was a simple dinner at home with his family and the cake I carried. He didn't even like me to buy him anything. Of course, I always did. The last birthday of his we were together I bought him a new motorcycle helmet. Little did I know he wouldn't need it for all that long. Such tender but guilt-ridden feelings surrounded him selling his motorcycle to purchase my engagement ring. I'm sure he had cursed me over it a time or two. Maybe he still did.

I carefully held the cake in one hand while I knocked on their door. I didn't even think about it this time like before when I brought the biscuits. I knew what I wanted, and I was going for it. It didn't take long for the door to swing open. There Bobby Jay stood shaking his head and grinning from ear to ear at me. It was still weird for me to see him all dressed up in business attire. He looked so grown up, which sounded silly, considering he was older than me.

"Ryder," Bobby Jay yelled, "you have a special delivery." Bobby Jay waved me in with a wink.

I stepped into the bachelor pad. One thing that hadn't changed was that these boys were messy. Pizza boxes and beer cans littered the coffee table and the kitchen counters. It made me glad to see the mess. It gave me hope that not everything had changed. I hoped that included Ryder's love for me. Surely he could find it again.

Ryder walked out from the back loosening his tie as he went. Though I missed the blue jeans and T-shirt, there was something to be said about the sex appeal that oozed off the dressed-up version of him.

"What are you hollering—" Ryder caught sight of me and stopped mid-sentence. "Shelby." He rubbed his neck.

I held up the cake. "Happy birthday. Your momma gave me her recipe."

His eyes widened. I was surprised too. She guarded that recipe like she would a child.

Bobby Jay looked between the two of us. "I think I'm going to change."

I gave Bobby Jay a grateful smile before he headed Ryder's way. Bobby Jay punched Ryder's shoulder as he walked past him. "Don't be a prick."

Ryder scowled at him before he braved approaching me. "Momma said you had talked, but she didn't mention the cake."

I wondered what she had mentioned, but I didn't ask. Instead, I held up the cake and handed it to him. "She wanted to make sure you were taken care of, and I don't think she trusted Bobby Jay's abilities."

Ryder cracked a smile before relieving me of his cake. "Seeing as all he knows how to do is warm up a can of pork and beans, that was smart on her part."

I laughed. "I suppose it was. Well, anyway, I just wanted to wish you a happy thirty-fourth. I hope this is a good year for you." It took all I had not to kiss him, but I made myself step back. "I should get going."

He stared at me, unsure, but didn't say a thing. That, unfortunately, was my cue to turn around.

"Good night." I reached for the door handle.

"You expect me to eat this all by myself?"

I grinned to no one but me. "I'm sure Bobby Jay will be more than happy to help you out," I spoke to the door, my hand still on the knob.

"Stay, Shelby. Please."

My heart did a little dance before I turned around and played it cool. "All right, if that's what you really want."

"I wouldn't have asked if I didn't." He turned and headed toward their small kitchen. "Make yourself at home. I'll cut us each a slice."

"You will do no such thing. It's your birthday." I took the cake back from him. "You sit down, and I'll see if I can find a place to put this cake in all your mess."

He chuckled. "I guess we should tidy up."

"Cleaning was never your forte."

"Been busy." He cleared away several takeout boxes, giving me room on the counter to put the cake.

"That's what I hear. How's the new update going?" I searched the kitchen drawers for a knife.

Ryder came behind me and got some plates for us. "There are always setbacks when it comes to software. You fix one bug and discover three more. I need to hire more developers, but that takes time too."

"Don't you have a project manager to do that?"

He set two plates next to me. A tired grin played on his face. "I should, but I haven't wanted to give up that control yet. And honestly, I still feel more comfortable acting as a developer than the boss."

"I can understand that." I plunged the knife into the three-layer cake. "But it can't be good for you to work so many hours and wear so many hats."

He shrugged and with it came an unwelcome change in his demeanor. "It's been a good distraction."

I had said the wrong thing. I wanted to kick myself; instead, I tried to smooth it over. I placed a large piece of cake on one of the small plates before lifting it up and presenting it as a peace offering. "Here's to you getting some better distractions this year." I used my, *why yes, I'm talking about me* voice and I would be very happy to distract him right here and now.

He eyed me carefully before taking the cake. The tension eased from his face. A smirk even appeared. "Thank you." He took the cake.

"You're welcome. I'm sorry I didn't bring any candles. I could still sing to you."

In his eyes, I could see the memory play of the last time I sang "Happy Birthday" to him. It was a private setting in the back of his truck after his family birthday party. I wished him happy birthday in my own way.

He drew closer as if inviting me to replay that night, but he paused. "That sounds like trouble, Miss Shelby."

I wished he would call me Chief, but Miss Shelby was better than Miss Duchane any day. "You always said a little trouble was good for the soul."

"You've always been a lot, darlin'." He ran away from me and landed on his couch.

I internally sighed and cut myself a small piece of cake. I hoped Emma would forgive me for cheating without her. I sat down with my cake on the plaid chair, away from him, wondering what it was going to take for him to warm back up to me.

He cast me a furtive smile as if he himself knew how silly it was for us to be sitting so far apart. After his sneaky grin, he dove into his cake. One bite in and pleasure filled every nook and cranny on his gorgeous face. "Dang. I think this is better than my momma's."

I smiled, pleased. "Let's not mention that to her." She prided herself on that cake.

He chuckled. "Good idea." He started shoveling it in as fast as he could while keeping some manners intact.

I took small bites and savored every bit knowing it would be a while before I had sugar again. Tomorrow I was back on the detox wagon. "I was thinking you should talk to Jenna and Brad Kacinski. They own High on Laughs, a comedy club in Edenvale. It's really popular among the college kids there. It would be a great business to add to your app."

He gave me a crooked grin. "You trying to take over Bobby Jay's job?"

I bit my lip. "I'm just trying to be helpful."

"I see that." Sexy undertones accompanied his response.

I set my cake down on the pizza box in front of me and leaned more toward him. "I was also thinking that maybe you should meet me there on Saturday night. It's comedy sports night. Several teams compete against each other to see who's the funniest. It's a lot of fun." I tucked some hair behind my ear. "And, you know, I could introduce you to Brad and Jenna. It could be strictly business."

He lowered his fork. "Business, huh? Is that what you want?"

I shook my head. Sexual tension lingered between us like fog after a Georgia rain, thicker than chicken and dumplings. Unfortunately, Bobby Jay came in like a fog light, laughing at us.

"Y'all need help. Why in the world are you sitting so far apart? I thought I'd come in here having to tell you to take it to the bedroom." He let out a heavy breath. "Since you're still being stupid, I guess I'll get some cake."

I sat back in the chair, disappointed, until Ryder said quiet-like, "What time on Saturday?"

"Seven." I smiled.

"Save me a seat."

My heart soared so much I wanted to fling myself onto his lap. The knock on the door prevented me from being foolhardy. It also gave me some pause. Bobby Jay answered the door with cheeks stuffed full of cake. On the other side of it were two beautiful bombshells, Macey holding a large bouquet of brightly colored happy birthday balloons, and Marlowe looking put out, as usual. I gripped the chair, not sure what to make of it. Ryder stood, looking between me and them. Was he trying to decide who to choose?

Macey ran in all smiles and avoiding my gaze. "I heard it was your birthday!"

Marlowe rolled her eyes. Was that because she wanted Ryder, or she thought, like me, that Macey was an imbecile? Marlowe also gave me an appraising sort of look. If I wasn't mistaken, it was almost as if she were sorry. That more than anything threw me off.

Bobby Jay put his arms around both women. "Now that you're here you can join us all for cake. Miss Shelby has made the finest cake in the history of the world."

"You know, I better get going." I stood.

Bobby Jay's head dropped.

Ryder looked unsure as to what he should do or say. I took matters into my own hands. I shimmied around the coffee table to get close to the man I loved. I took one moment to peer into his eyes and say with my own what I really wanted to. Tenderness filled his, letting me know the message was received. It gave me courage to lean in and press my lips against his warm cheek. I only lingered for a second. "Happy birthday," I whispered. "I'll see you Saturday."

He placed his hand on the cheek where my lips had just been and nodded.

I turned and gave a dazzling smile to everyone else. I took note of Macey's dropped jaw and Marlowe's impressed grin. "Good night, ladies. See you at work tomorrow."

Translation—keep your hands off my man.

Chapter Twenty-Two

"He'll be here." Emma patted my arm after I'd looked toward the entrance at High on Laughs for the hundredth time.

I had emailed him yesterday with the address and reminding him of the time, thinking that would be cute and spark some sweet memories of us. I took a chance that he still had his old email address. He did and he emailed me back saying he was looking forward to it. He still didn't call me Chief, but I was hoping we were getting there.

"Don't count on it," Aspen disagreed. "There is one thing you can and should count on, and that is that men will disappoint you as often as they can. Take Leland, for example. See, I thought he would stay out of mine and Chloe's life forever, but no, the pig called me this week after three years of hearing nothing from him, not even a birthday call to his daughter. And you know what he told me?" Her voiced cracked. "He informed me he got remarried and has a new baby, another daughter."

Everyone in our group who was standing around the DJ booth gasped, even Sawyer and Brad.

"That's right." Aspen was doing her best to fight back tears. "Not only that, he might have a job opportunity that will bring him back to Colorado and he wants to know what he can do to make things right between us so that he can see Chloe. When I told him there was nothing he could do, he said he'd take me to court if he had to."

"No!" Emma reached into her bag and handed Aspen a tissue.

"That d-bag," Jenna hugged Aspen. "Doesn't he owe, like, thousands of dollars in child support?"

Aspen nodded against Jenna. "Unfortunately, that doesn't bar him from seeing her. Though he could be jailed or fined for it. I could only hope. I don't have the money to fight him in court."

"We'll help," Sawyer put his arm around Emma. Emma beamed up at him as if he were finer than frog hairs.

"That's kind of you." Aspen dabbed her eyes. "But he's never followed through with any promise, so hopefully he won't now. You know what kills me the most? He said his new wife taught him how important family is and what love feels like. What were Chloe and I to him? I did love him and tried my best to make us work despite the odds. I begged him to stay." She crumbled into Jenna's arms.

My heart ached for her. No wonder she was so disillusioned about men and relationships. I knew she was only nineteen when she got pregnant and married. So young to have your heart ripped into shreds. Having a child, I'm sure, only made it harder. She didn't even get the chance to graduate from college until this year. I thought she was remarkable. Her twelve-year-old daughter, Chloe, was the sweetest, smartest kid I'd ever met. I attributed that to Aspen being such an attentive and hardworking mother. She talked tough about men, but she was all soft when it came to her girl.

"Baby, we've got to get ready and start the show," Brad gently reminded Jenna.

Jenna gave Aspen one more big squeeze. "We'll figure this out together."

We all nodded.

I put my arm around Aspen. "Let's go find some seats." I took another peek at the door before we took up a section in the second row. I saved a seat for Ryder on the end, telling myself there was still ten minutes before the show started so I shouldn't worry.

We all talked about Emma's soccer team she coached to pass the time. They'd had a game today. It brightened Aspen up since her daughter, Chloe, was the goalie and she had made some spectacular saves, from the sounds of it.

Seven came and still no Ryder. While Brad and Jenna jumped on stage to welcome the crowd and get them hyped up, I pulled out my phone and checked my email. Sure enough, there was one from Ryder.

Sorry this is last minute, but something has come up and I need to attend to it. I'll catch you later.

I shoved my phone back into my purse.

"Everything okay?" Aspen whispered.

"Yeah. Maybe you're right. I should have expected to be disappointed."

Aspen grinned wickedly. "I can order another cockroach."

"I'll let you know."

I arrived home just after midnight. After the show at the club, we all decided to do a late dinner together to celebrate yet another Jenna and Brad sports night comedy victory. That, and it meant baby snuggles for me. Jenna and Brad picked up Elliot from Brad's dad's house before they met us for dinner. They couldn't stand to be away from him for too long. I couldn't blame them.

While Elliot was not the man I hoped to be snuggling for the evening, he was a great substitute. Though as cute and cuddly as he was, he didn't take my mind off Ryder. We discussed Ryder at length. The women were for naming a cockroach on his behalf, but the men said we women were reading too much into it. Brad and Sawyer sympathized with starting a new business, as they had each done it. Regardless, it was disheartening.

Not as disheartening, though, as when I walked into the mostly dark house. The only light came from the large flat screen in the family room. A movie I didn't recognize played on it, but a distinct sound I hadn't heard in a long while was louder than the surround sound. Bobby Jay's snoring was unmistakable. It sounded like an opossum had gotten stuck in a garbage disposal. What was he doing here? I'd asked him if he wanted to come to the comedy club tonight, too. I suggested he bring his mystery lady, but he said he and his girl had plans already.

I tiptoed into the family room and discovered I was right, Bobby Jay was there sound asleep sitting up on the large leather couch with his big mouth hanging open.

Not only was I right, but I was dead wrong. Wrong to ever have any hope of Ryder and I getting back together. He slept on the couch too, right between Marlowe and Macey. A girl for each shoulder. They all looked cozy—boy, girl, boy, girl—under the afghans that normally hung on the back of the couch. I guess something had come up, all right. Why didn't he just tell me he had a date? With which Carrington twin I had no idea; they both looked like a candidate with how contently they slept on him.

I ran from the room and held in the sobs that wanted to erupt from my chest until I made it to my bedroom. Once behind the safety of its door, a cry so gut wrenching escaped me that it had me sliding down the door until my head fell into my knees. There I cried a river down my bare legs.

An ache worse than the one I felt after getting those godforsaken pictures filled me. I had my answer. It wasn't what I wished or hoped for, but there it was handed to me in a cruel manner. Maybe this was his revenge. One cowardly act for another.

I eventually cried myself to sleep there. I woke up on the floor to a damp spot on the carpet. The morning light was barely filtering in through the blinds. I sat up and felt like that time my cousin Arlene had given me the whiskey and cigarette. My head pounded, but it was clear, and I knew what I had to do after I showered. My body needed the warm water after a night of sleeping on the floor and crying.

I let the water wash over me, wishing all the hurt could wash down the drain, but it was ever present. Nevertheless, I was determined to finally move on from Carroll Ryder Prescott. I was going to start by giving back his ring and searching for a new place to live. I had no intention of seeing him gallivant around with Macey or Marlowe.

I wasn't even sure I wanted to see Bobby Jay again. He had to have known. All that talk about us being family was just a lie. Maybe I could talk Mr. Jacobsen into renting me the yellow house this summer. We could do a rent-to-own situation. And maybe Macey and Marlowe could find new employment at Prescott Technologies because the first person to say Ryder's name at the boutique was getting fired.

I got ready for church, because if ever I needed Jesus, today was the day. I put into practice the code of all Southern women: I did my hair and makeup and threw on some high heels. Meanwhile, I was dying inside. Opening my nightstand drawer and reaching for his ring almost made the makeup all for naught, but I held back the tears. I had shed my share throughout the night and for the past year. I threw the ring box in my purse, resisting the urge to look at the vintage byzantine ring one more time. It wasn't mine anymore. And I didn't care how early it was, I was giving it back first thing this morning. I could no longer carry the emotional weight of it.

I took the back stairs that led into the kitchen. It was so early not even Mr. Carrington was awake. My heels landed on the hardwood floor and echoed across the kitchen. I clacked my way across the floor not paying attention to anything except making it to the front door as if it were the key to my freedom. There was an obstacle though. A gorgeous one running his fingers through his mussed hair, looking dazed and confused as he headed toward my escape route.

My heels alerted him to my presence. He faced me in his wrinkled dress clothes, blinking as if he were trying to focus.

Why hadn't I thought he might have spent the night? Because I was an idiot. That much was obvious. Well, at least he was going to save me a trip in my heels down the rocky path to his cabin.

"Shelby." He rubbed his neck. "I didn't expect you to . . . I mean, about last night—"

"I know. You don't need to say anything." I tried to keep my voice steady while reaching into my purse. This was it. I was moving on. I could do it. Why, then, was my hand gripping the box as if it was begging me not to let go? I had to. I approached him near the door and pulled out the wooden ring box. His eyes widened when he recognized what I held.

Tears pooled in my eyes against my wishes. "I know you don't want to hear this, but I am sorry for everything." I took his hand and placed my ring, his ring, in it. "I should have given this back to you a long time ago."

He stared blankly at the small box.

I leaned in and breathed him in one last time before kissing his cheek, leaving not only a lipstick stain, but some of my tears. "I will always love you, Ryder Prescott. I wish you all the happiness in the world. Good luck with Marlowe, or is that Macey?" Either way he was going to need it, but I didn't wait for his reaction or response, not that I was expecting one. I fled as fast as my heeled feet would take me. I didn't even bother to close the door behind me.

By the time I made it down the porch, I heard Ryder call out to me. "Shelby, wait."

No. I was done waiting. I wasn't going to wait any more for him to forgive me. I was awarding myself custody of my heart.

Chapter Twenty-Three

I WALKED AS fast as my heels would allow to the garage. Once I got in my car, I tore out of the Ranch like I was late to Nordstrom's half yearly sale. I blared my breakup mix through the sound system, crying and singing along to every sad lyric. I made it to church in no time. I parked in front of *my* house. There I took a moment to breathe and pull myself together. That was, until I turned and saw the For Sale sign in front of my house.

What? I jumped out of the car to get a better look. This had to be a mistake. Mr. Jacobsen promised he wouldn't put it on the market until the fall. I walked up the cobblestone path and, sure enough, the house was for sale. I grabbed one of the informational brochures and had to swallow my heart down. The asking price was well above what he and I had discussed. What had changed? It appeared I was meant to lose everything today.

Solemnly, I walked toward the church on the lonely sidewalk staring at the brochure, trying to think of any way to afford the house. Even selling my car wouldn't get me where I needed to be. Now what was I going to do? I had to get out of Carrington Ranch. I couldn't watch Ryder fall in love with another woman.

I was so early to church there was no one at the door to greet me. I was grateful for it. It allowed me to sneak into the chapel unnoticed and slip into the back pew. As soon as I was seated, my emotions heightened and the tears came with it. What was it about church that made you cry so hard or smile so wide? It was like being in God's presence made you more aware of everything. Like my heart and mind realized the full impact of the loss I had incurred this morning.

With head bowed, I quietly let it all out while I silently prayed to God to help me. To let Jesus take that wheel and direct me. I needed Him to now more than ever. I had never felt so lost or alone.

Amid my silent pleas, I felt someone sit next to me. At first I was irritated that in an empty chapel they would choose to sit near me, but then the scent of sandalwood tickled my nose right before a warm, strong hand took my own and held it between both of his. My eyes fluttered open as if I were dreaming, but this wasn't a dream. I turned and faced Ryder, who was still dressed in his wrinkled clothes with mussed hair.

"What are you doing here?" And why was he holding my hand and looking at me so tenderly.

He squeezed my hand. "Isn't this where proud bastards come to seek forgiveness for their prideful behavior?"

I tilted my head, still confused. "Well, yes, but—"

"Shelby." He reached up and wiped away some of my tears. "I could never stand to see you cry, especially when it was my doing."

I looked down at our clasped hands that belonged together, then back up into his misted eyes. "Aren't you with Marlowe? Or Macey?"

"Why would you think that?"

"I saw you last night on the couch sleeping with both of them."

He grimaced before groaning. "Darlin', I didn't mean to fall asleep there. I came looking for you last night to apologize about standing you up when Bobby Jay and Marlowe invited me to watch a movie with them while I waited for you."

I blinked rapidly, trying to comprehend. "Wait. Wait. Did you say Bobby Jay and Marlowe?"

He flashed me a crooked grin. "They've been seeing each other."

I shook my head, astonished. "That can't be. He's not her type. She'll eat him alive."

"That's their business." He shrugged.

"What about Macey?"

"What about her?"

"You were together last night."

He scooted closer to me. His lips rested on my forehead, filling me with warmth and a comfort only he could provide. "Shelby, I'm not with Macey. I've only been trying to come to terms with all that has passed between us. I know that's hurt you and for that I'm sorry, but you don't know what you did to me, leaving like you did." He leaned back. There was no malice in his eyes, only hurt.

I squeezed his hand. "If I could go back and change it all I would. At the time, it all made sense. Something had changed between us."

He let out a heavy breath. "I know."

"Why did you keep Worlds Collide a secret from me?"

He thought for a moment. "Will you go on a walk with me?"

I nodded.

We stood together, our hands clasped as if we were holding onto every ounce of hope we had. We walked out into the warm morning sun in silence, but together. My heart could hardly believe it. Was there a chance for us? We naturally drifted in the direction of the park a block from the church, our clasped hands swinging between us.

"Shelby," he breathed out when we passed the church's parking lot, "remember when you tried on your wedding dress for me?"

I nodded with a smile.

His face, on the other hand, was filled with consternation. "You never looked so beautiful or happy."

"You make that sound like a bad thing."

He squeezed my hand. "No darlin', I never wanted you more, but it hit home that day that unless I did something different, I could never afford to give you that moment."

I tugged on his hand and stopped. "Ryder, it was you who gave me that moment. Do you think I was that happy when I tried the dress on with my momma, who criticized everything about it from the cut of it to the fact that it wasn't white?" Not to mention who I was marrying, but I left that bit out. "But the way you looked at me in it and knowing that it was the dress we would become man and wife in," emotion bled through my voice, "that's what made me happy."

"But Shelby, I couldn't buy that dress for you."

"It was never about the dress. It could have been any dress."

Red crept up his neck and face. "You kept saying things like that, but how could you know for certain, never having to do without? The more we planned our wedding, the more I realized what you were really giving up."

"I only ever looked at what I was gaining by marrying you," I sighed and kept on walking. "I wish you would have believed me."

"Shelby, it was never a matter of believing in you. It was believing in myself. I wanted to do right by you."

"You could have told me about what you were doing."

"I could have and probably should have, but I couldn't stomach the thought of failing you and I knew it was a long shot. I didn't want to get your hopes up."

I stopped and peered into his eyes. "My only hope was for us was to go through life together and raise a family." Tears trickled down my cheek.

He reached up and gently wiped the tears away with his thumb. "Then why, at the very least, didn't you confront me, or at the most, why didn't you trust me?"

The ache in his voice killed me. I closed my eyes for a moment, part of me wanting to hide from him, the other trying to put it all into words. With a deep breath out, my eyes opened wide. He deserved at least that from me.

"I guess it all comes down to I couldn't think of anything besides another woman that would have kept you away from me. You had always been so attentive, and then suddenly it was as if you loved someone more than me. When I got those pictures, it broke me. I couldn't bear you telling me that you were in love with another woman."

His eyes bordered between understanding and ire.

I held onto his hand with all I had. "I'm not making excuses; I'm just telling you why and where my heart was."

"It never occurred to you that your parents," he spat out, "were behind it all?"

I shook my head. "It should have, but I never thought they would be so cruel to inflict that kind of pain on me. I know you've been hurting, and I take the blame for that, but don't think for a second that this past year hasn't brought me to my knees. I've shed a river of tears for you, for us. Now, to know it was my own doing, you don't know what that has done to me. I'm so sorry," I cried.

He pulled me to him and enveloped me in his strong arms. I sobbed against his chest, not caring that we were out in public or that someone from my congregation might see me. All that I could focus on was that Ryder was holding me. I was where I had longed to be for months. I had come home.

Ryder stroked my hair. "Shelby, I'm sorry for keeping things from you and for being a stubborn bastard. Please don't cry." He kissed my head. "You know I can't take it."

"Too bad," I blubbered into his chest.

He pulled me tighter, holding on for dear life. "I've missed you."

"I've missed you so much." The tears kept on coming.

"Your parents deserve to be shot and hung. If I ever see them again, they are going to wish they never lied to me or you."

I leaned back. "Lied to you?"

He narrowed his eyes, confused. "I came looking for you at your momma's and daddy's and they gave me some tired story of how you came to your senses and thought it would be less messy to end things this way. They told me to move on and forget about you."

I blinked and shook my head. "Wait. They told me you never bothered to come."

A deep growl rumbled in his chest. "Damn them." His jaw tightened but he took a deep breath and let it out slowly, his anger dissipating. "I never stopped looking for you."

"Really?"

"Really." His warm hand caressed my cheek.

I leaned into it. "How did you find me?"

He flashed me a crooked grin before taking my hand. "Let's go sit on that park bench. Those heels have to be killing you."

I grinned down at my nude peep-toe heels. "These? I could mow the lawn in them."

He gave me a look I had been longing for that said, *that's my girl,* before leading us toward the bench. He made sure to help keep me steady as we walked through the grass. One of the things that made me love living in Colorado was that the grass here was so green and soft. Back home it was vine-like and coarse. Ryder helped me sit down before joining me. He put his arm around my shoulder. I rested my head on his chest. For a minute, we both took in the view without saying a word. The park was filled with metal sculptures of children at play. They were whimsical and sweet.

Ryder's fingers glided down my bare arm. "Your memaw told me where you were."

My head popped up. "I don't believe it. She was furious with you."

He shrugged. "She also drinks too much at bridge club and," his lip twitched, "I do know how to charm a lady."

"You seduced my grandmother?"

His face scrunched. "No," he said, disgusted. "I only persuaded her."

"She never mentioned talking to you."

He grinned wickedly. "She said it would be more fun that way."

"What does that mean, and didn't she at least yell at you about the pictures?" I hesitated to mention them.

"Like I said, she was tipsy, and I caught her unawares while her driver was helping her into her car, though she mentioned I was a bad, bad boy and if I wasn't so good looking, she would feed a certain body part to her dog. I wasn't sure what that was all about, but now it makes more sense."

I rolled my eyes. Memaw was something else. "What else did she say?"

He swiped my bangs to the side. "She said your momma deserved the vexation and if I was ballsy enough to track her down outside of her bridge club then maybe I deserved a second chance."

"Is that what you were looking for? A second chance?" My heart begged for him to say yes.

He paused and thought. "I was so angry, I didn't know, but I knew we had unfinished business. I wanted you and your family to see that I had made something out of myself."

I rested my hand on his stubbled cheek. "Men are not made in boardrooms. They're made at their momma's knees and working with their daddies in hay fields."

He took my hand and kissed my palm. His warm breath on my skin excited me. A sultry expression danced across his handsome face. "There are some other things I enjoyed more in that field."

I blushed thinking about those "other" things.

"I didn't mean to embarrass you, Miss Shelby."

"We never did anything that I'm embarrassed about."

"I'm relieved to hear that." He kissed the tips of my fingers.

I could hardly breathe, his touch had me so wound up. "What now, Ryder? Where do we go from here?" My heart beat furiously, hoping for the best.

He leaned in and rested his forehead against my own. His unspoken thoughts hung heavy between us. "Let's start over, Shelby. See if this new you and me can make a go of it here, away from your family."

The thought made me soar, but doubt crept in. "What if we find we don't like each other?"

"Darlin'," he kissed my nose. "I don't see that being a problem for me. I like you more now than ever."

"I was hoping you would finally realize that." I laughed and cried all at once. So many emotions coursed through me.

"Believe me, it's taken everything I have since our first run-in here not to take you into my arms and show you *everything* I like about you."

Oh, Mylanta.

His strong hand brushed through my hair. "What do you say, Shelby? Will you give us another chance?"

"I would love that more than anything," I choked out.

"Promise me something."

"Anything."

He cupped my face and leaned away enough to look into my eyes. "Promise me if you ever have any doubts about how I feel or where we stand, you'll come talk to me before you go running off."

"With all that I am, I promise. Will you promise not to go off and start a company without telling me?"

"Deal." He leaned in. I held my breath waiting. Waiting for and anticipating *the* moment, but his lips lingered inches from my own.

"What?" I whispered when the kiss I expected didn't come.

"You're wearing the same look as you did right before I kissed you for the very first time. Like you're worried."

I reached up and fulfilled my wish of running my hands through his hair. Did it ever feel good. "It's not worry. I just know now, like I knew then, that my life was about to change forever."

With that, he waited no longer. He brushed my lips gently, once, twice. The third kiss had his warm, wet lips lingering on mine. I closed my eyes and let him seep into my soul. His slow hands trailed silkily down my arms, leaving a path of raised skin. When I shivered, his tongue skimmed my lips, begging for them to part. I leaned in, allowing him access. He took the invitation but didn't rush. He let me savor his taste. It was like warm milk and honey, sweet and hot, infusing all my taste buds. He was all home and comfort until he deepened the kiss. Suddenly sweet became spicy and the hot turned to fire filling my soul, making me gasp and him groan.

I wanted to evaporate any space between us, but all too soon his lips left mine. He took a breath while I tried to catch mine. I was right. My life would never be the same again. This time, though, I wasn't going to let go of him.

His forehead rested against mine. "Did I mention I missed you?"

My hands rested on his chest. His heart was pounding as hard as mine. "I think so." I could hardly think.

"Do you think I can get your number?"

I giggled. "Is this where I give you my email address again?"

He brushed my lips. "No. This time I'm not leaving without your phone number. I'm not wasting any more time."

Chapter Twenty-Four

BOBBY JAY AND I sat on the front porch together on Monday at twilight while he waited for Marlowe to finish getting ready for their date. I was waiting for Ryder to pick me up for our second first official date.

Ryder and I were having dinner with his investor and his wife who had come into town. Ryder seemed awful pleased that he could share this moment with me. It was sweet, and I hoped it was the first of many things to come that we would share, including last names someday, but I admit it was a little strange for me. It felt reminiscent of, I hated to even think it, all the dinners my parents attended while I grew up. Just like Momma, I sat there dressed to the nines in a little black dress with my hair done up waiting for the CEO, my corporate beau. I never thought this would be Ryder and me. Not that there was anything wrong with it. I knew Ryder was nothing like Daddy. Ryder wanted to share the moment with me, not treat me like his accessory.

I was still trying to wrap my head around it all. Who would have imagined Ryder and me, here in Colorado? Not only that, we were together. And then there was Bobby Jay. I kept staring at him in amazement. While Ryder had a certain refinement and charm, Bobby Jay was loveable and clunky. Not the kind of man I had seen Marlowe with this past year.

Bobby Jay laughed at me and nudged me like we were two kids swinging on the front porch swing. "Quit looking at me like that, girl."

"It's just . . . I mean, how did it happen?"

He stopped the swing and looked down his nose at me. "What are you trying to say, Miss Shelby?"

"This is not an indictment against you. I'm just worried. She's always acted put off by you."

"Nah." He waved his hand in front of us. "She digs me."

"Are you sure?"

He flashed me a wicked grin. "Believe me, darlin', I'm sure."

My eyes widened, thinking of all the possibilities I prayed he wouldn't voice. "I don't want you to get hurt, especially after what Leigh Anne did to you."

He put his arm around my bare shoulders, and with the push of his leg we were swinging again. "I appreciate that, but for now we're just having some fun. Unlike another couple I know who were tangled up on the couch last night."

Heat seeped through not only my cheeks, but my entire body. I wanted to tell Ryder good night last night when he got back from work, and I did it with my lips, for hours. I didn't even know Bobby Jay was home. "We were having fun too."

"I saw that, darlin'." He chuckled.

"How long has this thing with you and Marlowe been going on?" I changed the subject.

"Since our first night here."

I leaned away. "Really?"

Bobby Jay sat up, proud like. "When I left here after talking to you, she was coming in. I worked my charms on her and took her for a drive."

"But the next day at church she was with Ryder."

He grinned. "She told me she was still going for him. I warned her it wasn't going to happen and she was only asking to get hurt chasing after a man who was in love with another woman. Told her you and Ryder were written in the stars. It didn't take her long to see I was right. Her sister, on the other hand." Bobby Jay shook his head. "Foolish girl."

Poor Macey could barely look at me yesterday at the boutique. I did my best to give her some space. I even let her go home early.

"Don't take this the wrong way, but do you have anything in common with Marlowe?"

"She likes to talk about herself and I love to look at her while she talks."

I rolled my eyes.

Bobby Jay chuckled. "Don't worry about me, girl. We get along. She can't resist my Southern charm and I can't resist her beauty; it all works out."

Speaking of the beautiful creature, she walked out in a blaze of glory. Her legs-for-days were on display in her Daisy Dukes. Her tank top showcased the rest of her nicely.

Bobby Jay jumped up looking mighty pleased. "Gorgeous." He reached for her hand and she took it, to my surprise, though she gave me a look that said she didn't want to hear a word about it.

Mr. Carrington came out and smiled at the two of them before saying, "Take good care of my girl."

"Yes, sir," Bobby Jay replied.

Marlowe rolled her eyes. "Dad, I'm not in high school."

"I probably should have had a few more talks with those boys and some of the men you've brought around since then."

Marlowe tugged on Bobby Jay's hand. "Good night, Dad."

Mr. Carrington laughed and waved. He took Bobby Jay's empty seat next to me. "She's always been so pleasant," he teased, making me laugh. "I like that Bobby Jay, though. I met with him last week. He and his cousin have created quite the business."

"I'm real proud of both of them."

Mr. Carrington gave me a knowing smile. "I'm glad to see the other cousin came to his senses."

I bit my pink tinted lip. "Me too."

Mr. Carrington patted my knee. "You have a good night. I'll leave a light on for you."

I took his hand and squeezed it before he stood. "Thank you."

He squeezed back tenderly. So like a father. He reminded me of Ryder's daddy and of what my own lacked. Mr. Carrington left me alone there to contemplate how truly terrible my own father was.

Since yesterday, I'd been so overjoyed about my reunion with Ryder, I hadn't had much time to stop and think about the wicked game my family had played with us. The levels they'd sunk to were astonishing and heartless. I was giving up on calling them. At this point, I was fine with never seeing my parents again. Memaw and I would eventually have some words. I couldn't believe she told Ryder where I was and that she had spoken to him and never mentioned it to me. It was as if she was playing her own game. I refused to be part of any games anymore.

I sat there and swung, waiting for Ryder in the warm evening air daydreaming about the day when I had my own porch and little ones at my feet. It, unfortunately, wasn't going to be at my little yellow house. Not sure where I was going to live now, but I absolutely knew who the daddy of those future babies was going to be. It was the man who pulled up in his shiny black sports car five minutes late and skidded to a stop on the driveway in front of the house.

Ryder jumped out in a dark suit, his tie undone and slung around his neck. He rushed up the porch steps. I stood ready to tease him that he'd never been late picking me up, but he froze on the steps, eyes fixed on me. I looked at my attire thinking maybe something was amiss. When I couldn't see anything, I met his eyes. They were still zeroed in on me.

"What?" I asked nervously.

He sauntered toward me. "I'm speechless, darlin'. You are a vision."

I smiled and approached him. I lifted the collar of his shirt and placed his tie under it, around his neck.

He gave me a sultry smile. "I always knew you were the kind of woman who would tie her man's tie for him."

"Is that so?" I began tying a full Windsor knot. "See, I never pictured you wearing one."

"Times change." He leaned in and brushed my lips.

"I see that." I finished the knot, centered it, and fixed his collar. "You're all set, handsome."

"Thank you." He took my hand. "We need to get going; we're

late." He led me quickly to his car and opened the passenger side door. He had to help me in more than normal. Sports cars weren't friendly to women wearing tight, short dresses. I tried to be as ladylike as possible, but still Ryder got a show. Not that he minded.

He ran around to the driver's side and slid in before taking off like we were on fire.

"I could have met you at the restaurant."

He shifted gears and kicked up a dust storm, barreling out of the Ranch. He glanced at my bare legs. "Then I couldn't see those pretty legs of yours."

"Is that the only reason?"

He took my hand and kissed it. "Shelby, this is our *first* date and I want everything to be perfect tonight. Besides, I couldn't wait to see you."

"Better." I took my hand back hoping he would use both to steer the car.

He laughed and shifted gears again.

I gripped my seat and swallowed.

"What do you think of my new car?"

"Um . . ." I looked around at all the fancy features while holding on for dear life. "It's nice."

"Nice? Listen to it purr." He increased his speed once we hit the main road outside of the Ranch.

I wanted to say I preferred the rumble of his old truck. "Would you mind slowing down?"

He immediately eased off the gas and glanced my way, noticing how uncomfortable I was. "Sorry, darlin'. I forget sometimes how much power this baby has."

"It's fine." I rubbed my lips together. "Do you still have your truck?"

"That pile of junk? I couldn't even give it away. I sold it for scrap metal."

"Oh."

"You sound disappointed."

"We made some good memories in it."

His lip curled up. "We sure did." His warm hand landed on my thigh and caressed it. "We'll make new memories in this car."

I nodded, knowing it wouldn't be the same. There was something about the back of a truck. "Remind me of the name of the couple we are having dinner with."

"Wes and Deidre Halstrom. Wes owns a VC firm in Florida. He's one of the people who I was meeting with when . . ."

We both grinned sheepishly, not wanting to revisit that particular part of our past.

"It's difficult to get VC investment—his partners must have really believed in you and your product," I tried to smooth it over.

"They did, but he ended up personally investing. After hearing what his company did and how much of a chunk it would take of mine, I wasn't too keen on going that route. When I told him so, he still wanted in."

"I'm impressed."

"I'm glad, darlin'. Your opinion matters the most to me."

I reached over and ran my hand down the back of his head and rubbed his neck. "I've always been proud of you."

"Mmm," he groaned at my touch. "You haven't seen anything yet. I've got big plans for us."

"Big or small, as long as we do it together, that's all that matters to me."

"Think big, Shelby." Such excitement accompanied his words.

I'd always planned on small, but big could work as long as we stayed grounded and didn't let business consume us like my family had.

We pulled into Chandlers, the most expensive restaurant in Carrington Cove—and that was saying something considering everything was expensive in Carrington Cove. This little place was nestled up in the mountain and looked more like a bed and breakfast than a restaurant, but it boasted one of the top chefs in the world from Europe. Macey and Marlowe loved this place. Their goal was to get their dates to take them here. For some reason, I hoped Bobby Jay never did. I couldn't picture him here. To be honest, I couldn't picture

172

Ryder here either. He used to make fun of these hoity-toity places, as he liked to call them. He used to say he'd rather buy a whole cow than pay $75 for a steak.

Ryder looked out at the white house with black shutters surrounded by a white picket fence. "Have you been here before?"

I shook my head.

"Really? I thought for sure you had. This place has you written all over it."

I could understand why he might think that, but even when we were together before and I had lots of disposable income, I wouldn't ever expect or even want him to take me to such a place. "It's pricey and—"

"We aren't worried about price tonight." He took my hand and held it between his own. "You are worth it all."

That was sweet but, "You know I don't expect to be taken to fancy restaurants."

He leaned over and skimmed my lips. "I know, but I've always wanted to be able to do this for you."

I ran my hand across his cheek. "Ryder Prescott, you are a sweet man."

He pulled me to him for a brief kiss before whispering against my lips, "If you knew what was going through my head right now looking at you, you wouldn't think so."

"You should hear what I've been thinking about you."

"Mmm," he groaned. "I'm going to need to step out of this vehicle before I give in to temptation and make us very late."

"If you must." I leaned away from him.

He, on the other hand, drew me back to him and pressed his lips against mine for a stirring moment before pulling away and jumping out of the vehicle. He ran around to my side, opened the door, and offered his hand to help me out. I noticed he purposely averted his eyes when it came to my legs.

We walked hand in hand under the trellis dripping in lilacs to enter the property. Not only did the scent of lilacs linger in the air, but the smell of divine cuisine wafted on the light breeze. It was all picturesque with hanging lanterns in the trees and a lighted brick-paved pathway. I noted how pleased Ryder looked that he could afford to take me to such a place. I never realized how much of a concern that truly was to him. But I was honest in saying I didn't need this. What I cared about was that we were together. He could have taken me to Burger Shack for all I cared. I was just as happy to share fries with him as I would be to dine on filet mignon. But I leaned into him, happy he was happy.

He kissed my head. "What do you think of this place?"

"It's nice."

"Nice, she says." He chuckled.

The Halstroms were already seated when we arrived inside the exquisite little place made of stone walls and plank wood floors. The low lighting made it feel even cozier.

Wes and Deidre both stood when we arrived at the small table near the hearth that did not bear a blazing fire but glowed from the hundreds of twinkle lights within. They were an attractive couple, probably in their mid to late forties. Wes was tall with an athletic build and Deidre was petite with a crown of auburn hair. Both, though, looked welcoming and greeted Ryder as if he were an old friend. Wes gave him a hearty handshake and Deidre hugged him and kissed his cheek.

Ryder was quick to introduce me. "This is my fian . . . Shelby Duchane," he corrected himself. I was taken aback by him almost introducing me as his fiancée. I hoped that meant he was thinking along those lines. I knew we were starting over, but I already knew where I wanted to end up.

Wes and Deidre offered me warm smiles. Deidre was obviously an affectionate person and wrapped her arms around me. "It's so nice to finally meet you."

Finally? Had Ryder talked about me with them?

"The pleasure is mine," I responded.

Wes shook my hand once his wife released me. "It's nice to meet you, Shelby. I'm glad to see Ryder's move out here has proved to be more than just financially equitable."

Ryder gave me a crooked grin before pulling out the heavy rustic wood chair for me. Once everyone was seated, Wes announced, "This calls for a toast." He hailed the waiter dressed in a suit and tie and ordered a very expensive bottle of champagne. I recognized it as it was one of my mother's favorites. She loved the hint of lemon and berries in it. As soon as the order was placed, Wes directed his attention toward me. "Before I start to grill Ryder here about how my investment is going, tell us what you do."

"Currently I own and run a clothing boutique in town, M&M'S on Main."

"Ooh," Deidre squealed to my right. "The concierge at our hotel suggested I visit your store. I had no idea you owned it."

I smiled, happy to know the store was being touted. "Please do. I should be there all day tomorrow."

She pointed at my dress. "Is this something you carry in your store? I love it."

"This is from a line we carry, but this particular dress we had in stock last year."

"Well, I know where I'll be going tomorrow while Wes hits the golf course to meet with potential clients. We're using our anniversary trip for business and pleasure."

I wanted to say how nice, but honestly it was awful. It was something my father would do to my mother. Anniversary trips should be strictly pleasure, in my opinion.

"How long have you been married?" I asked.

"Twenty years and four kids later," Wes answered, beaming at his bride.

"How old are your children?" Kids were a favorite topic of mine.

"I'll let Dee do the bragging while Ryder and I get down to business."

Oh. I wasn't sure what to think about that. Suddenly I felt very much like my mother, as if I were here to play a part, not be a part of it. Not like I knew a lot about software, but I did own my own business and was well educated.

Ryder took my hand under the table and gave me a strained smile as if he knew what I was thinking. Before any verbal communication could pass between us, I found myself being sucked into the world of the Halstrom children while Ryder and Wes talked strategy, reaching other verticals, and staying ahead of the technology curve. I tried to glean what I could from their conversation while I listened to Deidre lament about how their daughter Giselle had failed the driver's examination four times already and their son Oliver was cut from his high school basketball team. Between all that, a quiet voice pricked my senses, and it brought up a poignant point.

The same two worlds were colliding again. Would the outcome be any different this time?

Chapter Twenty-Five

THE DRIVE HOME started out quiet, other than the country music that hummed in the background over the incredible sound system in his car. I was happy he still liked the same music and bands.

Ryder's warm hand landed on my thigh while he drove us home at a much slower pace. "Thanks for coming. I'm sorry Wes dominated my attention. He's only in town for a few days and he likes to keep tabs on his investments."

"I understand. It was nice talking to Deidre." That was the truth. She was a lovely woman who obviously loved her children and supported a lot of great causes. We had traveled to many of the same countries, so we had plenty to talk about.

"The food was great," Ryder added.

"It was nice." Albeit weird seeing Ryder order roasted chateaubriand and pommes puree like he did it every day. It was really a fancy version of meat and potatoes. And wasn't he the one who said we should serve beer at our wedding reception instead of champagne? It was a lot cheaper and tasted better, to quote him.

He gave me a wry glance. "Was there something wrong with your salad?"

I took his hand and held it. "I enjoyed it."

His loud exhale indicated my answers dissatisfied him. I felt bad

177

for that. I was just trying to mentally reroute my expectations, is all. I don't know why I assumed we would pick up right where we left off. Ryder was right—we had both changed over the last year. They weren't bad changes, but we were different. More than I had anticipated.

Ryder walked me up the steps to the front porch. We hadn't had a porch scene in what felt like forever, and for some reason this one felt awkward like the first time. We stood there smiling at each other like we didn't know what we should do.

I leaned in and breathed in him before kissing his cheek. "Thank you. I had a—"

"Let me guess, a *nice* time?" He grimaced.

I bit my lip. I guess I had used that word a lot tonight. I fell into him, wanting to be held. He picked up on the cue and wrapped me in his arms. The comfort I felt in them hadn't changed. That lifted my spirits. I snuggled into his chest. We said not a word for several minutes. I took the time to soak him in and listen to the steady beat of his heart. He eventually kissed my head. "Shelby, I hate to go, but I have to finalize a presentation that Bobby Jay and I are giving at the college tomorrow."

I was reluctant to let go, so I tilted my head up to gaze into those pools of chocolate that allowed me access to his soul. In them I could see it was still beautiful and alive and well. The passion he always had for me burned bright, making me feel so much better, but not as good as when his warm lips came down on mine, urging my own to part. While our tongues slow danced together, his hands ran through my hair and then down my curves. Every contented sound that escaped me urged him to dance longer and hold onto me tighter until I shuddered from the pleasure of it all.

He tore his lips from mine, breathing hard. His hands cupped my face. "Darlin', I need to go."

"If you're sure." Seduction wrapped around every syllable in hopes he would change his mind.

"You don't play fair." He kissed my forehead and forced himself away from me. "I'll see you tomorrow night."

"Okay," I sighed, not used to him turning down my advances.

He made sure I was in the house before he walked away. I shut the door, exhaling louder than I meant to.

Mr. Carrington, who I didn't realize was sitting on the recliner in the living room reading a book, startled me when he said, "I recognize that sound." He set his book down in his lap. "Do you want to talk?"

I smiled and joined him in the living room. I sat on the loveseat and sank into it. "We had a nice time."

Mr. Carrington took off his reading glasses. "Nice? That's the kiss of death for men."

I laughed. "I think Ryder would agree with you."

He leaned forward, ready to listen. It hit me that my own father had never waited up for me. Daddy was never present or involved enough to know whether my dates were all I had hoped they would be.

I rested my head against the loveseat. "I guess I was hoping for old times, something simple like a picnic by the lake or maybe a dinner that didn't have a thousand-dollar tab."

Mr. Carrington scrubbed a hand over his scruffy face. "This reminds me of the first time I took Shannon out." The smile I associated with his wife spread across his face. It was a smile that spoke of the greatest love and loss of his life. "I was so nervous to make a good impression after being friends for so long. And I felt I had to live up to Anders, which was no small task. He was the best man I ever knew."

That had to be weird for him to date his best friend's wife.

"Anyway," he continued, "I thought it would be smart if I showed her exactly what I could offer her. I started with picking her up in a limo."

I giggled.

"I know, honey, it gets worse. After that I whisked her away to the most expensive restaurant in Edenvale. We couldn't pronounce anything on the menu and what we did order was terrible. We both left hungry and I think she left a little unsure of me, or maybe a lot after I hired a helicopter pilot to take us on a tour. I didn't know Shannon wasn't fond of flying and she vomited."

"Oh, goodness no."

Mr. Carrington shook his head at himself. "Thankfully we ended up laughing about it and I came to my senses and took her to a drive-in movie where I paid the limo driver to leave us for the duration. She loved to tease me about my misguided ways."

"Sounds like a sweet memory."

"It is," he sighed. "I'm just glad she saw past my nervousness and ego and didn't hold it against me." He gave me a little wink.

"Are you trying to give me advice?"

"I'm just telling you that I think your young man's heart was in the right place and I wouldn't be surprised if he's kicking himself right now."

"I don't know. His job is keeping him real busy. He left to get some work done." My phone started vibrating in my purse.

Mr. Carrington gave me a sly grin. "I think you might want to get that."

I slid my hand into my small purse and retrieved my phone. My heart skipped a few beats when I realized who it was. I smiled at Mr. Carrington before I answered. "Hey there. Is everything all right?"

"No."

My heart dropped.

"I want a redo."

"A redo?"

"I'll be there in ten minutes. Wear something comfortable. No heels," he specified. We'd had many conversations on how I found heels to be comfortable.

"I thought you had to work."

"It can wait, but you and I can't. I'll see you in ten."

I hung up feeling all sorts of wonderful.

Mr. Carrington stood, grinning. "What did I tell you? Good night, honey."

I jumped up and kissed Mr. Carrington on the cheek before I rushed to my room to change. I felt like a teenage girl who just had the cutest boy in school ask her out on a date. For the first time in a long time, I didn't overthink my clothes or try on several outfits to see which one made me look best because I knew Ryder would think I looked good in all of them. So maybe I went with the skimpy shorts and a tight T-shirt. He was definitely going to like those.

I slipped into some sandals and ran back downstairs to wait for him on the porch since it was late and Mr. Carrington had gone to bed. I sat on the swing, waiting for Ryder to appear in his car, but I heard the crunch of gravel on one of the paths that led to the cabins. Sure enough, it was Ryder.

I jumped up to meet him. It was then I noticed he was carrying what looked like a comforter he had ripped off his bed, and a bottle of wine and some paper cups, with his guitar case slung across his back. This was my Ryder. My Ryder was sexy too, wearing a plaid button-down that was undone enough to give me a peek at my name across his heart. And those jeans. Oh Mylanta. I refrained from fanning myself, but I surely felt the heat.

"Hey, darlin'," he held up the bottle of wine, "I brought a taste of home."

I loved strawberry wine, and even though it meant breaking the no sugar rule twice tonight, first with champagne, I knew Emma would understand. This was for a worthy cause. So maybe I wouldn't tell her. I knew she could think of several worthy causes to drink Dr. Pepper.

I planted myself right in front of him and stood on my tiptoes. "This is my favorite taste of home." I skimmed his lips.

"I hope you are planning to indulge tonight," he whispered in my ear, sending ripples of shivers down me.

I took the wine and cups out of his hands. "Deeply," I promised.

"Let's get out of here."

"Where to?"

"The lake?" he suggested.

"I have a better, more private place we can go."

"Lead the way, darlin'."

I held the bottle and cups in one hand so I could take one of his. Every time our fingers interlocked, I felt myself bleed into him until it was like we were one. I guided him toward the road that led to Shannon's Meadow. I knew Emma and Sawyer wouldn't mind if we made ourselves cozy among the tall grass and wildflowers back behind their temporary housing and their new housing that was being constructed next door. Last time I had been down this way the frame was mostly up.

I looked up at the clear sky and the millions of stars. The stars didn't shine this brightly in Georgia. "*Nice* night," I teased.

"No more using that word," he growled.

I laughed and leaned into him. "I'm glad you came back."

"Me too. Where are you taking me, by the way?"

"To a little piece of heaven on earth."

He pulled me closer to him. "I'm already there, Shelby."

He had me so choked up a reply escaped me. That was okay; in the silence I felt the truth of what he said and it was better than any old words. I was happy to see the lights were off in the King house and some progress had been made on their new home. It was now the proud owner of a roof. We carefully traipsed through the meadow toward the pond where there was a clearing we could nestle into. The pond didn't have the stark beauty of the lake, but it possessed a tranquil loveliness.

Ryder picked the perfect spot to spread out the comforter, not far from the water's edge. He carefully laid his guitar down before helping me sit. He settled next to me and I leaned my head on his shoulder, looking out at the tiny ripples in the pool of water. A sweet sigh escaped me.

"Do you like living here?" Ryder asked.

"I never thought I would, but I do. I especially love the summers here. No June bugs." I laughed.

He joined me. "I still remember the night you got one caught in your hair. I've never heard someone scream so loud."

"They make an awful noise and you were laughing too hard to get it out."

"You were such a city girl."

"I'm finding I like small town life."

"Do you now?" He pulled me onto his lap.

I snuggled right into him. "I like it a whole lot better now that you're here."

His arms tightened around me. "Do you plan to stay in Carrington Cove?"

I let out a heavy breath of disappointment. "That was the plan, but the house I was planning on buying is now out of my reach." I'd spoken to Mr. Jacobsen yesterday. He apologized, but his children convinced him to strike while the iron was hot and that it would be easier to sell in the summer. I couldn't blame him.

"That little yellow thing you showed Bobby Jay?"

"Why do you say it like that?"

"It doesn't seem like your style, and you weren't all that keen to live in my little house."

"You know it wasn't the house. I loved your place. It was the commute, and I wanted something more than a Piggly Wiggly to shop at."

He chuckled. "Carrington Cove does seem to have more of a selection."

That it did. "I love that little yellow house. It has charm and a big backyard for babies."

He nuzzled my neck. "You plan on having those babies by yourself?"

"If I have to," I stuttered out. Ryder was making it hard to breathe.

"I could give you some options," he groaned against my ear.

"Is that so?"

"Uh-huh." He started kissing his way up, speaking between the brushes of his lips against my warm, raised skin. "What do you think of moving to Edenvale once the summer is over?"

"Oh." I inadvertently sat up.

Ryder leaned back. "Did I say something wrong?"

"Not at all. I just hadn't thought about it. It's a long drive from Carrington Cove." Especially in the winter. I still hadn't mastered driving in the snow.

"That's why I've been looking at condos near my office up there."

"Condo?" My brow furrowed. "I never imagined you living in one."

He flashed me a wry smile. "It would only be temporary. But time is money, darlin'."

"I suppose it is. My boutique is here and, well . . ."

"Well, what?" He kissed my nose.

"There was something about that house. It called to me. I know it sounds silly, but I thought we belonged together."

In a fluid move, he laid me down, our legs tangled together while he hovered over me, resting on his arms. An alluring expression played on his face. "You and I belong together."

I reached up to where his shirt hung open. I brushed my name with my fingertips. His warm skin raised. The act had my eyes welling up with tears. "Thank you for keeping my name."

He lowered himself to where we were breathing each other in. His finger traced my face. "I love you, Chief."

The tears spilled over and down my cheeks. I had longed for him to call me Chief and to hear those three beautiful words come out of his mouth. "I love you, Ryder."

Chapter Twenty-Six

"SO HOW'S IT going with you two?" Jenna set her book down and took a sip of her lemonade.

We were having our Wednesday night book club at Sage Café, one of our favorite hangouts near the comedy club.

Emma didn't give me the chance to answer. "Well, I can report that a certain couple was found sneaking out of the meadow Tuesday morning before the crack of dawn. A guitar and an empty bottle of wine were involved, not to mention a large blanket." Emma nudged me and laughed while I blushed uncontrollably.

"Ooh, does he play the guitar?" Jenna asked.

"And sings." I smiled, thinking about how he serenaded me Monday night into the early morning hours. Between making my body sing with his kisses. Oh, how I had missed him.

Aspen forcefully dipped her chip in the salsa. "I hope he doesn't break your heart. You have to watch out for the gorgeous let-me-sing-you-out-of-your-panties men."

We all choked on our drinks. "Aspen!" Jenna smacked her arm.

"What?" Aspen feigned innocence. "That's how I found myself pregnant and married at nineteen and divorced before I was twenty-one. I'm just saying Shelby should use caution."

I tucked some hair behind my ear. "Ryder's not like that," I politely defended him.

"Are you and Ryder a couple again?" Jenna rested her elbows on the table and propped her head on her hands.

"Yes." I grinned.

"Are you engaged?" Aspen asked, worried.

"No. We have some things to iron out before we get there again."

"What things?" Emma asked.

I took a sip of my water and thought about how to word it. "It's funny how life works. Our roles have reversed in some ways. He's making more money than ever, and for the first time in my life I have to budget. And now that I'm ready to settle down in a small town, he's angling for life in the city because it's more convenient." I let out a sigh. "His work schedule worries me some too," I admitted quietly, out loud for the first time.

Emma tilted her pretty head. "What about it?"

I shrugged. "One of the reasons I fell in love with him was because he was so different from my daddy. Mind you he still is." Daddy would have never skipped working on a presentation to have an unforgettable night out under the stars. "But I worry about how much he has to work now, what if that doesn't end? What if, like my daddy, work becomes his mistress and he loves her more than his family?"

Emma rubbed my back. "Then he would be an idiot and I would be heartbroken for you, but I bet after this new release he'll be seducing you in my meadow every night." She grinned deviously while I giggled and blushed.

Jenna reached across the table and patted my hand. "If not," she looked between me and Aspen, who had been biting her tongue, "we feed him to the meerkats."

Aspen's eyes lit up. "Yes! Now we are talking."

I shook my head at the lovely women who were the best friends I could ask for. More than that, I was grateful they had made room for me in their tight-knit group. "Y'all are crazy, but I love you."

Our table erupted in laughter.

"Can we talk about Bobby Jay and Marlowe?" Emma asked.

"Ooo, yes," Jenna was eager.

"Bobby Jay is Ryder's cousin?" Aspen asked, not having met any of them yet.

Emma and I both nodded.

"He's the sweetest," I commented. "And no offense to Marlowe," I grinned at Emma, "but I am surprised."

"Me too." Emma returned my smile. "Believe me, I know how my sisters are. It makes me feel better, honestly, to know she isn't so shallow. Not to say there is anything wrong with Bobby Jay. He seems like a nice guy, which is why I'm surprised Marlowe is dating him."

I bit my lip. "I agree, but . . ." I paused, wondering if I should divulge what I overheard at work today. I didn't want to become that boss.

All the ladies stared at me in anticipation.

"I don't know if I should say."

"Of course you should." Jenna grinned.

Everyone else nodded, eager.

"Well . . . I did overhear your sisters talk at the boutique today and Marlowe, I think, might really like him. She said for once in her life she didn't feel like an object."

Emma leaned back with wide eyes. "I always thought that was her goal."

"Apparently she wants more. She even mentioned to Macey that she needed to get over Ryder," I kept any derision out of my voice, "and perhaps she should give Jaime a shot."

"Holy crap! Are my sisters finally growing up?" Emma asked, astonished. "My mom must be putting in some overtime in heaven to pull off that miracle. Speaking of miracles." Emma's face shone. "Sawyer's Dad and Bridget are finally getting married."

"Really?" Jenna, Aspen, and I said in unison. It was widely known that Sawyer and his father, Warren, had a rocky relationship after his parents divorced. He blamed a lot it of it on Bridget unfairly without knowing all the details. Anyone who had ever met Warren and Bridget could easily see how in love they were, but they refused to get married until they had Sawyer's blessing. Though Sawyer wasn't withholding it, per se, I think Warren wanted more than his blessing. He wanted him to be by his side through it all. He wanted his son back. Since Emma and Sawyer had been married, Emma had helped make that happen. She and Bridget were close, which meant the two couples spent a lot of time together. Though I didn't know Warren and Bridget well, I could say it would be hard not to like them. All my interactions with them had been genuine and warm.

"How does Sawyer feel about it?" I asked.

Emma let out a contented breath. "I think he is truly happy for them. His dad asked him to be the best man and he accepted."

"When's the big day?" Jenna asked.

"They are thinking in the winter on the ski slopes where they rekindled their relationship. I told Bridget I would love to see her ski in a wedding dress. And I would totally be down to join her in a bridesmaid dress."

I could picture it. That was Emma's style.

Aspen cleared her throat. "Fantastic, another love story. Can we get back to *How to Get Over Your Ex in Ninety Days*, which by the way, I am very disappointed in how it ended."

We all laughed at her, knowing she would be upset the couple ended up together.

"I mean, come on, she didn't need him." Aspen shoved a chip in her mouth and chomped furiously.

"But she wanted him," Emma countered. "Besides, everyone makes mistakes. Right, Shelby?" She winked.

"And learns from them," I added.

"That Jackson was sexy." Jenna wagged her brows. "Are all Southern men that way?" she asked me.

"Not all of them, but mine is." I smiled.

"You are all hopeless." Aspen reached into her bag and pulled out a book and set it on the table, tapping on it. "For our next book club night, we are going to read this."

Jenna picked up *Silent Stones*. The cover featured a misty moor with an ominous deserted castle. Jenna flipped over the book to read the back copy. She read it out loud. "For years, the abandoned castle on the hill—once home to Lord and Lady Alexander, an old aristocratic family all of whom died mysteriously—called to Isabella Jones. She had no idea why until the gruesome details of her father's death were uncovered and the diary he meant for no one to see found its way into her hands . . ."

Jenna looked up, wary. "This sounds like it could be gory."

Aspen waved away her concern. "It's a little bloody, but it's so intriguing you won't mind."

Emma grabbed the book from Jenna and took a good look at it before holding it up and pointing to the picture of the author on the back cover. "I think Aspen has a crush on this Taron Taylor—dark hair and stunning aqua eyes. And . . . he happens to be British. Imagine that." Emma smirked at Aspen.

Aspen snatched the book from her. "That has nothing to do with it. It's smartly written and for all the squeamish moments, there is a lot of wit."

"And romance, from what the back copy says," Emma taunted Aspen.

"There is some, but it's not nauseating or the focal point," Aspen defended herself.

Meanwhile, Jenna started googling Taron Taylor. "Ooo. He's not married and freaking hot. Check out these pictures." She held out her phone for all of us to see. There were several photos of Mr. Taylor in different poses, most of them casual, looking quite dashing whether signing books or playing polo.

Aspen pushed Jenna's phone down. "Who cares what he looks like?" Her pink cheeks said she did.

Sweet Emma put her arm around Aspen. "It's okay, you know, to be vulnerable."

Aspen made to say something, instead, she rested her head on Emma's shoulder. "I can't afford to be. Not with Chloe. She doesn't deserve another man to walk out of her life."

"Neither do you." Jenna smoothed Aspen's hair.

"That's why I stay away from men. It's easier that way."

"Is it really?" Emma asked, squeezing her tighter.

"That's what I keep telling myself. And with Leland rearing his ugly head again, it only solidifies my decision."

"Is he moving back here?" Jenna asked.

"I hope not," Aspen choked out. "But he called me again and wanted to talk to Chloe. She refused to. I can't blame her even though I've tried my best not to say anything negative about him around her other than it's his problem and not her fault that he isn't in her life. But he hurt her. When your father doesn't contact you for three years, that does something to you. Of course, he blamed me for poisoning her, not taking any responsibility for his actions, as usual."

"Chloe is lucky to have you as her momma. Every girl needs a strong woman in her corner, especially her momma." I tried to comfort Aspen.

Aspen sighed. "I don't know, sometimes I wonder if I'm all she needs. My parents try to fill in, especially my dad, but she sees her friends with their dads and I know she longs for that. She wants her own dad to take her to the daddy daughter dance they have at school every year. And I get it. I've read the books. Girls with good fathers go on to choose better partners. I apparently missed that memo." She laughed derisively to herself. "I have the best dad and I still ended up with a d-bag, so maybe it doesn't matter."

"You were young and let's be honest, Leland was pretty irresistible," Jenna offered.

Aspen closed her eyes as if she didn't want to think about it. "Lots of other women thought so too, and he found them more desirable than me and our baby."

"It wasn't you," Emma soothed her.

"Why didn't I go out with Sean Rawlings in high school? I ran into his mom the other day and she mentioned he just opened up his own orthodontic practice in Denver and he's married with two little girls and is the sweetest dad ever."

"Uh, you didn't go out with him because he popped his pimples in class and he wore his pants up to his belly button," Jenna said.

Aspen laughed. "There was that. I bet he's a solid husband and dad, though."

"Probably," Emma said, "but you can do better than Sean. I'm pretty sure at our high school reunion I saw him pop one of his wife's pimples on her back."

We all squirmed.

"That's disgusting." Aspen lifted her head off Emma's shoulder. "I think I'll stay single."

Jenna held up her phone and dangled it in front of Aspen. "I think you should give some serious consideration to Taron Taylor."

Aspen rolled her eyes. "Right, because I can afford to take a jaunt over to jolly old England. I'm sure he's been wishing for a single mom who makes twenty dollars an hour as a personal banker."

"No, but I bet he wants a hot babe like you." Emma wagged her brows.

"No more hot babe here. I started wearing granny panties for the fun of it. I have to say they are quite comfy." Aspen grinned.

Our table erupted in laughter.

Aspen's demeanor turned thoughtful. "I do love you, ladies. Thank you for putting up with my anti-man ways. How about this. I promise you if I ever meet Taron Taylor, I'll give him a shot."

"You're only saying that because you know you'll never meet him," Jenna called her out.

"You got me." Aspen smirked.

"Well, I believe in magic, Miss Aspen, and meant-to-be's, so I would be careful if I were you." I reached across the table and took her hand. "I have a feeling true love will come knocking on your door one day, and the man on the other side of that door will be the luckiest man in the world."

Aspen squeezed my hand back. "Hopefully when I'm not in my granny panties."

"If it's the right man, he won't care," I responded.

Aspen took a moment to let that sink in. "You're right."

Emma and Jenna added their hands to ours. A collective smile filled the table as if we each knew what a precious moment it was. I knew for me, it would be one I would never forget. It sparked an interesting thought. If it hadn't been for heartache and the awful mistake I'd made, I would have never had this moment or these wonderful women in my life. God never ceased to amaze me with what he could make out of a mess.

I prayed now that Ryder and I came out stronger and better for it too.

Chapter Twenty-Seven

"HEY, CHIEF," RYDER sounded exhausted when he answered his phone.

"Hi, handsome, are you still working?" It was already past 9:00.

"Yeah. I'm at the office actually. Our continuous build server crashed and I'm configuring a new server."

"I'm not exactly sure what that means, but I'm still in Edenvale. I would love to come and see your office since I haven't had a chance yet, and I would more than love to give you a reason for a break." I had just left the café after our book club and hoped to head straight to his cabin, but his office would do.

"Chief, I would love nothing more, but until I get this new server up, our integration testing is at a standstill."

"Don't you have anybody else who can do that?"

"I'm the one who originally set it up, so it falls on me. And I'm particular about it."

"I will let you get back to work then." I couldn't hide my disappointment.

"Hey, how about I make us breakfast in the morning?"

"I'd like that."

"Is 6:30 too early? We have our Scrum meetings in the morning, so I have to be in early."

"Do I want to know what Scrum means?"

He laughed. "It's just a development methodology."

"Oh. All right. I'll see you in the morning."

"I love you, Chief."

"I love you too."

"Good—"

"Ryder," I interrupted him. "It isn't always going to be like this, is it?"

"No, darlin'. I'll make it up to you. I promise. I need to run. Good night."

In an instant he was off the Bluetooth in my car and I was left to wonder in the silence how long these insane hours of his would last. I didn't get to think about it too much. My phone rang.

"Hello," I spoke out into the car.

"Darling, it's Memaw."

I would know her rich alto voice anywhere. "It's late where you are."

"No darling, it's early. I'm in Paris."

"You are? I had no idea you were traveling."

"That's the beauty of being my age and filthy rich—I don't have to tell anyone where I'm going or *who* I'm traveling with."

"Are you traveling with someone?"

"Perhaps, but that's my secret."

Was this someone a male? I wasn't sure how I would feel about that. Memaw had never been with another man since Granddaddy died, as far as I knew. That was a conversation for another day. I had other bones to pick with her. "You can keep your secret, but why did you keep from me that Ryder had been to see you and that you told him where I lived?"

"Like I told him, and from the sounds of it he told you, I thought it would be more fun this way."

My heart dropped. "Am I just a game to you too?" My voice cracked. I couldn't bear the thought of the one person I could count on growing up using me for some sick pleasure.

"Shelby," her voice turned somber, "you are the best thing that ever happened to me, darling. I didn't tell you about Ryder because I wasn't sure anything would come of it and I didn't want to injure you further after what he'd supposedly done to you."

"Supposedly?"

"I began to have my suspicions even more after he came to see me that perhaps all wasn't as it seemed. The look in that boy's eyes said he was every bit as hurt as you. That, more than anything, is why I told him."

"Why didn't you tell me about your suspicions? Do you know how awful it was for me to accuse Ryder to his face only for me to find out that I was the one who had made the mistake?"

"Don't you dare blame yourself for that. That was all your momma and daddy." She sounded livid.

"I do bear the blame, and it kills me." I still shuddered at the thought of all that I could have lost forever.

"And that's why I didn't tell you. I knew it would eat you up and I thought what was done was done. I was proud of you for standing on your own out there. I still am. And I'm happy you and the boy are back together."

I eased off the gas in my car. "How do you know?"

"Your parents know. I figured you told them."

A sick feeling washed over me. "I haven't spoken to them. They are too cowardly or don't care enough to return my calls. Are they spying on me?"

"Would you put it past them after everything you know?"

"No," I whispered. "But it doesn't matter," my voice increased, "Ryder is my choice and there is nothing they can do about it now."

"You keep that attitude, darling, because they will try to convince you otherwise."

"Why?" I cried. "I don't understand."

Memaw was quiet for a spell. "I've never understood your mother, to be quite honest. But this I know—she's never liked to lose, and whether she would admit it or not, she never wanted to lose you. I know you never felt like she loved you the way she should have, and I would agree with you, but when you were born, she used to look at you as she would a fine piece of art, her greatest creation made in her own image. She thought you, above all else, would love her more and better than anyone. But she did her best to push you away. Not intentionally, mind you."

"I wouldn't be too sure about that."

"Sugar, sometimes people can't stand to lose something or somebody so much, they hold on so tightly that it allows them to slip away, just like you."

"My parents only care about the control, not me."

"I believe they care about both. If not, they wouldn't keep trying to keep you in their lives."

I wasn't sure I believed her. "Well, if they think trying to separate Ryder and me again is a good way to go about it, they're dead wrong. We love each other and aim to stay together."

"Be on alert," she sighed.

"Did they say something?"

"No, but your momma is fit to be tied, and good never comes from that."

Didn't I know it. I gripped my steering wheel tightly as if it would brace me for whatever she had up her sleeve. "Thank you for the warning."

"We haven't talked in an age. Tell me how you and your beau are?"

"Well, maybe if you would answer your phone," I teased.

"Darling, at my age, I answer to no one. Besides, I've had my phone turned off ever since I've left the states. I find it unnatural that people can get ahold of you any time, day or night."

"I can understand that."

"You didn't answer your Memaw's question."

"We're happy to be back together."

"That boy has a lot of spirit, starting up a new company and following you out there."

"That *man* was crushed by the games my parents played with us and he's brave to want to be involved with any of us again."

"That *boy*," she refused to ever call him man, "would be a fool not to want you. You are the sweetest and prettiest peach Georgia ever produced."

"You're biased."

"I may be old but I'm not blind. So, you two getting hitched now?"

"We don't have any plans to."

"Take my advice and run to the nearest courthouse and start having me some great-grandbabies."

I laughed at her. "We'll get there, but we need some time to get to know each other again and decide where we want to live."

"I thought you were buying that house you were going on and on about."

"Not anymore. I'm not going to be able to afford it." Those words were still a new thing for me to say, but it's funny how I didn't find them as devastating as I thought I would. I had gone over and over the numbers yesterday, and even if the boutique kept doing as well as it was, it would take me several more months to afford the down payment. Then the thought of a large mortgage payment plus the business loan I had frightened me.

"Sugar, how much money do you need?"

"I don't want your money."

"For heaven's sake, why not? I've got plenty to go around."

"I appreciate that, but I want my home to be something that is truly mine. Never before have I had anything that I could say that about."

"Well, child, you have certainly made me proud. You better watch out or I might leave all my money to you after all."

I giggled.

"Darling, I must say goodbye. I have a hot date."

"Do you really?"

"No, but I love to mess with your momma. She thinks I've run off with a man named Pierre. I'm just here with some old biddies drinking wine and shopping until my bunions start barking at me."

"I love you, Memaw."

"I know, darling, that's why you are my favorite. If you change your mind about the house, let me know."

"I won't but thank you."

"Love you, sugar. Give your momma a run for her money."

Chapter Twenty-Eight

BEFORE I COULD even knock on Ryder's door early the next morning, I found myself being pulled in and wrapped up in Ryder's arms. It was exactly where I needed to be. I had hardly slept after my conversation with Memaw. Not only was I sick and worried that someone was following me, I was afraid of what my parents might try to do to tear us apart.

I nestled into his dress shirt and breathed in his sandalwood scent. I'd been wanting him all night but hadn't wanted to bother him while he worked.

Ryder stroked my hair. "I'm sorry about last night. I feel like I keep saying that to you. I have a lot on my plate right now. A lot of people's livelihoods depend on me."

"I can understand that." Though none of my employees would be in dire straits if the boutique closed its doors.

He leaned back and tipped my chin up. "You know I'd rather spend all my time with you."

I stood on my tiptoes, pressed my lips to his, and just stayed there soaking him in, holding his face in my hands. Anything to remind me that he was real and we were together.

"Chief," he spoke against my lips, "is everything okay? Are you upset with me?"

"It's my parents," I whispered.

Ryder's face immediately flashed red. "What the hell have they done now?"

I lowered myself back on my feet and released a heavy breath. "I talked to Memaw last night. My parents know we're together."

"Good. I hope they do." His jaw clenched.

I pressed my hands against his tight chest. His pounding heart spoke of how angry my parents made him. "Ryder, I didn't tell them."

His eyes narrowed before dawning appeared in them followed by hatred. "Damn them. They're spying on us."

I nodded. "It appears so."

He scanned the cabin as if he would see someone before grinning wickedly at me. "I hope they get a good look at this." He leaned down and hungrily captured my lips while his hands ran through my hair and undid my messy bun. When my hair fell around us, he deepened the kiss while his fingers glided down my spine, igniting tingles and silently begging me to press my body against his. My hands slid up his chest, up through his hair, drawing us closer, fulfilling his desire and mine. A low moan escaped him when his lips departed from mine. A tiny gasp escaped me before I could catch my breath. His forehead rested on mine. Our breath mingled together and the outside world melted away.

"I love you," he whispered before raising his head and shouting, "I love her!"

"Shh." I pressed my finger to his soft lips. "You're crazy."

He took my finger and kissed it. "Crazy for you." He looked around again as if we were being spied on. "Did you get that? I LOVE HER!"

"I know! Now shut up!" Bobby Jay shouted back from his bedroom, disgruntled from being woken up.

Ryder and I broke out into fits of laughter. I snuggled into him. "I love you. I'm sorry."

"Shelby, you don't need to apologize. This is all your momma's and daddy's doing. If they know what's good for them, they won't interfere this time, because I promise you there will be hell to pay if anyone tries to come between us again."

I nodded against his chest, taking comfort in him.

He kissed my head. "Chief, you and I belong together. You've been in charge of my heart from day one."

His words brought immense joy but a touch of sadness crept in. Tears filled my eyes, wetting his shirt. "Ryder." I sniffled.

He leaned back, confused and worried.

"I deleted all your 'Chief' emails."

A rush of relief filled his eyes and his mouth tugged upward. "Well, then, it's a good thing I saved them, darlin'."

"You did?"

He reached up and brushed away the tears that lingered on my cheek with his thumb. "I tried a hundred times to delete them, but I kept being drawn back to your responses. Wondering if that woman still existed and if she did, why did she leave me? I had to know one way or the other."

The heartbreak in his voice made me tear up more. I took his hand and held it between my own. "I'm so sorry I hurt you. Thank you for not giving up on us."

"Just promise me if any new pictures show up with me and a hot chick rolling around the meadow, you will one, know it's you, and two, you'll send them to me so I can have my own copies." He wagged his brows.

I smacked his chest, making him laugh.

He took my hand and pulled me to the small dining area. "Let's eat. I'm starving."

In the middle of the table sat a large bouquet of peach roses.

"Are those for me or Bobby Jay?" I teased.

He pulled out my chair for me. "I don't make midnight store runs for Bobby Jay."

"Midnight? What time did you get home?"

"One," he said as if it were no big deal.

"Why are you even up?"

"I would think that was obvious."

I rested my hand on his cheek. "This is all very sweet of you, but—"

"No buts." He took my hand and kissed my palm. "You are the

most important thing to me, and when this release is out, the two of us are going to get away. You name the place and we'll go."

I bit my lip and thought. "First, I want to go home to see your momma and daddy, and then I would love to go to our place." Visions of him and me at Rosemary Beach on the hot white sand made me feel all sorts of warm.

He leaned in and his lips played against mine. "This is why you own my heart," he whispered. His lips swept across mine. "Now sit down. Breakfast is getting cold."

I took my seat and he pushed me in before rushing over to the kitchen and bringing back two plates, each filled with a huge omelet and cut up tomatoes on the side. He set a plate in front of me.

"This looks divine. Thank you." I was also touched he remembered I was still on my no sugar kick. Emma was down five pounds and surprisingly hadn't had a drop of Dr. Pepper. But she warned me if she didn't get pregnant soon she would seek retribution against me.

"You're welcome." He took the seat next to me. "I'll say grace." He took my hand, bowed his head and closed his eyes.

I couldn't help but stare at him. It wasn't out of disrespect to God, but out of the admiration I had for the man who talked to God like He was a friend and thanked God for me. Was there anything more precious than a man thanking God for you? In his simple, heartfelt prayer, Ryder reminded me of all the reasons I was in love with him and wanted to raise a family with him. There in that moment, I saw the farm boy I fell in love with. Maybe Memaw was right. I should haul him down to the courthouse now and start in on that baby-making thing.

Ryder said, "Amen," and caught me admiring him. "What?"

I tilted my head and smiled. "I was just thinking about how much I love a man who can cook and pray." I had some other thoughts too, but I kept it ladylike.

He grinned before digging into his food.

"Did you get that server thingy fixed?" I asked.

He chuckled. "Integrated server, and yes, we should be back up and running today." Such relief flooded his voice.

"Is there anything I can do for you?"

He set his fork down and exhaled. "Be patient with me."

"I can do that."

He took my hand. "How about this? If I need to work late again, if I can, I'll bring it home so at least we'll be together. And let's do this every morning."

"I'd like that very much."

"Good, Miss Shelby, because I plan on having breakfast with you for the rest of my life."

Chapter Twenty-Nine

RYDER WAS GOOD to his word, which meant I spent a lot of time with him on his couch over the next week while he worked and I studied up on how to apply for my APN license in Colorado to allow me to practice midwifery again. I didn't want to sell the boutique, but I was ready to start doing what I loved in all aspects of my life. It also meant I had to move on from the not meant-to-be's in my life, namely my little yellow house, which meant I also was looking for a place to live.

I would interrupt Ryder from time to time while he was working to get his take on different properties. Like a fixer-upper in the old part of Carrington. I held up my screen and enlarged the tiny two-bedroom brick home that was in serious need of some TLC, but it was within my price range.

Ryder set his laptop down and took my tablet. He squinted his eyes at the home and me. "Darlin', why would you pay good money for this shack?"

I took my tablet back. "Because I love Carrington Cove and I promised Mr. Carrington I would move out in two months at the end of the summer." I knew Mr. Carrington would let me stay longer but staying felt backwards to me. I loved the Ranch, but it was a safety net that I needed last year when I was trying to deal with profound loss and get my footing. Now I had the direction I had longed for and the love of my life. It was time to move on.

He nuzzled my neck. "Do you really have your heart set on living here?"

"Yes," I breathed out. His lips grazed one of my favorite spots, the hollow of my neck, sending tingles through me.

"Then we will figure something out together." His hot breath played against my skin.

I closed my eyes and focused my senses on his touch. My hands ran through his hair. "I don't want your money." He, like Memaw, had offered to help buy the yellow house.

"Who said anything about *my* money?" He worked his way up to my ear and stayed a while, driving me nuts with his soft kisses.

"I did . . . I mean, what were we talking about?" My brain was going fuzzy.

He laughed low against my ear while brushing back my hair with his strong hand. "You're like putty in my hands."

I nodded, giving him permission to keep on molding me, but he only pressed a kiss to my bare shoulder "It will work out, I promise."

He went to reach for his laptop, but I had other ideas. I straddled his lap. "Hey, I wasn't done with you."

His brown eyes widened, but his smile said come and kiss me. I leaned in to do just that until Bobby Jay busted through the door with Marlowe.

"Oh my hell, you guys are here again? You've turned into an old married couple already."

I discreetly took my place back by Ryder's side, blushing a little. Ryder grabbed his laptop, disgruntled. I'm not sure if it was from being interrupted or called out. "I've got deadlines, brother, in part thanks to you."

"You can thank my record sales all the way to the bank." He put his arm around Marlowe, who was looking lovely in a floral jumper. "We are only here so I can change my clothes." He was still in his business attire. "Come with us to the bonfire."

I looked hopefully at Ryder.

His face fell. "I have to get this piece done tonight so it can be tested tomorrow. I'm sorry."

Bobby Jay rolled his eyes and grabbed Marlowe's hand. "Come with me, darlin', we'll leave the boringtons to themselves."

Ryder, I noticed, started to flip Bobby Jay a crude hand gesture until he thought the better of it in my presence. "He doesn't understand the pressure I'm under. He's not the one signing the paychecks."

I reached up and rubbed his tense neck. "I wish there was something I could do for you."

"You're doing it by being here. But if you want to go with them, you should. I feel awful, us spending all our time together like this."

"It's only temporary . . . right?"

"Of course." He went right back to work.

By the time Saturday rolled around, I was promised a date night I wouldn't forget. And not at his place. All I knew was it involved him borrowing Bobby Jay's truck, which excited me. Trucks and us equaled magic. Because of the night I was hoping for, I offered to make us a picnic dinner, which Ryder said would be perfect. All very promising.

Marlowe even volunteered to close the boutique for me so I could go home and get ready. Her thoughtfulness was appreciated, though I had to admit it was surprising. Bobby Jay was having quite the effect on her. She seemed more mature and less self-centered. I noticed another attempt to be thoughtful last night when she brought Bobby Jay a specialty beer he liked.

When I got home, I made all of Ryder's favorites, from fried chicken and biscuits to strawberry salad and, of course, sweet tea. I was a hot mess when I was done in the kitchen, so I headed straight for the shower. I was pulling up my hair as to not get it wet when my phone rang. It was Ryder's ring tone, so I answered it.

"Hi, sugar."

"Hey, Chief." A heavy breath accompanied his greeting.

"Everything all right? I was about to jump in the shower after fixing dinner. I hope you're hungry."

"Listen, darlin', I hate to do this —"

With that one sentence, all my hopes disintegrated. "Let me guess, you have to work."

"Shelby, it's not like that. We started getting several complaints that our app is running slow and come to find out we are under a distributed denial of service attack. I don't have time to go into what that means, but it's serious and my team and I have to fix this before the app crashes." His through-the-roof stress levels came through loud and clear. "I'll make it up to you. I love you." He hung up.

I sat on my bed, stared at my phone, and sighed. My first instinct was to be put out. My second was to be hurt. But then reason kicked in. This was an emergency and he had made every effort since we were together to spend every waking moment he could with me, despite it costing him sleep. But I would be lying if I said I wasn't concerned. Now wasn't the time to voice it. After this crisis, though, I would. In the meantime, I would show him how much I loved him. The man still needed to eat, and I hated to see all that food go to waste.

I called Bobby Jay, who was beside himself too—apparently, this distributed denial whatever was a big deal, and with social media the way it was, Bobby didn't want complaints of service to start popping up all over for potential customers and partners to see. He decided he better head into the office to see what he could do to help as far as mitigating calls or messages that came through customer care. This way he would have real-time updates from Ryder. I asked to follow him over so he could let me in since their offices were technically closed on the weekends except for their support center.

It wasn't the circumstances I'd hoped for to see his office for the first time. I was hoping for more of a tour that ended up with us in his office, locking the door, and us making work a whole lot of fun. Maybe another time. I pulled up to the modern red brick building with big windows and several floors. Prescott Technology was one of many tenants in the large building. Bobby said sales and support took up the third floor and the development and executive offices were on the fourth. He let me in with his keycard and gave me directions to Ryder's office.

I had to admire the work space. It was open and instead of a lot of offices, there were work stations of different varieties, some had standing desks, others had half-moon shaped desks. I smiled at the ping pong and foosball tables in the middle of it all. There were even arcade games to the side and a soda machine. No one was playing today. All I saw were heads down and the worried expressions of the women and men on Ryder's team. A few lifted their heads as I walked by carrying my picnic basket. A couple gave me odd looks. I got it—it was no time for picnics and girlfriends.

Ryder's office was toward the back. I admit I was bummed to find all but one of his office walls were made of glass. That nixed my future fantasies and the goodbye kiss I had planned for him today. It also ruined the element of surprise. He looked up from his large, curved monitors and noticed me. He stood, surprised, and waited for me to walk in.

"Chief, what are you doing here?"

I held up the basket. "I thought you might be hungry."

He ran his hand through his hair. It looked like it had been thoroughly run through all day long. "I just ordered pizza for everyone."

"Oh."

"I don't have to eat pizza." He gave me a tired smile.

That was enough to propel me forward and place my basket on an empty space near the edge of his desk. "In that case, I brought you all your favorites." I went to open the basket.

"I appreciate that, darlin', but I don't have time to eat right now. I will later, though."

My eyes met his red, gritty ones. Somewhere in there I saw the Ryder I fell in love with. The one who would have taken me up in his arms the second he saw me or would have made me sit down and insisted we at least eat together. I wondered, though, if he would appear again. "I'll let you get back to work." I turned and walked away.

"I love you," he called to my retreating figure.

I gave him a wave of acknowledgment, not returning the sentiment. It's not that I didn't love him. I did. And I truly understood this is where he needed to be. But I remembered all the excuses my daddy had of why he couldn't make it to recitals or even my high school graduation. He had to fly to New York or meet with Hobbs Inc.'s largest vendor. Work always came first.

I was tired of being last.

Chapter Thirty

MY SULLEN MOOD left me in no mood to deal with the unwelcome guests who had apparently arrived moments before me in the rented Jaguar in the driveway. Emma hadn't even had time to call me. She and Sawyer were at the main house visiting with Mr. Carrington when my parents and, unbelievably, Barrett Chapel arrived. It was bad enough my parents showed up without any warning, but to bring the man they had deemed worthy of me with them was inexcusable. But why should I have thought any less of them? The way they had treated me my entire life, and especially recently, was beyond inexcusable.

All heads turned toward me when I walked in. Everyone was standing in the foyer. Momma's expression caught me first. I could tell already she was disappointed in my attire. In a rush to comfort Ryder, I hadn't changed after making dinner. My dark T-shirt was marked with flour and my linen shorts were more than wrinkled from the long drive in the car. Momma, on the other hand, was dressed as if she were headed for dinner at the club in a form-fitting white dress with gold accents. I had to hand it to her, she wore her age well. People always said we looked more like twins than mother and daughter. Daddy and Barrett looked as if they came off the golf course in pressed slacks and expensive polo shirts. Both distinguished men in their own rights. Mr. Carrington, Emma, and Sawyer were all standing back with wide eyes waiting for the show to start.

Momma played her part and walked like a runway model toward me in her heels. "Darling, there you are. Isn't it so lovely that we surprised you?" She wrapped me in her arms but was careful to keep her distance. Heaven forbid she get anything on her white dress.

I wouldn't use the word lovely. Stunned. Appalled. Suspicious. Those were better words. I pulled away from her. "What are you doing here?"

Momma waved over Daddy and Barrett as if this had been rehearsed and they had missed their cue. "I told you Barrett was coming to town for a visit and we thought this would be the perfect time to visit our precious girl." Wow, she was laying it on thick.

Daddy played his part and put his arm around me. Unfortunately, it felt unnatural for both of us. "How are you, Shelby Katherine?"

"Fine, Daddy."

Barrett extended his hand. "It's been too long, Shelby. You look as beautiful as ever."

I caught Emma's eyes that said that was too bold. I agreed.

I took Barrett's hand and meant to shake it briefly, business like, but he kept ahold of it. "I hope you don't mind the unannounced visit, but I couldn't stay away knowing you were so close by."

Momma patted him on the back as if he played his part well.

I pulled my hand away. "That's nice, but I'm sure my parents have told you that I'm in a *serious* relationship."

The show had begun.

Momma pressed her lips together and I could tell she was count-ing to ten in her head and telling herself not to make a scene.

Barrett was unabashed, as if he knew he had my parents on his side. His pale blue eyes said he was sure he could charm me. To be sure, he was handsome with his dark, styled hair, a few strands of gray to enhance the character of it. He was nicely built, but he didn't love me and I certainly would never love him. Daddy gave me a look that said he wished he could send me to my room to think about what I was doing to all of them. If I would only think about what merging the Duchanes and Chapels would do for Hobbs Inc.

Mr. Carrington cleared his throat and stepped in. "Would you folks like to sit down?"

"That will be unnecessary," Momma said while looking around with her nose up. How could she not think this was a beautiful home? It didn't drip in opulence, but its rustic charm was gorgeous. "We'll be taking Shelby out to dinner after she changes."

I stood straight as a pin, astonished. "No, I don't believe you will be." I wasn't going anywhere with people who were spying on me. Not to mention who lied and manipulated me.

The Kings and Mr. Carrington all gave me appreciative smiles. Emma even giggled.

Momma's hands with razor sharp nails painted in a shade of taupe clenched. "Shelby, you are making a scene, darling."

They hadn't seen anything yet. I was about ready to unleash my list of complaints against them when the doorbell rang. Since I was right there, I answered it. Another surprise waited for me on the other side. This one was at least more pleasant, though I had to say I had some mixed emotions about the man who barged right in once I opened the door. "Ryder?" What was he doing here? I thought his company was in peril.

He took me into his arms before he noticed the unwelcome guests. "Chief, I—" His arms dropped, but he took my hand and pulled me close as we both faced my parents and Barrett. "What in the hell are you doing here?" Ryder dispensed with any pleasantries, not that I blamed him.

Emma and Sawyer particularly were loving how this was all playing out. I swore Emma looked like she might take a seat and grab some popcorn. I noticed Mr. Carrington move closer as if he wanted to protect me from my parents if he had to. I loved that man.

My parents didn't take kindly to Ryder's greeting and stiffened. "I see you still haven't learned any manners," Momma spat at him.

"I find it rich that you're lecturing me about manners when you spy on your own daughter and lie through your teeth."

Momma placed her hand across her heart. "How dare you accuse me of such untruths."

"I think you should leave." Daddy stared down Ryder, trying to intimidate him. "This is a private party between my wife, myself, my daughter, and Barrett here."

Ryder was not someone to be intimidated. He sneered at Barrett. "I remember Shelby mentioning you." He grinned wickedly at me. "I can't remember, darlin', did you say he kissed like a dead fish, or was that a limp noodle?"

Emma burst into laughter and exited to compose herself. Sawyer followed her, shaking, trying not to openly laugh.

I had no words.

Barrett clenched his fist like he might throw a punch, but after sizing up Ryder, decided his best course of action was to stomp out. "I didn't sign up for this. You told me she was available." He slammed the door. Where he was going, I had no idea, nor did I care.

Momma reached for my free hand. "Shelby, look what you've done. You need to fix this and go after him."

I was beginning to think my mother had a mental disorder. I shook my head. "Momma, listen to yourself. I don't care for Barrett. I never have."

"But you could. You would be so good together. We only want what's best for you. Why can't you see that?"

That was the last straw. I dropped Ryder's hand and stood tall on my own looking between my parents. In a sense, they were strangers to me. "For once, we are going to be honest with each other and you are going to let me have my say. You have never wanted what's best for me, only for yourselves."

Momma tried to argue, but I held up my hand. "It's my turn to talk." She shut up, but it was all she could do.

"You've lied to me and manipulated me," I continued. "You callously tore me away from the man I love, not thinking at all about how much that would devastate me or him. You say you want what's best for me, but how could you, considering you don't know me?"

They both looked thunderstruck.

"Why so surprised?" I directed my attention to my father. "Daddy, when is the last time you called me?"

He swallowed hard and thought. "We talked over the holidays."

"No, Daddy, you were too busy wining and dining business associates. Business has always come first."

I inadvertently looked at Ryder, who hung his head.

I wasn't finished with my father. "I would guess you don't even know when my birthday is." My voice trembled with emotion.

"It's in February," he stumbled, trying to think of the date.

Momma elbowed him. "It's Valentine's Day, Montgomery."

"I knew that." He refused to make eye contact with me.

"Maybe once upon a time you did. Believe me, I know how little I have meant to you in your life." Tears streamed down my face.

"That is not true," Momma cried desperately. "You are the apple of our eye. Our pride and joy."

I shook my head. "No, I'm a status symbol, like the expensive car you drive and house you live in. You only wanted something you could show off, and it killed you when my choices weren't the sparkling ones you hoped for. So you punished me by taking away the person who always used to put me first. Who showed me what real love was and that success had nothing to do with your job, but how important you made the people around you feel."

I met Ryder's eyes. Sorrow swirled in his. He reached out and took me into his arms. There I fell apart and cried into his chest.

"I'm sorry, Chief," he whispered in my ear. "After you left, I kept staring at the picnic basket and thinking what an idiot I was. You're the reason I started this company in the first place, and I already lost you once because of it, and I'll be damned if I let that happen again. I'll close the doors tomorrow if I have to."

I leaned away and peered up into his misty eyes as if only he and I existed, not caring we had an audience. "Ryder, I don't want you to lose your company. I'm so proud of what you've built, but I've told you from the beginning that I wanted something different from what I grew up with." I grabbed his shirt and pulled him closer to me. "I didn't fall in love with you because of the things you could buy me. I fell in love with you because you gave me all the things money can't buy. And . . . I like the way you kiss." I gave him a come and kiss me right now grin.

He flashed me a sensual smile before leaning in, but unfortunately, the audience wouldn't stay silent.

"Shelby Katherine, mark my words, you are going to waste your life away with this boy," Momma screeched.

In Ryder's arms and together, we faced my parents. "No, Momma, I'm going to live my life with this *man*, a real life, and I suggest that you don't get in the way of that."

Momma's skin blotched red with anger as she realized she couldn't control me. Daddy was assessing Ryder with his stare but not saying a thing.

"What about us?" Momma cried. "We are your parents. Your blood."

I shrugged. "If you can't accept Ryder and me, then you can go to heck."

"She means hell," Ryder clarified through his chuckle.

Mr. Carrington, who had been keeping watch over me, laughed at my manners.

Momma squared her shoulders. "Well, I see there is no reasoning with you."

"Not even a little." I smiled at her.

Momma pointed at Ryder. "He has had a wicked influence on you."

I gazed up at Ryder. "Wickedly good, I would say."

Ryder leaned in and brushed my lips with his.

That did it for Momma. She click-clacked her way out the door, acting like a two-year-old throwing a hissy fit because she didn't get her way.

Daddy stayed for a bit longer, looking at me as if it was the first time he ever saw me. Maybe it was. The businessman who could command a room with his words and presence seemed at a loss for what to say or do. He finally let out a heavy breath and approached us. He awkwardly kissed my head and said, "I'll call you," before he rushed out. I didn't even have time to respond, but I found I didn't care. I was where I wanted to be—in the arms of the man I loved.

Mr. Carrington, in contrast, was not awkward when he came and kissed my forehead. "You did good, kid."

"I'm sorry you had to see that."

He waved away my concern. "Honey, I'm sorry you had to live through it." He directed his attention toward Ryder. "See that she always comes first in your life."

"Yes, sir," Ryder responded.

Mr. Carrington nodded and wandered off toward the family room.

Once we were alone, Ryder cupped my face with his hands and pressed a kiss to my lips. "I am sorry, Shelby," he whispered between us. "You make my life worth living. I love you."

"I love you too."

He leaned away enough for me to see the glint in his eye. "I'm happy to hear that because dang, woman, you're sexy when you get all riled up."

"Is that so?"

"Yes, ma'am. I think we should capitalize on it. I just happen to have Bobby Jay's truck and a picnic basket full of delicious food made by the most beautiful woman on God's green earth. Not to mention a bottle of sweet strawberry wine and a blanket or two." He flashed me his most wicked grin

"That all sounds perfect, but what about the distributed attack thing? I meant what I said—I don't want you to lose your company."

He tenderly ran his thumb across my cheek. "I'm not going to lose my company. I'm going to trust my people and hire a project manager and more developers so I can spend more of my time doing what I love most."

"And what would that be?" I asked coyly.

"This." His hands ran down my curves until they took hold of my hips. He pulled me flush against him before taking a moment to gaze into my eyes while his lips teased mine, so close but never touching. The pressure of his hands increased on my hips as the tension mounted between our lips. Each breath between us became heavier and deeper before his warm lips came down upon mine. There they teased more before his tongue slid across my lips and into my mouth. He tasted like home and everything good in my life. With every sweep of his tongue, my pulse raced, making my body tremble with delight.

I pulled away only enough to catch my breath. "I think my momma was right about one thing. You are wicked."

He groaned before picking me up and carrying me out into the night. "I plan to show you how right she is."

Oh Mylanta.

Epilogue

"ARE YOU SURE you can't see?"

"I'm sure." I touched the blindfold Ryder had placed on me before we left the Ranch. I wasn't sure where we were at, but I could feel the late August sun beating down on me and it smelled like someone was barbecuing. "We're going be late signing the lease," I told him.

Ryder convinced me that leasing a condo in Edenvale until we could find the perfect home made the most sense. And I suppose he was right, especially since my little yellow house had a big fat Sold sign on it.

"We're not going to be late, darlin'." He called out to me. He had left me standing who knows where, but I heard the jangling of keys and what sounded like a door opening.

I stood there twisting the vintage wide-band byzantine diamond ring on my finger. Ryder had placed it there almost immediately after my parents left town. I hadn't taken it off since.

"Okay, are you ready?" Ryder spoke in front of me.

"Ready for what?"

He swept me into his arms. "You'll see."

I instinctively wrapped my arms around his neck. "What are you up to?"

He planted a kiss on my cheek. "Trouble, as always."

"That's what I thought, Mr. Prescott."

"You are right, Mrs. Prescott."

I loved that name more than any other, even though it had only been mine for a short time. We decided not to leave anything to chance and wed at the Ranch under the pergola that was rumored to bring good luck and a lasting marriage, in front of our friends and, of course, Bobby Jay. My parents had refused to come and his couldn't, but they gave their blessing. My daddy did send a check, though, as a wedding present.

It was a simple affair. Me in a white chiffon dress from the boutique and he in jeans and a white button-down. It didn't matter what we wore. All that mattered were the vows we spoke and had been living up to. He repeated the same ones he had written so long ago before we were torn apart.

Shelby Katherine Duchane, I haven't been the same since the day our worlds collided. You brought out the man in me. You made me think more of someone else than I did about myself. Your happiness became my own. I live to see you smile. When you take my hand, I never want to let go. Today you take my name. There is no greater honor I could receive. Today our two worlds more than collide, they become one, as it was always meant to be.

Ryder walked us up some steps. Wood creaked beneath us. "I'm going to have to fix that," he grumbled.

"What are you going on about?"

Instead of answering, he carefully removed the blindfold, making sure not to drop me. I immediately recognized where we were. The yellow house with the wraparound front porch and cute white shutters. I looked out toward the yard. The For Sale sign was still there with the big Sold sign across it.

"Why did you bring me here?"

He flashed me a crooked grin. "To walk my bride across the threshold."

"Wait, what?"

"We aren't going to be late signing that lease because you're already home."

"You bought the house?" Emotion filled my voice.

"I did, even though I never thought I would spend so much money on a fixer upper."

I squealed and squeezed him tight. "I love you." I tried to hop out of his arms, excited to go inside *our* home. We had been living at the cabin together, which had been glorious, but even with Bobby Jay moving out into an apartment in Edenvale it hadn't quite felt like home, more like an extended honeymoon, which, like I said, I had no complaints about.

"Hold on, Chief." He held me tightly and walked us across the threshold. We entered the open-floor-plan house. It was already furnished with my things that had been in storage for months. There sat my white living room furniture arranged in front of the stone fireplace. My rustic wood dining room table sat to the left of us with boxes piled on top of it.

"When and how did you do all this?"

"I put an offer on the house not long after it went on the market."

"Why would you do that when we were barely together?"

"Because I could tell how much it meant to you, and whether we ended up together or not, I was going to offer it to you. But I knew I wasn't ever going to let you go again."

I ran my hand across his cheek. "You are the sweetest man."

"I did have some help. Bobby Jay, Sawyer, and Brad helped me move your stuff in last night."

Now it made sense that Emma asked me out to the movies last night even though the poor dear was suffering from morning sickness. I was so glad she got pregnant, or my life might have been on the line. Though she was ticked that Dr. Pepper made her want to throw up now.

I kissed my husband and jumped out of his arms. I couldn't believe this place was ours. Before I could explore, a large, white box resting on the farmhouse style coffee table caught my eye. "What's this?" I walked toward the box.

Ryder took my hand and led me the rest of the way. He sat down on the couch and pulled me onto his lap. "Open it, darlin'."

I reached for it and placed it on my lap. It was heavier than I expected. I lifted the lid and pulled back the tissue paper. Tears immediately filled my eyes. I ran my hands across the silk organza lace bodice. "Ryder, how did you? Why did you? We're already married."

He gently set the box to the side. His eyes met mine while he caressed my cheek. "I swore I was going to be able to buy you that dress one day."

I started to say I didn't need it, but he placed a finger on my lips. "I know what you're going to say and you're right, *things* don't matter, but you matter to me and I know that dress makes you happy. And my momma and daddy were hoping you would wear it when we come to visit. They'd like us to have a wedding there."

"I would love that." I took his face into my hands. "But we are going to have to hurry."

He narrowed his eyes. "Why?"

"To make sure the dress fits."

"The lady at the boutique said we might have to alter it even though they still had your measurements on file."

"That's all well and good, but I don't think she was talking about the kind of alterations I'm going to need."

"What kind might you need?" His grin was hopeful.

I rested my forehead on his and took a deep breath before I rocked his world. "You. Are. Going. To. Be. A. Daddy."

My Not So Wicked Boss

DON'T CRY. DON'T cry. Don't cry. It wasn't the end of the world. I stared at the email from the vice president of the bank who didn't have the decency to tell me in person that he wasn't going to be promoting me to the position of client services manager. Even though I'd jumped through all the hoops and had been an employee longer than Stephen. Stephen who I trained to be a personal banker like myself. Stephen who barely knew the difference between a credit card and a debit card. Stephen who was walking toward my desk in his new suit wearing a gloating smile and a ridiculous combover to hide his balding spot. Stephen who had a huge piece of spinach wedged between his two front teeth.

"Aspen, I just wanted to say that going against you was stiff competition, so this win means even more to me."

Wow. For that, I wasn't going to mention the spinach. Or the coffee he had dribbled on his white shirt.

"In the end, the best man won. I hope there will be no hard feelings. Especially since I'm your new boss." He guffawed to himself.

I pressed my lips together, not knowing what to say. He wasn't the best *man* for the job. All he had was a degree from a highly-touted university and a mother who was on the bank's board of directors.

He waited for my reply, but I had nothing. All I could think of was my daughter, Chloe. I wanted to be able to finally move us out of our tiny apartment and to say yes more to the things she wanted, even needed, like braces. I almost had to take a loan out just pay for her junior high school fees.

Don't cry.

When I said nothing, he blankly stared at me for a moment longer. "Well," he clapped his small, oddly shiny hands together, "now that we've cleared all that up and moved on, I need you to help out today in private banking." He smirked. "Now."

I wasn't surprised. I knew he would be the worst sort of boss—authoritative without any skills. He would make himself look good on the backs of others. My back. I stood without a word, only taking the time to log out of my computer and grab my satchel before I marched across the marble floor to take the elevator to private banking on the second floor. It was rubbing salt in my wounds to have to help the wealthier part of our customer base today. At least the solo ride on the elevator gave me time to compose myself. Tears pricked my eyes, but I stifled them with shallow breaths.

Evelyn, the sweet receptionist who was old enough to be my grandmother and planned to work at the bank until her dying day, greeted me with a smile on her cute, chubby aged face as soon as I stepped off the elevator. "I was hoping they would send you up here today when Valerie called in sick."

"Thanks, Evelyn. Should I take the floater's office?"

"I have it ready for you."

When I walked past her desk, she stood and took ahold of me. "I heard the news," she whispered in my ear. "I can't believe they promoted that little brownnoser over you."

"Me either." I had to stave off the tears again. I was afraid I was never going to catch a break.

She tipped my chin with her crinkled finger. "You keep your chin up. Better doors to open wait for you. I just know it."

I sighed, not sure. I was told if I finished my degree that the job would be mine. Now all I had to show for my degree was student loan debt and the long hours I spent late into the night doing homework and taking online classes so that I didn't take time away from my baby.

I settled into the desk chair, at least thankful I had an office today. Downstairs we were in cubicles. Apparently, if you didn't make a lot of money it was okay if you discussed your financial needs and private information for the world to hear. I reached into the desk drawer and grabbed my extra nameplate and set it on the mahogany desk and logged into the computer. While the computer started up, I stared at the framed picture on the wall in front of me of a beautiful mountain scene with our bank logo and slogan obscuring it, "A Better Bank for a Better Life." *Lie,* was all I could think.

I didn't have time to wallow. Before I knew it, Evelyn was bringing back my first customer of the day. I sat up tall and plastered on a fake smile when I saw her coming. Evelyn was fanning herself as she walked toward me with a Cheshire grin. I wondered why until I saw a man trailing behind her. Not only *a* man, but *the man*. At least, I thought it was him. If not, I was going to start believing in doppelgangers.

I stood, and for the first time in forever my heart raced. And not because I opened the electric bill. This was a different kind of pulse, one I had forgotten existed. You see, I didn't like men as a general rule, unless I was related to them or I was friends with them circa high school. I made a few exceptions if my friends happened to be married to them and were bearing their children, which was happening more and more lately, but beyond that, I didn't have much use for men. But this man I had kept by my bedside for over a year now. No one knew that.

Evelyn made it in before him. The man in question happened to have a little someone with him. That little someone was giving him fits as little people often do. But what a cutie the whining boy was. He had curly dark hair like the man who was now kneeling in front of him. Did he have a son? For all my admiring of his picture and reading the book he wrote more times than I was willing to admit, I had forced myself not to learn more about him except that he was single and loved to play polo. I only knew those tidbits because of my friends.

"Listen, mate, if you're good here, I promise we will go get ice cream afterward. Does that sound good? Can you do that?" The man in question's sexy British accent wafted my way making my pulse tick up even more.

The handsome little boy dressed like a tiny royal in shorts, a sweater with a collared shirt underneath, and dress socks up to his calves nodded and took the man's hand. The man was also impeccably dressed in dress slacks with a dark blue button-up that brought out his aqua eyes.

Those eyes I'd stared into too many times.

Never did I think I would get the opportunity in real life. Not that I wanted it. Okay, maybe I thought of having dinner with him a time or two, but it was only to discuss how brilliant his book was. I wanted to know how he dreamt up the complex character of Isabella Jones. She and I had bonded. I felt this odd connection to her, almost as if I knew her in real life. We shared similar backstories, both middle children, once upon a time uninhibited, but life had gotten to us making us much more reserved in nature and maybe even a tad snarky. I also wanted to know when the sequel to *Silent Stones* was coming out. It had been two years. How long could it take to write a book?

Evelyn, still fanning herself and red like she was having a hot flash, cleared her throat. "Aspen, this is Miles Wickham—"

I shook my head, not sure I heard her right. Miles Wickham? I expected her to say Taron Taylor. I guess I was wrong. He wasn't the man on the cover of my book that held a place of honor on my nightstand. I told my heart it could stop racing, but Mr. Wickham's piercing eyes caught hold of mine. They widened as if he were surprised to see me as if we were already acquainted. Then he tilted his head and began studying me from every angle. I wasn't sure what to make of it, but I reminded myself I was at work and to focus back on Evelyn.

"—he's here to open a checking account. I thought you would be perfect to help him." Evelyn gave me a covert wink. She was always trying to set me up with someone, including most of her grandsons.

I walked around the desk a bit shaky and held my hand out. "It's a pleasure to meet you, Mr. Wickham." I had to stop myself from smiling. All I could think of was wicked Mr. Wickham from *Pride and Prejudice.*

Mr. Wickham held out his own masculine hand, still studying me. He swallowed hard. "The pleasure is mine, Ms.—?"

"Parker," I stuttered like an idiot. Men weren't supposed to have an effect on me. It was the British accent, I told myself.

"Ms. Parker." He spoke my name with reverence while keeping my hand in his. "I feel as if we have met before."

I looked at Evelyn, not sure how to respond. Not sure if I could. There suddenly was less oxygen in the room, or so it felt. Evelyn's excited eyes said to say something flirty. I didn't remember how to do that. More importantly, I shouldn't be doing that. I was a professional and I didn't like men, I reminded myself.

I found some air and pulled my hand away from his. Oddly, it made him smile as if that's what he expected. "I think I would have remembered if we had," I finally managed to say, which, unfortunately, did sound flirty even though it was true. I would have remembered him if we'd met before. To cover up my blunder, I knelt carefully in my pencil skirt in front of the little guy who had to be all of three. "And who are you?" I asked.

"I'm Henry," he replied. Forget the sexy British accent, his adorable one was ten times better. He held up his bear. "This is my teddy, George." His teddy bear looked well-loved with matted down fur and his askew bowtie.

I shook George's paw. "It's nice to meet you, George."

Henry giggled, making me wish Chloe was a toddler again, or for another little one running around. I would have had another baby in a second if I could afford to and, you know, if didn't involve the opposite sex.

"We are going to get ice cream," he said so grown-up like.

"That sounds yummy. What kind of ice cream do you like?"

"Butterscotch." He smiled.

"I'll have to try that flavor."

Henry nodded and I stood to find Mr. Wickham gazing thoughtfully at me. He was not helping with the pulse racing thing.

"I'll leave you to it." Evelyn wagged her brows before exiting.

"Please have a seat." I waved to the chairs in front of my desk, trying to maintain my composure.

Mr. Wickham took a seat, but Henry had other ideas; he followed me to mine.

"Henry, come sit next to me." Mr. Wickham directed kindly.

Henry grinned mischievously while shaking his head no. He held his arms out to me. One look at his big brown eyes with lashes to die for and I could hardly refuse. "Do you mind?" I asked Mr. Wickham.

"Not at all. My nephew is . . ." he swallowed. "Is a precocious tyke."

I don't think that's what he was going to say, but no matter. I picked the little guy up along with his bear and set him on my lap and wondered why he had his nephew with him. Bringing a toddler to a bank wasn't always a wise choice.

"He's adorable."

"He gets that from me." Mr. Wickham grinned.

I started to respond with my normal sarcasm toward the opposite sex, but I stopped myself. "What can I help you with today?"

Mr. Wickham leaned forward as if he were trying to get a better look at me. "I'm going to be in the States for a while and my financial advisor recommended I open an account here to make things easier."

"We have a few options. Let me get you a brochure and we can go over those and see what best fits your needs."

Henry didn't want to be forgotten. "I'm three." He held up three fingers.

I wanted to kiss those cute fingers but thought that was even more unprofessional than holding him on my lap. "You are a very big boy for three."

He puffed out his chest.

I reached into the desk drawer for the brochure. "What brings you to the States?" I tried not to stare at the handsome man. I couldn't get over how much he looked like Taron Taylor. He was even British which was odd. I had to say, though, that I was relieved he wasn't my favorite author. I had promised my girlfriends if I ever met him, I'd try to get to know him. I knew the odds were in my favor of that never happening, so I agreed to appease them. They worried I was going to die an old maid. The odds were highly in favor of that, considering I hadn't been on a date since my ex-husband left me and our daughter twelve years ago.

"I have some personal and business matters to attend to." He kept it vague on purpose given his stiff body language.

It didn't offend me that he didn't divulge anything personal. I could relate. I slid a brochure of our different account types across the desk. "Here are—"

"My mummy and daddy are gone," Henry wailed unexpectedly.

My head shot up and caught Mr. Wickham's defeated eyes. He sighed and hung his head. Meanwhile, I tried to comfort poor Henry, who began to cry into my bosom. I wrapped my arms around him, hoping his parents were on vacation or something, but Mr. Wickham's demeanor said otherwise and it broke my heart.

"My sister and her husband were in an automobile accident," Mr. Wickham spoke low, refusing to finish the rest. I could guess. "Come here, Henry." Mr. Wickham stood to retrieve his grieving nephew.

"No!" Henry refused, snuggling further into me.

Mr. Wickham looked at a loss of what to do. "I'm new at this."

"It's fine. I don't mind keeping him, if it's all right with you."

He sat back down relieved. "I was only supposed to be the fun uncle."

"I'm very sorry for your and Henry's loss." I stroked Henry's dark curls.

"Thank you, luv. Do you mind if we move along? I have several appointments to attend to." He suddenly seemed uncomfortable.

"Not at all." I kept one arm around Henry, who was shuddering against me. Poor baby. I used my free hand to point at the brochure. "If you could tell me a bit about your goals and profession, I can make a solid suggestion on the right account for you."

He grinned, albeit subdued. "Would you believe I'm an international bestselling author?"

I gasped.

"Are you all right, luv?"

"Yes," I squeaked. "You wouldn't happen to use a pen name, would you?"

His left brow raised debonairly. "As a matter of fact, I do. Taron Taylor."

The bated breath I had been holding came out in a rush. "Oh."

His aqua eyes danced. "Have you heard of me?"

I nodded and unfortunately, I was blushing. I could feel my cheeks burn.

"A fan," he said, ever so pleased and as a statement not a question. "I love fans."

"I never said I was a fan," came rushing out of my mouth before I could stop it. I didn't want to be rude to him. It was a conditioned response to men. A defense mechanism, if you will.

Weirdly, he didn't believe a word or seem to take offense. "Which book is your favorite?" He flashed me a disarming smile.

It was enough to almost make me blurt out how much I loved *Silent Stones*, but I stopped myself. "I think our platinum premium account would suit you," I suggested instead of answering.

He laughed this deep, rich laugh. "Aspen, was it? I like you."

I tucked my long, brown hair behind my ear. "Um, the account has a competitive APY, no fees, online and mobile banking—" I started to ramble, amusing him more.

"Sounds brilliant."

"I'll need your passport, individual tax identification number and—"

His phone rang, interrupting me. He held up his finger. "One moment please. I must take this." He answered and walked out but kept me and his nephew in his line of sight. He kept smiling at me and shaking his head like he couldn't believe this was happening. I had the exact same thoughts but wondered why he felt so. And why did he think we had met?

Henry had cried himself to sleep against me. I stroked his baby-soft brow. "I'm so sorry," I whispered. I had to keep myself from tearing up. When I looked back up, Mr. Wickham or Taylor or whoever he was, now pacing, running his hands through his gorgeous hair, I mean, his hair. It was just hair.

"What in the bloody hell am I going to do now? I don't have time for this." His voice, while raised, was still discreet given he wasn't in private. I still couldn't believe he was here and I was holding his sweet nephew. I shifted him on my lap, trying to get more comfortable. It was amazing how much heavier they felt as they slept. I missed these days, though Chloe and I did snuggle on the couch when we watched our favorite shows and stuffed our faces with popcorn.

Mr. Wickham paced and paced some more, talking more quietly. "Stella, I can't just pick someone off the street." He glanced at me and his nephew before abruptly stopping. His lips curled and his eyes brightened. "Let me call you back. I think I have a smashing idea." He hung up without another word and shoved his phone into his pocket. He walked back in, his lips pressed together, assessing me even more than he had previously done.

"Ms. Parker, do you like your job here?"

That was an unexpected and uncomfortable question given the morning I had had.

"Um . . ."

"Hesitation," he said, pleased. He shut the office door and leaned against it.

I couldn't help but stare at him. The picture on his book cover didn't do him justice. Which was ridiculous. Because my second thought was this was inappropriate. Closed doors had become something of a taboo. You'd be surprised at some of the salacious stories that had circulated around the bank.

I bit my lip. "Mr. Wickham."

He pushed off the door. "Please call me Miles." He took his seat back, grinning between me and his nephew, who he was obviously fond of by the tender look he gave him. "You see, Aspen, I'm in a bit of a bind. I came here because of my sister's last wishes and to work on my novel."

I wanted to say it was about time—I needed that book—but instead I attentively listened.

"She loved Carrington Cove," he said wistfully.

"I grew up there. It's a beautiful place." My parents still lived there while Chloe and I lived in Edenvale because it was cheaper and closer to work.

He clapped his hands together. "Splendid. I think a bit of kismet is at play here."

"I'm not following you."

He gave me a charming grin. "I'm in need of someone who can be both a nanny to my nephew and a personal assistant to me."

I laughed, startling Henry who I quickly soothed back to sleep. "You're kidding, right?" I looked around for a recording device. "Did my new boss put you up to this?"

"I assure you, I'm not having a laugh at your expense. I'm in earnest here, and somewhat desperate."

I blinked an inordinate amount of times. "No. No. I'm not a nanny." And I certainly could not be his personal assistant.

He stared down at his sleeping nephew. "You seem to have a magic touch when it comes to wee ones."

I shrugged. "I wouldn't say that, but I have a daughter."

"How old?" he asked.

"Twelve."

His brows raised. I knew what he was thinking. *You look too young to have a child that age.* He was right, but I would never regret it even if it meant having the most worthless ex-husband in existence. Chloe was the best thing that had ever happened to me.

He cleared his throat. "Excellent," he stammered as if he was unsure what to say to that. "You have plenty of experience then. Exactly what Henry and I need."

"Listen, Miles, you don't know me. I have a degree in business management, not child development."

"I would do a background check on you, of course. And I need a savvy business mind."

"I don't think I'm the right person. Maybe I could ask around for you." I looked down at sweet Henry and my mother's heart wanted nothing more than to see that he had the right person to take care of him.

"Whatever you are making here, I'll double it." Miles slapped his hand on the desk.

My head popped up. Our eyes locked.

"What do you say now, Ms. Parker?"

Oh. Wow. I leaned back, stunned. "Can I think about it?"

If you enjoyed *My Not So Wicked Ex-Fiancé,* here are some other books by Jennifer Peel that you may enjoy:

All's Fair in Love and Blood
Love the One You're With
Facial Recognition
The Sidelined Wife
How to Get Over Your Ex in Ninety Days
Narcissistic Tendencies
Honeymoon for One- A Christmas at the Falls Romance
Trouble in Loveland
Paige's Turn
My Not So Wicked Boss

For a complete list of all her books, visit her Amazon page.

ABOUT THE AUTHOR

Jennifer Peel is a *USA Today* best-selling author who didn't grow up wanting to be a writer—she was aiming for something more realistic, like being the first female president. When that didn't work out, she started writing just before her fortieth birthday. Now, after publishing several award-winning and best-selling novels, she's addicted to typing and chocolate. When she's not glued to her laptop and a bag of Dove dark chocolates, she loves spending time with her family, making daily Target runs, reading, and pretending she can do Zumba.

***

If you enjoyed this book, please rate and review it.
You can also connect with Jennifer on social media:
Facebook
Instagram
Pinterest

To learn more about Jennifer and her books, visit her website at
www.jenniferpeel.com

Made in the USA
Monee, IL
04 August 2021